D1392724

PENGUIN BOOKS

ONE FOR SORROW

THE MAGPIE SOCIETY

ONE FOR SORROW

THE
MAGPIE
SOCIETY

ZOE SUGG
AMY McCULLOCH

PENGUIN BOOKS

PENGUIN BOOKS

UK | USA | Canada | Ireland | Australia
India | New Zealand | South Africa

Penguin Books is part of the Penguin Random House group of companies
whose addresses can be found at global.penguinrandomhouse.com.

www.penguin.co.uk
www.puffin.co.uk
www.ladybird.co.uk

Penguin
Random House
UK

First published 2020
This edition published 2021
001

Copyright © Tiger Tales Limited and Zoe Sugg, 2020, 2021
The moral right of the authors has been asserted

Set in 10.8/14.8pt Sabon LT Std
Typeset by Jouve (UK), Milton Keynes
Printed and bound in Great Britain by Clays Ltd, Elcograf S.p.A.

The authorized representative in the EEA is Penguin Random House Ireland,
Morrison Chambers, 32 Nassau Street, Dublin D02 YH68

A CIP catalogue record for this book is available from the British Library

ISBN: 978-0-241-40235-1

All correspondence to:
Penguin Books
Penguin Random House Children's
One Embassy Gardens, 8 Viaduct Gardens, London SW11 7BW

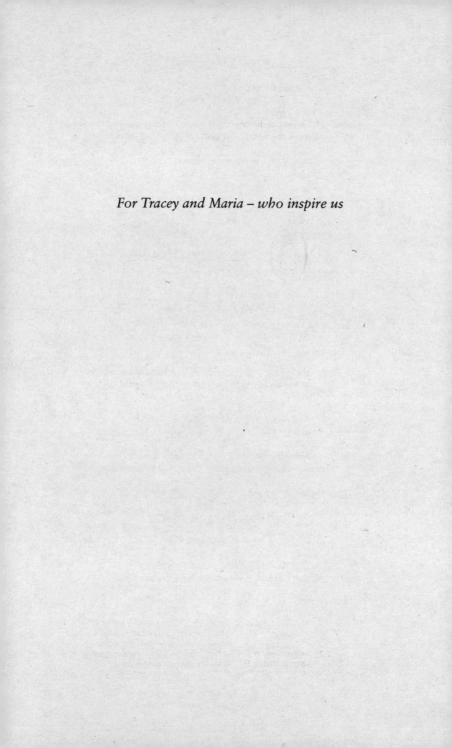

For Tracey and Maria – who inspire us

PROLOGUE

The night she died, all our phones were turned off.

The police didn't believe us.

Kids don't go anywhere without their mobile phones, they said. *You expect us to believe you weren't Snapfacing or Insta-booking or whatever it is you kids do these days at your end-of-term party? That not a single person took a selfie or boomerang or video?*

We all had the same answer: *No.*

They checked our phones anyway. Logged into our clouds. But there was nothing to find.

The detectives discovered a scrap of paper at the scene. It was one of the posters that had been stapled to the driftwood gate that marked the entrance to the steps down to the beach. It said in big, bold letters: **NO PHONES, NO CAMERAS, NO SOCIAL MEDIA, NO EXCEPTIONS!**

As if anyone at the party needed a reminder. Because that was the whole point: we'd *wanted* a chance to switch off. To have a party that wouldn't be documented, to dance the night away in blissful anonymity, to have memories that couldn't be fact-checked by photographs and videos. No one broke the rules. No one wanted to. We all had eagle eyes when it came to spotting the telltale glow of a smartphone screen, or the glint of a camera lens.

Some of us might break a law or two, if we felt compelled. But disobey the rules of our end-of-term party? No one would dare.

The police officer rolled his eyes as he interrogated us one by one. *You mean to say you all followed these rules? I don't believe you.*

But we had nothing to show him. That was the truth. So he asked us to tell him instead.

The beach was alive that night. The bonfire was lit, the flames leaping up into the sky. Some of the logs flashed green as they burned, choked with salt from the sea. As we danced on the beach, our shadows stretched up the chalk cliffs looming over the horseshoe bay so that it looked as if the cliffs were moving. Waves crashed in the distance, the low tide leaving the sand littered with seaweed and shells. The summer evening was warm, the start of another British heatwave.

And, of course, it was rammed with *us*. Out of uniform, it was harder to tell who was who. Ironic, wasn't it, that a uniform designed to make us all look the same actually became a blank canvas on which we could showcase our individuality? Now, in our normal clothes, we looked like regular teens. But we weren't.

We were students of Illumen Hall.

That's what made this party different. At other times of the year, students from nearby schools would come to our events – our Samhain party was legendary and if you missed our Christmas Extravaganza, you might as well say goodbye to any semblance of a social life.

But the end-of-term beach party was ours. We lived together for the whole year and, whether you enjoyed your time at school or not, separating for the summer suffused everyone with a sense of melancholy. No matter how hard you tried to avoid it, if you were one of the chosen 600 who attended Illumen Hall, you were woven into the fabric of the school. Summer split us apart and this party was a final memory to sustain us through two months of enforced separation.

The smell of charcoal permeated the air. The logs snapped and crackled with the heat, sending up blisters of embers into the rapidly darkening sky. Combined with low house beats and swaying bodies, it was intoxicating – or maybe that was just the copious amounts of alcohol that flowed into our paper cups.

The tide crept in as the hour grew later, until the bay was almost cut off and the only way out was back up the rough-hewn steps cut into the cliff face. It was all beautiful: us, the sand, the waves and the fire.

A blood-curdling scream sliced through the music. The crowd of writhing bodies froze. Then there was a surge, a ripple of panic that leaped from person to person. The screaming continued, the music snapped off, and we rushed as one down towards the water.

The screaming was coming from the sea. A figure was standing by the water. The sun had disappeared from the horizon, but there was enough ambient light to see by.

A body lay on the sand, waves lapping at the soles of her

feet. She was on her front, but her head was tilted to one side, her lips tinged an unnatural blue.

Pale skin, blue lips, tangled strands of hair, twisted limbs.

And, on her back, an elaborate tattoo of a magpie, every detail intricately laid out across her shoulder blades, which jutted out on either side of her spine as sharp as knives. The bird's wings were stretched out so that the edges of the feathers curled across on to her collarbone, and the tail feathers disappeared beneath the back of her dress.

A voice. 'Go back to town and call the police. She's dead.'

1

AUDREY

Is there anything worse than starting over at a new school?

Turns out there is. Starting over at a new school when it's lashing down with rain and a hurricane-force wind is blowing. In just a few months, I've managed to go from a warm, inviting red-brick high school in sunny Georgia to what looks like a lame-ass version of Hogwarts on an isolated peninsula somewhere in the south of England, and in the worst weather I've ever seen. The windshield wipers of my dad's Merc are moving at lightning speed, the engine still running, the sound mirroring my pounding nerves.

'Be good, Audrey,' he says, without turning around from the front seat.

Be good. Have words ever been so loaded? What he really means is, *Don't screw this up – don't make things worse – only two more years until you're no longer our responsibility and we can wash our hands of you once and for all.* But, of course, none of those things are *actually* said. They're in the tightness of my dad's shoulders and the fact that Mom isn't here at all, but away with Jason, my younger brother, in the south of France. Edison, my older brother, is at college in New Haven, and so no help there either.

I don't answer Dad. Instead, I take a deep breath and stare out the window. If I thought it looked ancient on the website, *IRL* Illumen Hall makes me feel like I've stepped back into a different century. It looks positively medieval. Like it wouldn't be a surprise to see the severed heads of bad students staked between the turrets, *Game of Thrones*-style. Still, I'd risk the wrath of the Lannisters over staying in the car with my dad for a second longer, so I open the door, clutch my Chanel bag to my chest and brave the rain.

He shouts something as I run towards the entrance of the school, but his words are swept away by the wind.

I make a spectacular entrance, tumbling through the doors as they open smoothly, and, before I know it, I'm dripping rain on to a polished hardwood floor.

The noise of the storm outside is almost completely swallowed up by the building as the doors close softly behind me, and the quiet is disconcerting. I slowly lift my eyes, trying to take everything in. My gaze stops at a huge portrait of an imposing woman dressed in an elaborate emerald silk gown. She's staring down at the door as if she's judging every person who enters. I feel about two inches tall – which is surprising because I'm five eleven and normally tower over everybody.

'Intimidating, isn't it?'

I spin around to see a woman dressed in a smart pale-pink suit with matching low-heeled pumps.

'Yeaaah.' My Southern drawl echoes round the atrium. *Ugh.* I've never managed to *sound* as out of place as I feel.

'You must be Miss Wagner?'

'Oh, uh, just Audrey is fine,' I say.

Her lips pull into a tight smile – she doesn't look like she takes too kindly to the idea of casual greetings. 'I'm Mrs Abbott, headmistress of Illumen Hall.' She extends her hand and I shake it weakly. 'I saw you and your father pull up in the courtyard – I'm sorry I didn't come out to greet you, but . . .' She shrugs, and gestures to the puddle I'm making on the floor. 'Your things have arrived safely, so I'll show you up to your room.'

I raise an eyebrow. I know my dad's company is big and important, but is it normal for the principal – *head-mistress* – to act as tour guide? 'Where is everyone?' I ask.

'Most pupils won't be here until this afternoon, in time for the welcome assembly.'

She's walking away before her sentence is even finished, and I scramble to keep up, my flip-flops squelching on the wood floor. I bump my hip into the banister, only just stopping myself from cussing. *Klutsy, loud, foul-mouthed American* isn't the first impression I want to give Mrs Abbott. I'm never this awkward back home, but here I can't help craning my neck to gawk at the lofty ceiling with its intricate carved stonework, or at the gigantic paintings that almost completely cover the walls. I've never been in a place like this that wasn't a museum or a gallery.

'We've put you in Helios House,' says Mrs Abbott, climbing the stairs. 'You'll be sharing a room with one of our top pupils, Miss Moore-Zhang, so you can direct any questions that you have to her. She'll give you the full tour once you're settled in.'

I take a deep breath. I really hope that my new room-

mate and I will be good friends. I want a fresh start here –
new country, new school and a whole new set of friends.
Brendan, my then-boyfriend, laughed when he found
out I'd be sharing a room. *You? Princess Audrey?* A good
reminder of why he's now an ex-boyfriend.

We turn down a hallway on the second floor where we
need to step over a fairly large pile of rubble. Mrs Abbott
tuts loudly at a gaping hole in the ceiling.

She sees the frown on my face. 'We've had some building
work done over the summer that I've been *promised* will
be finished by tomorrow.' She raises her voice as she says
that last part. I think I catch an answering grunt from
deep inside the cavernous ceiling. I wonder if Mrs Abbott
thinks I'm gonna report back to my dad. *As if.*

I try not to get too much dust on my bag as I follow Mrs
Abbott down the hallway. 'Did you bring your ID card?'
she asks me as we stop by a pair of double doors.

'Oh, um . . .' I dig through my handbag, knowing I put
that stupid school pass somewhere. It's the size of a credit
card, and apparently my key to all different areas of the
school – including my accommodation.

Mrs Abbott waits a few seconds and, when my searching
becomes even more frantic, lets out the tiniest huff of
annoyance. She takes her own pass out from her suit
pocket and swipes us in. 'You must keep your card safe –
without it, you'll have trouble getting around.'

'Here it is!' I say, finally prising it free from between a
make-up compact and my AirPods case. I make a big show
of putting it in the front zipper of my bag. We pass by
something that looks like mailboxes, covered by a glass

window, and I catch my name written underneath one of the shelves.

'Here we are.' We're outside room number seven. 'Your home for the rest of the year. Sorry I have to dash off – as you can see, there's a lot going on that needs sorting out before the chaos tomorrow. I'm sure Miss Moore-Zhang will be along shortly. In the meantime, settle yourself in and unpack. And, Miss Wagner – welcome to Illumen Hall.'

'Thanks,' I say. About a billion questions bubble to the surface, but Mrs Abbott doesn't hang around to hear them. I take a deep breath, steel myself and push open the door.

The first thing I notice is a deep bay window, right opposite the door, framed with voluminous white voiles and heavy brown velvet curtains. Across it sits a little bench covered in forest green satin. It looks like the ideal reading nook – even I might be tempted to curl up with a book once in a while – and even though it's stormy outside I can tell the window will bring a lot of light into the room in nice weather. The walls are panelled in rich cherry-coloured wood and there are two single beds pressed up against the walls on either side, along with two matching wardrobes, two desks and two dressers. It's as if a mirror has been placed down the centre of the room.

There are some loose boards in the hardwood floor that rattle as I step on them, but nothing a good rug won't cover. With a few pictures to warm up the wood, some ornaments dotted around . . . it won't be so bad. I smile to myself and take out my phone to send a picture to Lydia, my best friend back home. She's obsessed with interior design so will have plenty of ideas about how to jazz it up.

My boxes and suitcases are in the hallway outside, but I'm in no rush to move them in. Still, the first thing I take out is my school uniform, which is pressed and fresh in its bag from the dry-cleaner's. I unzip the bag and stare at the uniform – my new outfit for the rest of the year. The blazer is a deep navy-blue wool, with gold buttons in the shape of stars. The pleated skirt is the same, accented with stitches in gold thread. It's not so bad.

I jump as a voice comes from behind me. 'Don't get too comfortable. This room is cursed.'

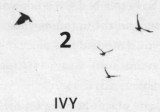

2

IVY

'This room is cursed,' I say, pushing my way round the tall, white, blond, slightly fragile-looking new girl in the doorway.

Be kind. Mum's words ring in my ears. Lola's awful accident at the start of the summer is already making this year difficult enough. But it's hard to be kind when I'm about to meet the girl I'm giving up my privacy for.

And it's especially hard to be kind when everything about her screams that we won't get along. In one hand she's got an oversized smartphone with a pink, fluffy case, and over her shoulder is a flashy designer bag. It must be freezing outside, but she has *flip-flops* on. I don't like to pass judgement on someone before talking to them, but she's making it too easy.

She darts round at the sound of my voice, her big blue eyes widening with fear. 'Oh my God, you scared me. Hi, I'm Audrey!'

Oh, it gets worse. She's American.

She hangs her dry-cleaning on the back of the door and extends her arms towards me, a grin showing off her perfect white teeth. 'So pleased to meet you!' she says.

I dodge her hug. 'Oh wow ... too soon,' I mutter. Ignoring her pained expression, I walk past her and place my battered leather satchel down on one of the beds to claim it. It's the better bed – the one with the view out of the bay window and the brand-new mattress, things you'd only know if you'd studied this place inside and out, like I have. 'I'll take this side,' I say – stating the obvious, but then she probably needs that.

Shrugging, she places her bag on the bed opposite. She sits down and the ancient springs creak. I wonder which dusty storage room they dragged it out of – turning this spacious single room into a cramped double.

'So, you're my new roomie,' she says.

'Your powers of deduction are marvellous,' I respond, putting on my poshest-sounding voice. 'I'm Ivy.'

She frowns, picking at the edge of a baby pink, manicured fingernail. I turn my back on her, feigning interest in the contents of my bag, but feel a twinge of regret. It's not *her* fault I'm in such a terrible mood. Well, OK, it kind of is. But she doesn't know that.

I've been dreaming of this year ever since my first night at Illumen Hall – staring at the ceiling, listening to other girls toss and turn and snore in shared accommodation – because finally, *finally*, I'd get to have my very own room. I've been grafting, working every angle, on my very best behaviour, so that I would be the *one* lower-sixth student in Helios to earn the privilege of having their own room. When it was confirmed at the end of last term, it was better than any prize.

Because Illumen Hall is my home. Much more so than my mum's tiny council flat. And the time had finally come where I didn't have to share that home with anyone else; I was going to get my own space – Lola's old room. I'd always envied it, and I hoped, in the aftermath of her passing, it would help me feel close to her.

That was until Mrs Abbott asked me to volunteer to share that space with Audrey Wagner. The American.

It wasn't really a request – it was a demand and, if Mrs Abbott demands, you do not contest.

'How long have you been coming to school here?' she asks my back. I exhale loudly through my nose as I continue to empty my bag. When I don't respond, she keeps going. *Ugh, can't this girl take a hint?*

'I don't know how *y'all* can live in a place like this. I feel like I'm in a freakin' museum.' Her accent grates on my nerves, but I'm curious enough that I turn round to face her again.

She smiles really widely so that I can see every tooth in her mouth. Her teeth are extremely symmetrical and almost glimmering white; I'm a little jealous. Her eyes are a shade of blue that reminds me of a china doll and, although her hair is down and rained on, it's tousled and beachy and looks effortlessly boho.

She seems so innocent and earnest. Is this what they mean by Southern charm? I realign myself. I don't need to be friends with this girl, but the history of Illumen Hall is one of my favourite subjects and I can't resist. 'This part of the building is actually pretty new – Victorian, I think.'

Her jaw drops. 'Isn't that, like, a hundred years old?'

I roll my eyes. 'You want old? We've got a building here that dates back to 1487.'

'Wow. We have some buildings from the 1800s in

Savannah – that's the town I'm from – and that's considered . . . really fucking old.'

I suppress a smile. Maybe not so sweet and innocent after all.

I spin round abruptly. I came here to claim my bed and I've done that now. I have too much work to do this year, too much to focus on, and plenty of friends like Harriet, Tom, Max and Teddy; I don't need another. She's already ruined my year by turning up, and I don't *want* to like her. I plan on us just sharing space and being civil to one another. I walk towards the door, but, as soon as I do, she's on her feet.

'Hey, well, maybe you can show me around? You seem to know a lot about the place. And I promise I'm a great room-mate. I can make killer s'mores with a candle and a fork . . .'

I frown. 'What's a s'more?' I ask, despite knowing full well.

'Oh, you don't have those here? They're delicious. Toasted marshmallow and chocolate between two graham crackers . . .'

'Gram crackers?' This is too easy.

She trips on her tongue. 'Like, uh, a kinda cookie-type thing?'

I wait, one eyebrow raised.

Her shoulders slump. 'You don't have those either?'

I shake my head. 'But that sounds like just the kind of skill you need around here – you'll fit right in,' I say, my voice dripping with sarcasm.

'You're hilarious,' she says, her eyes tightening at the corners. Our senses of humour are clearly very different. This interaction is starting to feel awkward even for me.

This girl really has no idea what she's letting herself in for. I know the reason Mrs Abbott asked me to offer up my room is because she thought I'd take her under my wing and make sure she's buckled up for the ride that is sixth form. Maybe last year I would have. But that was before the horrifying event on the beach a couple of months ago. Before Lola. Before my privacy became more important to me than ever before.

Be kind. Mum's words ring in my ears again. I grit my teeth. 'I'm sure s'mores are great,' I say with an exaggerated sigh. 'All this talk of food has made me hungry. Want me to show you how to get to the dining hall? We have a welcome assembly in a few hours, so you've got time to grab something to eat first.'

'Are you sure?' She tentatively picks her bag up off the bed. Maybe I really put her off with that s'mores banter. She pauses, her eyes scanning the room.

'You coming or what?'

She bites her lower lip. She looks afraid and it sends a shiver down my spine. *What does* she *have to be afraid of?*

'You said something when you first came in. That this room was cursed? What did you mean by that?' She's staring at me now.

I take a deep breath, working hard to maintain my calm exterior. I don't want her to feel comfortable. I want her to leave. 'Oh, that . . . didn't Mrs Abbott tell you? The last girl who lived in this room drowned.'

3

AUDREY

Well, *that's* morbid. I shudder. We lock eyes for a few long moments. She's already in her school uniform, a shiny badge with the letter P engraved on the front pinned to her lapel. With her tanned summer skin, neatly trimmed dark bob and slight frame, she might look unassuming at first, but her words pack a punch.

And I definitely don't need to hear any more about a drowning.

'You know what? I think I'll find my own way around. I mean, it's a school. Not exactly an escape room. See you later.'

I don't think this is what Ivy expects. Her shoulders tighten. I've never seen someone go so still. But, just as quickly, she shrugs. 'Suit yourself.'

I expect her to at least point me in the direction of the dining hall, but she flounces off without another word. I take a deep breath. Without knowing it, I've been picking at the edge of my nail polish and, if I continue, it will lift off – along with the top layer of my nail. I force my hands apart, curling my fingers inside my palm. This chick – this *school* – does not get to mess with my manicure.

It can't be too difficult to navigate my way around this place. There's an old-fashioned lock on the door in addition to the hotel-style key-card entry, but I wasn't given a key, so I slip my laptop underneath the bedsheets and close the heavy door behind me. With no real point of reference, I choose to walk in the opposite direction to the one I came from with Mrs Abbott.

God, I really hope everyone in this place isn't as unpleasant as my room-mate. I'm used to being popular – I *want* people to like me. I can already feel myself trying to think of ways to earn Ivy's friendship. Her bag was pretty old and shabby, and I have at least three like it back home I could bring her to replace it . . .

No, that was the old Audrey. The one who bent over backwards for people like a master yogi of friendships. And where did that get me? Contorted into knots that proved impossible to untangle. I'm not gonna do that again.

When the hallway opens up into another grand atrium, with staircases leading off in different directions, I open Snapchat to send Lydia a selfie. I pose, leaning up against the polished banister, trying to get as much of the grandeur of the hall in as possible (while still looking cute). I add a series of heart-eye emojis to the image, and hit send. There's a heavy weight on my chest. I miss her so much.

Well, I miss the Audrey and Lydia of six months ago. Before everything changed. I shake my head. This is my fresh start.

The sound of voices drifts up from the stairs below, which I guess means other students are starting to arrive. My stomach flips at the thought of meeting new people. It *has* to go better than it did with Ivy, or else this is gonna be a very long final two years of high school – or sixth

form, as they call it here. I check my image in the screen.
My eye make-up, carefully applied this morning, is
smudged at the corner. I dab at it with my ring finger.

'Better not let the housemistress see that, or you could
be in a lot of trouble.'

The deep voice makes me jump and my cellphone slips
from my hand. I squeal, the inevitability of what's about to
happen registering even though I know I can't react quick
enough to stop it. The phone bounces on the gleaming
steps once, twice . . .

It comes to a stop at the feet of the guy who interrupted
me. I stumble down the stairs after it, my flip-flops slapping
loudly. He drops to one knee and scoops it up, then presents
it to me in an exaggerated manner. 'M'lady,' he says. 'Your
iPhone.'

I don't even have time to register whether he's hot or not
(normally my first priority). I snatch my phone from his
open palm, ignoring his wry grin, and turn it over.

I groan and slump on to the step. A spiderweb of cracks
splays across the top corner of the screen, with one jagged
line spreading down to the bottom. Even though I know
it's stupid, that it's just a phone – easily replaced with a
quick email to Dad – I have to bite down on my bottom lip
to stop tears welling up.

The guy sits down next to me. 'I hear that's seven
months of bad luck.'

I roll my eyes. 'That's mirrors, not phone screens. And
don't you mean seven years?'

'Seven years is for an *actual* mirror. This is a digital
version. Moves faster.' He waits for a beat – maybe

expecting me to laugh or something. But I'm still in shock. 'You know, I could fix that for you,' he says.

Now he has my attention. I blink as I take him in for the first time. He *is* hot, a white guy with a thick mass of brown hair, warm honey-brown eyes, sharp cheekbones and a chiselled jaw. He's wearing his school blazer over a shirt and jeans, which already makes him better dressed than any of the Georgia boys I'm used to hanging out with, who were never out of board shorts and loose T-shirts. His eyelashes are so long the tips brush his brow bone. I smile. 'You can?'

'Well, new girl, this actually makes things easier.' He reaches into his inside blazer pocket and pulls out an old iPhone in a cheap Pokémon cover. 'Take this. We can change the cover,' he adds.

I arch an eyebrow. 'What are you, some kind of black-market phone dealer?'

He laughs, and the sound echoing off the grand atrium walls is so loud it makes me cringe. The school feels almost like a church, so it's as if his laughter is desecrating its sanctity. But he doesn't seem to notice. Maybe, once you're used to this place, you can be as loud as you want. 'Not like that. Here, we've done this all wrong. I'm Theodore.'

I smile. 'Audrey.'

'Ah,' he says.

'What does "Ah" mean?'

He blushes, and the pink from his cheeks seems to spread all the way up into his hairline. It's cute. 'You're Ivy's new room-mate.'

'Oh, so you know Ivy?'

'Everyone knows Ivy,' he replies. His lip quirks at the

edge. 'So, let's say fifty quid for the phone?' He waggles the Pikachu device at me.

I stand up, suddenly uncomfortable. I'm not gonna buy some crappy old phone from this guy. I grip my broken one like a shield. 'I'm good. I'll keep this one.'

'Oh no . . . you don't get it. Everyone needs a –'

'I'll be fine.' I move down a few stairs.

'Well, if you change your mind, I hang around in the SCR most of the time.'

I nod, but I have no idea what or where the SCR is. I just wanna get out of there. So far, at Illumen Hall, I've met three people – and they've all weirded me out. This is not what I expected.

I race down the stairs, only to be engulfed by a wave of students entering through a set of heavy double doors.

I dart one last glance back up, but Theodore's gone. *For the best*, I think. After all, my break-up with Brendan is still fresh. In fact, I have a voice note from him I haven't listened to . . .

I shake my head, dispersing thoughts of the hot English boy I just met and the even hotter guy I left behind in the States. This is supposed to be my new start.

No drama with guys.

No bitchy friends.

And *definitely* no more drownings.

4

IVY

'Enter each row from the left-hand side, please, and fill the seats all the way to the front . . .' I gesture towards the wooden chairs by the stage as students bumble into the assembly hall, one behind the other, whispering and gossiping. There's a low buzz of excitement in the air from the new intake, mixed with first-day-of-school nerves. Everyone else is more sombre than usual, especially when they see what's on the stage. It's enough to shut up even the chattiest of people.

I try to keep my eyes off it, and remain focused on the task at hand.

Being a prefect, you're entitled to a lot of perks, but they come with eye-wateringly boring responsibilities – like overseeing the students filing into assembly every week. I know . . . surely able-bodied humans are capable of taking a seat in an orderly fashion? Well, turns out not so much. If we left them to it, it'd be chaos. It's exhausting watching the newbies wobble around like lost sheep, and having to herd them like a sheepdog is really draining my bank of enthusiasm on this gloomy evening.

When I snap loudly at a first year who decides to jump a chair like he's practising his hurdles, Mrs Abbott gives me one of her 'looks', her piercing grey eyes narrowing as she watches how I control the situation. I send her a sharp smile back, making sure to give my most flattering and charming teeth-baring grin, which is then acknowledged with an eyeroll. Mrs Abbott and I have a very complex relationship. I don't think she approves of my background – but she can't deny that I earned my place here. We grate on each other like bickering relatives, but I always manage to win her over somehow.

The new Year Sevens are pretty funny to watch. They gawp at the size of the hall, the faded gold-etched names of the head boys and girls and their prefects listed on mahogany plaques around the wall, going all the way back to the mid-eighteenth century. My name is up there this year under 'Prefect', etched in sparkling new gold leaf. But one name is conspicuously missing from this year's head girl spot. And Araminta Pierce's is there in its place.

Instead, Lola's full name is written beneath a large photo projected on to a screen at the back of the stage. Even in black and white, you can see her skin glowing and her eyes sparkling. Lola would have hated that photo. She's perfection personified in it, right down to the stray perfect curl in her blond hair that looped just above her ear. But, by the end of last year, she'd shaved an undercut into her long blond locks, and her eyes were rimmed with kohl so black it made her light blue irises seem translucent. And then there was that magpie tattoo.

Everyone – even her best friends – had been shocked by that.

The words underneath the photo read:

DOLORES RADCLIFFE
FOREVER IN OUR HEARTS

They make me catch my breath. It still doesn't seem real. In all my years at this school, we've never been struck by any sort of tragedy – not of this magnitude.

There's an easel onstage too, draped in a red velvet sheet. I half expect Lola to burst out from underneath it, laughing, like it was all a big prank.

If she was still here, everything would be so different. This assembly would be joyful, not sombre. I'd have been by her side, running her errands, while she did her head-student duties. I never minded grabbing her coffee in the morning or helping her with her coursework because it meant I got to spend time with her – and being around Lola instantly increased your credibility. She was so alluring, so effortlessly beautiful that basically everyone fancied her. But it wasn't just her aesthetic that made her so magnetic. She was warm and charming and every word that rolled off her tongue left an impact. Her laugh had you smiling so hard your jaw would ache. Being in her orbit was a joy as pure as being on the beach, listening to the waves, sand between your toes and a cold cider in your hand.

It all feels so empty without her.

I turn round, blinking, and usher the last of the older students into their seats. It's been weeks – an entire summer – since Lola's death and many sunsets, hook-ups, break-ups and tropical Kent showers. Time carries on ticking.

I feel a stab of jealousy at the sight of fellow students

who appear fine. Smiling and greeting each other like it's a normal first day back, as if Lola's death hasn't shattered them like it has me. My vow had been to try and start the school year without letting it affect me too much. But it's clear, from how I feel seeing Lola's face once more, that's not going to happen.

I take my own seat at the end of a row, next to Teddy. He's the other prefect for Helios House – and my boyfriend. Sort of. He gives my knuckles a squeeze and I brush his fingers, but don't make eye contact. That might just send me over the edge, and I don't want to break down right now.

There's a clip of heels on the wooden stage, and I close my eyes for a second.

Mrs Abbott walks to the centre of the stage and fiddles with her microphone. I watch as Araminta and the new head boy, Xander Tamura, stand beside Mrs Abbott like her bodyguards. A student is playing 'Stuff We Did' on the piano at the side of the stage. The song is from the Disney film *Up*, one of Lola's favourite films, and a really beautiful, delicate piece to play. I've played the piano since I was old enough to sit at one and now I teach other boarding students at weekends.

Teddy whispers, 'Didn't you and Clover play this song together once? That kid isn't doing it as well as you two.'

'Yeah, we did.' I smile at the mention of Clover. She's two years below me – my fledgling – and I've taken my task of mentoring her very seriously. She'll be somewhere backstage, adjusting the lights and pulling on cables, probably wearing some outspoken, sweary T-shirt under her blazer. How she gets away with that I don't know, but I admire her gutsy attitude. Everyone knows Clover. If there's a protest on the grounds about the amount of water the school uses or the fact that the canteen doesn't provide enough plant-based options, you can guarantee Clover will be fronting it, with some sort of elaborate signage, and sometimes – on the rare occasion it's not locked in her office – Mrs Abbott's megaphone.

We're very different people, Clover and I – she likes meditation, singing in the choir, and will go for days without shaving her armpits and legs just to prove that women shouldn't conform to societal expectations. She's a bit Marmite – you either love her or hate her – but she doesn't give a damn either way. I admire the passion she pours into everything she does. In that way, we're kindred spirits and, as a result, we're friends.

Mrs Abbott's voice brings me back to the present. 'Welcome back, students of Illumen Hall. It is only fitting that we begin our year by taking a moment to recognize a huge loss for our small community: Dolores Radcliffe, or as many of you knew her, Lola.' Mrs Abbott shifts on the spot. Her voice wobbles. 'I also want to take this opportunity to thank those of you who helped the police with your statements and eyewitness accounts. I can imagine it's been a very hard summer for many of you.'

Sniffling starts up in little groups across the hall and tissues are passed round liberally. Lola's close friends, Jane and Heloise, are just to the right of me, holding in great heaving sobs by gulping loudly and blowing their noses. She really was loved by everyone. She had this ability to make people feel like they belonged at the school – even though she could trace her family's attendance at Illumen almost all the way back to its inception, she didn't hold that above anyone else's head.

Lola had seen something in me. It's hard to explain our relationship – I wasn't one of her best friends, but I looked up to her and she mentored me. I felt like I knew her – maybe even more so than the people she hung out with. The official cause of death from the police is 'by misadventure', since there was no note left for her family. But we're all warned over and over about the danger of walking near the cliffs, especially at night. To go there deliberately, to walk so close to the edge . . . The word 'suicide' floated round the edge of everyone's speculation, and I suppose you never know what demons people are hiding.

I've been gripping my hands together so tightly I've left little half-moon indents in my palm. Dr Kinfeld would not be happy – maybe I'd have to book another therapy appointment with her, even though I'm officially signed off.

'But, although we mourn and try to learn how to live with our feelings of loss and sadness, we must also remember that Dolores Radcliffe would not have wanted us to think of her only with tears, because she was a source of light and beauty in our lives. It's why I'm delighted to announce that, with the support of Lola's parents, Mr and Mrs Radcliffe, we'll be renaming the swimming pool in her honour this year.'

The hall breaks out into thunderous applause as Mrs Abbott points to Mr and Mrs Radcliffe, who I can see now are sitting in the front row. Mrs Radcliffe is still dressed in funereal black with a shock of red at her neck in the form of a scarf. Mr Radcliffe looks solemn by her side. Next to them is Lola's handsome older brother, Patrick, whom I haven't seen since he went off to uni years before. He'd been head boy when I first started at Illumen Hall. The Radcliffes were IH royalty. Even their parents met at this school.

Lola would be the only one who never got to graduate.

'We also have a beautiful portrait of Dolores, which I will ask her parents to unveil at the end of today's assembly. It will be hung at the entrance of Helios House, where she spent so many happy years. If anyone needs to speak to the school counsellor, please arrange it through your form tutor or come to me,' Mrs Abbott continues. 'Help is available to anyone who needs it, so please don't suffer in silence.'

She moves on to the standard part of her speech now, the one we hear every year. Now this is more comforting. It's part of the bubble of life at Illumen Hall. The safety net. I actually feel myself relax, my muscles melting into the chair. I hadn't realized how much all the talk about Lola's death had set me on edge.

'Moving forward, I want to welcome our new students! I'm sorry your first day has begun like this, but Illumen Hall welcomes you with open arms and we're all so pleased to have you here . . .'

Just as Mrs Abbott is about to move on to why Illumen Hall is the best place to learn and grow, there's a thunderous bang – and the electricity goes out. The room is plunged into darkness. Gasps and cries ring out, and Mrs Abbott's voice shouts over the din, 'Keep calm, everyone!' Without the amplification from the microphone, she might as well be trying to calm a herd of wildebeest preparing to stampede. There's a growing energy in the room, some kind of urge to run, to move, and wind rushes on to my face like someone's opened a door to escape.

It only lasts a couple of breaths before there's another pop, and the lights come back on. 'Sorry,' says a voice from the back of the room. Like meerkats, we all turn our heads at the same time, spotting a grizzled handyman in dark blue overalls wiping his hands down his front. 'Blew a fuse. All fixed now.'

'Settle down, please,' says Mrs Abbott, barely able to contain her irritation. I wouldn't want to be in that man's shoes. 'As you all know, we're having some work done in the school that should be finished soon, but in the meantime there may be some . . . unexpected disruptions.'

But the buzz in the hall grows again. Teddy nudges my shoulder. 'Did you give this to me?'

He holds up a rectangle of neon-orange paper, a flyer. I shake my head. 'No, of course not.'

'Oh, you've got one too,' he says.

I look down at my lap. Sure enough, there's a flyer sitting there – a rectangle of dayglo pink that wasn't there a few minutes ago. Frowning, I pick it up and turn it over.

I KNOW WHO KILLED LOLA . . .
AND ONE OF YOU IS NEXT
http://whokilledlola.com

5

AUDREY

Damn. So *she's* the reason my room is cursed.

When I close my eyes, all I can see is the black-and-white photograph of that girl staring down at us. Dolores Radcliffe. She must have really meant a lot to the school, because there were students crying all over the auditorium.

And then there was that flyer drop. It scared the shit out of me. But there's no way I'm visiting that website. I came here to get *away* from drama like that.

'You OK? You look a little pale.'

I look up, my heart racing. I've been sitting in my chair for so long the auditorium has almost emptied out all around me. I find myself face to face with two girls, both in immaculate school uniforms. I recognize the girl closest to me – she was one of the students on the stage next to Mrs Abbott.

'Oh yeah, sorry,' I reply.

'I don't think we've been introduced yet? I'm Araminta Pierce, head girl this year.' She smiles brightly at me, her long blond hair swaying in its high ponytail.

'And I'm Bonnie,' says the shorter white girl standing just behind her. 'I'm in lower sixth, like you.'

'You're Audrey Wagner, right?' Araminta asks, sitting in one of the empty chairs in front of me.

'Oh –' I blink several times, taken aback. 'That's me. You got it.'

'Oh my God, your accent is so cute! I feel like I'm on the set of *Nashville*.'

'Well, aren't you a darlin',' I say, doing my best Dolly Parton. I get an appreciative squeal from Araminta.

'I'm so sorry I didn't greet you when you arrived. I try and do that with all the new people. But I'm sure Ivy's been showing you the ropes! She's just so smart, isn't she?'

'But maybe not so good at sharing,' says Bonnie with a wink.

Araminta laughs. 'Good point! How are things with the two of you in that room?'

'Um . . .'

The longer I pause, the wider she grins. 'Oh, silly me! Being head girl makes me so interested in everyone. You'll have to get used to seeing a *lot* of me around here, nosying about in all your business.' She waggles her finger at me and laughs.

'Well, it's real nice to meet you,' I say.

'How are you liking the school so far?'

Her eyes are so wide, her face so earnest, that I find it difficult to lie. 'It's great!' I say, through slightly gritted teeth. Maybe it's just my accent, but she doesn't notice.

'It's impossible not to love it here,' she says, while Bonnie nods in sage agreement. 'But there are a few things you should know.' She leans in conspiratorially. 'There's a hierarchy in the school. The younger kids – we call them fledglings – help out the sixth-formers. Run round the school, doing our errands, that kind of thing.'

I wrinkle my nose. 'Bit weird, isn't it?'

'I suppose it is if you're not used to it. But then you're going to find a *lot* of things are like that at Illumen Hall. Fledglings mostly support the prefects anyway.'

'Prefects?' I ask.

Araminta slaps her forehead in an exaggerated manner. 'Of course! American – you wouldn't know. Prefects are like . . . school enforcers,' she says with another laugh. 'You'll recognize them because they wear these little badges.' She pulls out a bright yellow badge in the shape of a shield, with a black letter P embossed on the front. 'Mine's a bit different – as you can see.' It's a bright red star embossed with the gold letters HS.

'It used to say HG for head girl, and HB for head boy – that's Xander. But our Clover in Year Ten petitioned to make them more gender neutral – so we're head students now. I still call myself head girl though because that's how I identify!'

I barely listen as Araminta drones on about how prefects have to 'help with the smooth running of the houses' and 'supervise activities for the younger years', which sounds a lot like hard work to me. At least now I get the badge Ivy was wearing. My eyes drift to Bonnie, who's staring at Araminta like the sun shines out of her ass. I suppress the urge to giggle at that thought, before Araminta realizes I'm not listening. I'm sure she'd say that prefects were no laughing matter.

'So, have you had the full tour yet?'

'Not yet,' I reply, snapping my attention back.

'I wish I could do it myself, but Bonnie here knows so much about the school. And she's in your year, so it'll be good for you to have a friendly face in your classes. I'll leave you guys to it! I have to get all this mess sorted out anyway.' As she stands, she picks up one of the flyers, then tosses it back down on the floor in disgust.

I purposefully haven't touched one myself. I can see that a lot of students are grieving for their lost classmate, but I can't allow myself to get sucked in. I'm sure it's a sad story – and, from a brief glance at the wording on the paper littered all around me, there are lots of questions surrounding her death. But it's not my – well, not my business.

'Ready?' Bonnie asks me. When she smiles, little dimples appear in her freckled cheeks. She seems nice enough, and I remind myself that I shouldn't be afraid to make new friends. I'm sure they're nothing like the people back home. And not everyone will be as rude as my room-mate.

'Absolutely. Let's go.'

She leads me out of the auditorium, through long, meandering hallways to the cafeteria – or, as she calls it, the canteen. Artwork is hung on practically every wall, from paintings of trees and weird Victorian buildings to nonsensical abstracts. The way Bonnie leads me is warm and bright, but every now and then we walk past entrances to long hallways that seem to disappear into shadow. When I pause to peer into the darkness, the temperature seems to drop.

At this school, it isn't long before something new takes my breath away. The canteen is bright and modern, under an enormous domed glass ceiling, almost like a greenhouse, with a tree growing up through the centre. Bonnie explains that there's a more formal dining hall too, but most of the meals are taken here. My stomach rumbles – I haven't eaten since I arrived here and I refused Ivy's offer to take me to get something to eat. 'You're in Helios House, right?' she asks, once we've grabbed a takeout coffee and a slightly stale muffin from the 'tuck shop' in one corner of the canteen (I like this girl already).

'Yeah,' I reply.

'OK, that's cool – it's one of the oldest ones. I'm in Nova, the all-girls one. Do you know much about the houses?'

I shake my head. Bonnie grins, eager to share her knowledge.

'Well, Illumen Hall has six in total, all of them named after different stars. They were a sort of obsession of the Illumen Hall founder, Lord Brathebone – a super-rich merchant with an extraordinary interest in astronomy and astrology. Back then, there were only two houses – Helios and Polaris. But, as the student population grew, more houses were added to keep the small "family-style" atmosphere of the school. Nova House was added when girls were first allowed to come here. There's a portrait of the first housemistress, Lady Penelope, in the Nova House front room – I could show it to you another day, if you like?'

I smile. 'Thanks.'

There's an awkward pause where she waits for me to expand on my gratitude, I guess, but I don't know what else to say. I can feel her passing judgement, and I know I have to bring her over to my side. I don't want to isolate *everyone* I meet at this school.

'Wow. So much history. I don't think I'll ever learn my way around!'

'Oh, you'd be surprised.'

I know this type of girl. She wants to give me something – she's desperate to. I offer up the only thing I've been really curious about so far, and I hope it doesn't set the wrong tone.

'So, there is one thing ... I was kinda thinking of finding some place called the SCR?'

'Oh, I can definitely take you there. But first, do you play any sports?'

I shrug. 'Um, not really.'

'Hmm, well, they like us to pick some sort of physical activity – I'm on the hockey team.'

'I like playing tennis, I guess?'

'Great, let's go and see the grass courts before it gets too dark.' Bonnie grabs me by the hand, pulling me through a set of double doors and out into the grounds.

I feel like I'm on an Illumen Hall crash course as she fills me in on some of the rules and regulations and I get a tour of the grounds. Bonnie seems to know everyone – but then this school is a lot smaller than my old high school in Savannah. Only a few hundred students compared to a couple of thousand.

It turns out there are a whole bunch of sports teams I could join, clubs I could become a member of, basically every sort of extracurricular you could think of. Bonnie is sweet and friendly, and I find myself relaxing in her company. For the first time in a while, I'm laughing and chatting normally. I've been stiff as a board lately.

'OK, one last thing before we go to the SCR. It's a bit of a weird Illumen Hall tradition.'

'I've trusted you this far,' I say, laughing.

She grins at me and we head back towards the main school building. This part of the Illumen Hall grounds, just behind the school, is neatly manicured – all sculpted hedges and trimmed lawn. We stick to sandy, gravelled pathways, which wind their way through the gardens. Up in one of the topiaries, a scruffy-looking bearded guy in a close-fitting denim shirt and mud-stained trousers is pruning the bushes.

'Who's that?' I ask Bonnie.

She squints in the direction of the hedges. 'Oh, that's Mr Tavistock's grandson . . . Ed, I think? They're in charge of the grounds. They're both super creepy though, so I'd be careful not to get in their way. Mr Tavistock's wife disappeared in mysterious circumstances and they say the only reason her body hasn't been found is because he knows all the school's secret hiding places.' Bonnie shudders, but she has a grin on her face.

I don't find the rumour amusing, but I force a smile, so she'll think I'm easy-going.

The sun hangs low in the sky, casting an orange glow on the grey brick of the school. All around us is the sea, and the wind lifts my hair, tossing it around my face.

From this angle, the school is a mishmash of styles, thanks to all the extensions and additions. There's the glass dome of the canteen and a tower at the far end that looks straight out of a fairy tale. Bonnie catches me looking.

'That's the art wing. Well, the ground floor is.'

'Sucks I'm not taking art then!'

Bonnie shudders. 'Oh no, that doesn't suck at all. That place is freaky too. I swear if you walk by it at night it seems to hum like something out of *Black Mirror*. I avoid it whenever possible. OK, here we are! Do you have a fifty-pence piece or something?'

'A what?'

'Some change. Like a coin.'

We've come to a large pond, with yellowing lily pads and a gently bubbling fountain in the centre. As I look more closely, I see that the stonework that surrounds the pond, and the bottom of the pool itself, are carpeted with coins, bright pins and other shiny things. Bonnie balances a silver coin on her fingers and flicks it into the water. Then she crosses her fingers and says, 'I won't cross the magpies, and the magpies won't cross me.'

She turns back to me, her round face bright with expectation. 'So, do you have an offering?' she asks me.

'Um, sorry – no. Don't carry cash on me.'

'Anything shiny will do – a hairpin or earring or something . . .'

My hand flies up to my earrings – delicate hoops that were a gift from Brendan. As if I'd toss those into the school's water feature! Suddenly I yearn for Lydia. She would have laughed with me at how absurd this is. She'd cackled at the lady reading tarot cards in downtown Savannah. This tradition would be a step too far for her as well.

'I got nothing,' I repeat.

'Oh, OK then.' Bonnie's face falls. 'Don't say I didn't warn you. Everyone does it.'

She's not joking either. When we turn to walk back to the school, a small line has built up behind us. Students preparing to make their offering.

'I'll come back and do it another time,' I say, trying my best not to roll my eyes.

'I would,' Bonnie says. 'Because whatever else you do at this school you don't want to cross the magpies.'

6

AUDREY

After the creepy fountain incident, Bonnie takes me back to the entrance of Helios House. I feel wrung out from the effort of learning about this new school. It seems as if everyone is so entrenched in its traditions that it's like a second language to them. I'm left floundering without a translator. We didn't even get to the stupid SCR, so I'm still none the wiser about that either.

When I finally get back to the room, Ivy's there. She's been working hard: her side has been completely transformed. There's a new deep purple bedspread, so dark it's almost black, draped over her mattress, and her desk is piled high with books and lit by a beaten-up old angled lamp. Everything is neatly ordered and a calendar hangs above her desk covered in little coloured stickers.

She's clearly hyper-organized, which I am most definitely *not*. I'm no slob, but I get the sense she'll sneer at my occasional floor-drobe.

Ivy is sitting in the window seat, her back to me. She doesn't even look over when I come in. A cool blast of wind hits me from the open window, and there's even a damp patch on the floor where the rain from earlier has blown into the room.

'Can you close that?' I ask, suppressing a shiver and running my hands up and down my arms.

She doesn't move. Curious, I peer round her and see that she has one arm out the window. There's an empty plate at her feet, covered in crumbs. Finally, she speaks up. 'I thought I saw a nest outside the window. I wanted to leave some food out for the birds. It pays to be nice to them around here.'

'So I've heard,' I mutter. 'That's nice of you,' I say, a bit louder.

'I'm a nice person,' Ivy replies matter-of-factly. She pulls the window shut. The wind has shaken up her pin-straight bob and raindrops have settled on the dark brown strands like tiny beads.

'So . . . this place is weird,' I say, trying to start a new conversation.

'What did you expect? Didn't you get some kind of welcome pack?'

'Yeah . . . I don't read that crap if I can help it,' I say. 'I like to discover a place for myself, you know?'

She looks at me like I've announced I'm from Mars. 'No, I don't know. If I was coming to a new school, I'd want to know everything about it. I'd hate being ignorant.' She pulls back the bedcovers and settles in underneath her blanket. To my surprise, she speaks up again a moment later, face to the wall. 'Lights out is at ten. There'll probably be an inspection by the housemistress before then, in case you want to put stuff away.'

'Thanks . . . ?' I reply, my voice drifting into a question. She doesn't answer.

I sigh. I don't know if it's because I'm tired, or because I want to piss off my room-mate with the boxes for a bit longer, but I decide that it's too late to unpack.

I slump down on my bed, staring at Ivy's back. A wave of irritation washes over me. I didn't want it to be this way. I didn't want to start off on a bad note with my room-mate on the first day. I'd kinda hoped we'd be close. Especially because I've left all my close friends behind . . .

Good riddance, says a tiny voice inside my head and I know it's right.

This was supposed to be a fresh start. Dad kept telling me that Illumen Hall prided itself on its warm and friendly atmosphere, its moulding of the bright young citizens of the future. Bonnie and Araminta seem nice, but I just wish I knew what I'd done to get on Ivy's bad side so quickly. *Maybe we'll grow on each other . . . like parasites.*

What a thought.

I change out of my clothes, slip on my Victoria's Secret spaghetti-strap tank and shorts, and creep into bed. Instantly, I shiver. I might have to invest in some thermal PJs for life in this place.

I take my phone out, running a finger lightly over the cracks in its surface, my bottom lip poking out. The damage is only superficial, but it's super annoying, and tomorrow I'll have to email Dad and get him to send a replacement. Not exactly the 'pack your daughter off to boarding school to learn to be more independent' moment he was hoping I'd have here, but he'll get over it. I take a moment to scroll through the DMs, WhatsApp messages, Instagram Stories and Snapchats that I've received over the course of the day. It's the afternoon back home, and social media is a lot more active. It's strange to think that from now on, when my days are over, theirs will only be getting started.

But it's a trade-off. Leaving my old life behind means leaving my ghosts behind too, and that's definitely a good thing.

I hear a small cough, and turn to see Ivy sitting up in bed. I get the impression that she's been watching me, although her eyes are intently trained on the book in her hand: *The Handmaid's Tale*. Required reading for English class, I guess.

There's a very light knock on the door and a face peers round it. 'Everything all right in here, girls?'

'Fine, miss,' Ivy pipes up.

'Oh, Ivy – great to have you as house prefect this year, not that it was in any doubt! And in lower sixth too – I'm so proud of you.'

I resist the urge to roll my eyes. Why does everyone around here seem to worship the ground that girl walks on?

Then the teacher's eyes turn to me. She's smiling warmly, but a small frown appears between her eyebrows as her eyes flick between me and my bedsheets. I look down at my covers – they're not controversial at all, just my beautiful butter-yellow sheet set I bought from Anthropologie, decorated in delicate appliqué flowers. There can't be anything in the rulebook against adorable floral bedding, surely?

'Have we met yet? I'm sorry, my mind is a blur in the first days,' she says.

I shake my head. After a moment of hesitation, I swing my legs out of the bed and pad over to greet the teacher properly. If this is the housemistress that Ivy mentioned, then I want to get on her good side. 'I'm Audrey Wagner,' I say to her.

The frown falls from the woman's face, and she beams back at me. 'Our lovely new girl! Hello and welcome. I'm Mrs Parsons, the Helios housemistress this year. I think I have you for maths as well? You're doing the IB programme, aren't you?'

I nod. It was easier for me to transfer to do the International Baccalaureate than it was the strange GCSE/A-level system. At Illumen Hall, they prepare students for either.

'I am,' I say. 'Nice to meet you.'

'Now, you have full orientation tomorrow so I'm not surprised that you don't know our Illumen Hall rules yet.'

Mrs Parsons sticks out her hand, palm up. I look down at it, feeling stupid. She waggles her fingers at me and, when I still don't move, she sighs. 'No phones in school from Monday to Friday.'

'You can't take my phone!' I say, clutching it to my chest.

'I promise you it'll be perfectly safe – we keep them all locked up in a glass-fronted case so you can see them. In fact, come with me.'

I look over at Ivy for – I don't know – help? Support? But she's studiously reading her book. Mrs Parsons is already several steps ahead of me, so I jog to catch up with her. She stops outside a door with a small plaque on it that reads HOUSEMISTRESS. Just outside it is that glass-fronted shelving unit with our names engraved beneath each small box. Now I see that what I thought were mailboxes is actually a little zoo for phones.

'I know how you students treat these things like your own children! So here they are. It's for your own good too. Student productivity has increased by almost thirty per cent since we started this initiative. Think of all the reading you can catch up on in the evenings, just like Miss Moore-Zhang.' This time, when she holds out her hand, I place the phone in it reluctantly. Broken screen and all, it's still my connection to the outside world.

'We all have to do it,' Mrs Parsons says, gesturing to the case. Sure enough, on top of Ivy's name there's a slim black smartphone. I swallow hard, watching the housemistress lock my cellphone in the little cubby above my name.

'You'll have it back for the weekend, but make sure it's here, locked up in the case, by Monday. And, now that you know the rule, if I have to ask you more than once more, there'll be demerit points. But I'm sure we won't have that problem.' She must clock the stricken look on my face, because she places a hand on my shoulder. 'Life at Illumen Hall isn't like anywhere else. It takes some adjusting to, but you'll get used to it. And, if you have any problems at all, you know where I am.'

I turn on my heels and walk back towards my room. I feel like I'm in a daze.

'You could have warned me,' I say to Ivy, once I'm back in the room.

'I did warn you. Not my fault you chose not to listen.' She makes a deliberate show of putting her earbuds in.

'Bitch,' I mumble under my breath.

Then I frown. *What's Ivy listening to music on?* I glance over and see that she's sitting up in bed, texting.

On a phone. A brand-new iPhone.

'Where'd you get that?' I say, raising my voice. 'Hey!' I say again, when she ignores me.

'What?' She finally looks up, removing her earpods, her mouth twitching with irritation. Whatever. I need answers.

'Where'd you get that phone?'

Ivy frowns. 'My phone? I bought it in a shop.'

'Yeah, OK, but how come you have it? I saw your phone in that zoo thing outside Mrs Parsons' office.'

Ivy looks at me for the first time with what seems like pity. 'Oh, mate. *No one* hands in their real phone. Now please stop interrupting me. I have to listen to this.'

For a second, I almost call Mrs Parsons right then and turn Ivy in – but I know I won't do that. And Ivy knows it too. It's just another one of those rules that I'm gonna have to learn about this place.

Maybe Theodore was right. My seven months of bad luck might have just begun.

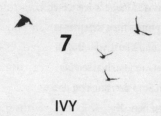

7

IVY

Audrey finally gives up the chat and rolls over with her back to me, pulling her twee yellow duvet up to her chin. I can't even imagine what that must have cost. I look down at my duvet and pick at a hem that's coming loose.

I sigh. Already life in the lower sixth isn't what I'd worked so hard for. Yes, I have the prefect badge and I'm really proud about that, but this was supposed to be MY year. The year I excelled in every subject, really put my head down and focused. A-levels are the stepping stone to the life and career I dream of. Being made to share is *really* shit. Kind of like my attitude right now. It's impossible to forget that Lola spent her final days in this very room.

I know that it must hold the echoes of her laughter, and I'm scared that one night I'll close my eyes and hear them. I try and think of something else. Nothing comes. My phone buzzes. I reach under my pillow and pull it out. It's Teddy.

> Hey, creeper. Just wanted to send you a little message. I know you're probably lying awake right now overthinking. If you need me, you know I'm here.

> Let's do lunch by the pool
> tomorrow? I feel like we haven't
> spent proper time together in
> weeks and I miss you. It was
> nice seeing you in assembly
> earlier. Stop overthinking and go
> to sleep now. X

It's frustrating how well he knows me. I go to send a reply – but notice he's typing again. Then he stops.

I wait a bit longer and stare blankly at the empty message box and the cursor blinking away. I lie back and stare up at the ceiling, the moon casting shadows on it through the gap in the curtains. Frustrated, I quit the message. Then I spot a corner of the dayglo-pink flyer I'd stuffed in my phone case. I unfold it, frowning. A message pops up from Teddy, his timing uncanny.

> PS Have you looked at the website yet?

I start typing.

> Just about to.

I take a deep breath, open up my web browser and type in the URL. It's a plain webpage, with just that creepy title – 'I KNOW WHO KILLED LOLA' – and a link beneath.

I shiver. I click on the link and it directs me to my podcast app. Taking Teddy's advice not to overthink, I hit 'subscribe' and click to listen to episode one.

THE <u>WKL?</u> PODCAST TRANSCRIPT

EPISODE ONE

[Intro] Quiet, low beats, like a heartbeat.

> ### VOICE UNKNOWN
> Welcome, curious ones, to the first episode of WHO KILLED LOLA? I'm your host, VOICE UNKNOWN, Vee for short, and I'll be spending the next few weeks with you, delving into the mystery of the death of Dolores Radcliffe, beloved student of renowned and mysterious boarding school Illumen Hall. Known as Lola to all her friends, her death was officially ruled 'by misadventure' by Kent police. But I have good reason to believe it was something far more sinister. And I also believe that whoever did it isn't finished yet.
>
> Subscribe and tune in as I hunt down clue after clue, working tirelessly to piece together this twisted jigsaw: the unsolved mystery of WHO KILLED LOLA?

[Interlude] Musical jingle plays for thirty seconds.

VEE

Where should I begin? I think it's fair to say that all of us – students and staff – at Illumen Hall were devastated at the beginning of the summer, when Lola's body washed up on the beach at the end-of-term party.

By now, most of you will have heard the story, but if you were living under a rock (or you were one of those poor students who had to head home before the infamous party), or if you're tuning in from outside the Illumen bubble, let me give you a bit of background.

Lola Radcliffe was one of Illumen Hall's shining stars. Seventeen, popular, beautiful, smart, with a head-student badge all primed and polished, ready for her final year. She had everything going for her. And surely someone who casts such a glow always leaves jealous eyes in the shadows . . .

The Illumen Hall end-of-term party is the highlight of the year, and kicks off the summer. No doubt Lola was planning to be there. We know that she left her house, dressed in a vintage Lanvin cocktail dress. We know that she got in her car, and that CCTV and traffic cameras picked her up as far as Winferne Bay, only a few miles from the party beach.

She'd sent texts that confirm she was planning to meet her friends by the fire pit, since no phones were allowed at the party.

But instead, at 11.47 p.m. exactly, it was just her body that ended up on the beach.

The police were called, everyone on the beach was interviewed, her friends and family questioned . . . and in the end the coroners ruled Lola's death as being by misadventure. They believe she fell from the cliffs, on that unstable ground that would have led fatefully to the sea. But how are they so certain? It makes no sense to those who knew her that she would risk a walk along the cliffs by herself in the dead of night. It's drilled into every student at IH how dangerous it can be. And Lola was far from stupid.

They often say that it's the boyfriend. But Lola was a social butterfly without one man to tie her down – and she was always attracting the eyes of men – even those who had no business loving her.

And friendships are sometimes even more dangerous than relationships. What about the public falling out that saw Lola crying in the sixth-form bathroom? Did jealousy push someone over the edge?

Or was Lola simply in the wrong place at the wrong time? Did you know that several suspicious persons were reported to have been near the cliffs that night? What do you think the police have to say about that?

I know that something doesn't add up. I'm not happy. I'm not satisfied. And I'm not going to let it rest.

[Interlude] Dramatic music plays.

We'll be talking to the detectives on the case.

A MAN'S VOICE
We left no stone unturned in our investigation. Now excuse me, I have serious work to do.

VEE
We'll be talking to Lola's family.

A YOUNG MAN'S VOICE
She had no history of mental illness. She was always so happy, like sunshine in a bottle. We can't understand it.

VEE
Her teachers.

ANOTHER MAN'S VOICE

She'd confided in me that she knew her parents
wanted her to go to university, but she wanted to
pursue her dream of acting, and I encouraged it.
She had a lot of potential.

VEE

Her friends.

A YOUNG WOMAN'S VOICE

I just don't get it. She had plans. Dreams. She
wouldn't have done this; I know it.

VEE

But do you think someone would want her dead?

THE SAME YOUNG WOMAN
[long pause]

Of course not. But she was so wild and carefree,
you know? She was a light. A beacon. But lights
attract bad things as well as good. And she loved
danger.

[Interlude] Quiet music plays.

VEE

Sometimes the police settle for the easy answer.
But those of us who knew Lola can't just stand by.
There are too many unanswered questions. Too
much that doesn't make sense.

And, of course, there's the question of that mysterious magpie tattoo ... What if her death had nothing to do with Lola at all, but with the very school she loved? Every student at Illumen Hall is warned about the dangers of 'crossing the magpies', but it's treated like a fun tradition, part of the school's charm.

What if ... it means something more?

And what if ... instead of a suicide, Lola's death was a murder?

[Interlude] Dramatic music plays.

                    VEE
Thank you for joining me for this introductory episode of the WKL? podcast, where we will get to the bottom of what happened to Lola Radcliffe – together.

Next week, I'll be airing my interview with the lead detective on the case, and sharing what I've learned about that magpie tattoo. Not everything is as it seems. Don't you want to know who's really been controlling these corridors? I can tell you it's not Mrs Abbott and her band of prefects ...

[Interlude] Sound builds.

Tune in next time for the second episode of WHO KILLED LOLA?

[End] Music plays.

8

IVY

Across the grounds, the morning dew has settled on the tops of the late summer flowers and clings to the neatly cut grass. A fresh mist hovers round the roofs of the buildings and the crisp air hits my lungs as I step out and take a deep breath in. I love being outside, come rain or shine, snow or sweltering sun. Just being able to look up at the sky and take in the fresh air has always been like a drug. An instant dopamine hit; there really is nothing like it. And when I've barely slept – like last night, after listening to that podcast – it helps me feel refreshed.

My feet pound along the woodland path that leads down towards the shoreline. My upper lip is salty with sweat, my heart beating wildly. Running here is so much better than running round the streets of London. Here, I don't even need to put music on (though I wear my earbuds anyway, in case anyone sees me – so they don't try to speak to me). It's much better to listen to the sound of the birds and to hear the waves crashing against the cliffs as I run closer to the shore. I love that feeling of the air rushing past my ears and through my hair, pushing my way forward with my arms, adrenaline pumping through my body. Aged nine, I lifted the first-place trophy for the Kent Junior Schools Cross-country Championships, beating every kid my age, and the older ones, in every school in our region. My mum kept all the medals and trophies as the years went on, although I'm pretty sure they just collect dust in a box somewhere these days.

I picked my favourite route this morning, round the science building, through the wood, over the narrow strip of land that separates the school from the mainland, then finally along the coast to an abandoned chapel. It's early, so it's really quiet. I'd left Audrey snoring in bed. I could tell she hadn't gone to the website on the flyer last night, unlike every other student. If she had, she couldn't have slept so soundly. I find her baffling. How could anyone be so wilfully ignorant?

I'd been unable to control my morbid curiosity. The podcast presenter was completely anonymous, the voice run through some kind of software to disguise it so I couldn't even tell if it was a man or a woman.

Of course, what Vee said must be completely wrong.

The police said it was an accident. Lola wasn't murdered, no matter what some anonymous randomer said. Only cowards hide behind a disguise, like trolls on Twitter with their little egg icons. In fact, that's exactly what this person was doing. Trolling the school. After listening last night, I immediately texted Harriet. Harriet and I have been friends for years. She was the first student in Year Seven who introduced herself to me. A bit brash, excruciatingly honest, but with a heart of gold. Sometimes she's as irritating as hell, never thinks before she speaks and gets herself into a lot of trouble, but we've been stuck together like glue throughout my years at Illumen Hall.

She agreed that the whole thing feels completely tasteless. A girl is dead – and this person is essentially just gossiping about it. I guess this anonymous creep is going to drag out Lola's death for as long as they can.

I pick up my pace, trying to outrun the images in my mind's eye . . . the ones of Lola's blue lips and that hideous tattoo. I really thought the new term was going to be the end of it. That I could forget about that night, and focus on my future.

The only person out at this time is Mr Tavistock, the groundsman. He's pushing a wheelbarrow along the path with his slow, slightly wobbly walk. I don't know who's holding who up at this point. He seems to be as eternal as the stone walls, destined to wander the grounds long after I've graduated. I pass his tidy little cottage, one of a series of dwellings dotted round the outskirts of the school grounds, homes for some of the teachers and their families or other school caretakers. Of course there's a beautiful Tudor cottage for the headmistress, its walls almost as ancient as the oldest building in Illumen Hall.

Old Mr Tavistock took me under his wing when I first started here. I'd often take walks around the grounds on my own and we eventually started chatting; he'd even join me occasionally. He taught me about the different flowers blooming through the seasons and the bugs and wildlife flourishing in the school grounds. One of my favourite things to do is report back to him about the birds I've seen on my walks or runs. His face always lights up when I pretend to be excited by a woodpecker. I think he's a little lonely – this stupid rumour circulated about him not having a wife because he murdered her and threw her body in the lake. School rumours can get so ridiculously out of hand. I know he's harmless and very sweet-natured, and his wife died of breast cancer fifteen years ago. I know this because we talk about our families a lot. I know that Mrs Tavistock's favourite flower was a peony and her favourite bird a robin. I often spot him talking to the robins and I'm convinced he believes they're her, just checking in on him.

Mr Tavistock lifts his hand and I wave back. In a way, he's like a grandfather to me. His family have been tending the grounds for generations, so he knows Illumen Hall inside out.

Once I'm past his home, I don't bump into anyone else and there's no sound but the crunch of twigs beneath my feet and the sway of leaves above my head. I savour the peace and quiet. By the time I get back from my run, the other students will be waking up for their first official day of term. Everyone will want to discuss the podcast, so I have to clear my head. I have to be ready.

My jog takes me through Brathebone Wood, and I duck under branches as long grass licks at my knees. The trail is faint at the start of the school year, not yet trampled down under the feet of hundreds of cross-country runners. I like making my small mark on this place. I've seen firsthand how the grass regrows, the branches creep back in, the ground grows wild again over the brief summer months. The school will forget me as soon as I graduate, unless I do something truly drastic in the next two years.

Like rob a bank. A lot of money might buy my name on one of the wings, or one of the facilities. The Ivy Moore-Zhang Library. Has kind of a nice ring to it. And it would be a change from all the boring old white men's names that adorn most of the halls and classrooms.

The track narrows as I cross over the bridge on to the mainland. I stick to the wood, keeping to higher ground, not following the road that would lead to the nearest town, or the footpath as it swerves down towards the beach.

I close my eyes briefly and, as I open them, a magpie shoots out from the tree just above me. Dipping and diving its way through the branches, it follows me for a short while. I salute it as it crosses my path, and watch as it disappears into the trees. I always give a magpie a salute if it crosses my eyeline, something my grandmother used to do to ward off bad luck. And that's definitely something I want to avoid right now.

I'm just approaching the field with the abandoned church when my heart drops and my breath catches in the back of my throat. I have the horrible feeling that someone's following me.

It's then that I hear a crunch on the ground that didn't come from my feet. Instead of turning to look who's following me, my instinct is to reach down and grab a small rock.

'GOTCHA!' says a male voice as he grabs my shoulders.

I fling my body round, every muscle tense. When I register who my assailant is, the rock tumbles from my fingers. I rip the earbuds from my ears. 'Teddy, what the hell?'

He kisses me on the lips even though my body is as rigid as a board. 'Sorry, I thought you heard me. I yelled your name.'

'Headphones,' I say. I narrow my eyes, because I don't think he did yell my name. I would have heard it. *He* doesn't know that my music was silent. I wonder what game he's trying to play. 'You scared the absolute shit out of me. Why on earth are you out here? Have you followed me the whole way?' I shake out my arms and brush my hands together to get the mud off them. My adrenaline is still pumping, so I walk on. He follows alongside me.

'As if I could ever keep up with your ridiculous pace. No, I know your favourite route. I knew you'd be coming past, as you always do, so I just thought I'd wait . . .'

'Well, that's not *at all* creepy . . .'

He shrugs. 'I mean, now that I've said it out loud, it does sound a little . . . much? But honestly, Ivy, I didn't know how else we would get to talk. I feel like you're avoiding me. You didn't reply to my texts last night after you went to the website.' He stops and grabs both my hands, bringing them into his chest. He stares at me with his intense, rich brown eyes. I immediately feel uncomfortable.

'Did you listen?' I ask him. I don't have to clarify.

'Yeah.'

'What did you think?'

'That this Vee person is full of shit. The police seem pretty sure no one else was involved and I'm more inclined to believe them over some random. What about you?'

I sigh. 'What I think is: are you finally going to tell me

where you were that night?' I hold his gaze, so I can catch his reaction.

He looks stricken, like I've reached out and slapped him across the face. 'I told you, I –'

'You said you were with your family, but Mia says you left after dinner and didn't come back until she'd gone to bed.'

This is the same conversation we've had all summer. Teddy won't tell me the truth. And his little sister Mia has no reason to lie.

He hangs his head. At least he has the decency to look ashamed rather than defiant. 'I swear I was on my way, but once I got to the party it was already over. The police were there.'

'It doesn't matter. You weren't there. You weren't with me when . . .' The rest of the words choke up my throat. *When her body washed up on the beach. On the worst night of my life.* He doesn't have that image seared into his brain. He can move on.

'So I guess I *am* avoiding you. I thought I made it pretty clear over the summer that I wasn't looking for a serious relationship anyway.' I pull my hands away and carry on walking.

'Ivy, we spent many a night together over the summer – are you telling me that meant absolutely nothing? If you're saying you just want us to be friends with benefits, I'm down for that. But can you just let me know?'

I start jogging as I feel my blood begin to boil, and Teddy has no choice but to trot alongside me, even though he's wearing white Converse, which are now covered in mud.

'That's not what I'm saying. I like you, you're great and yes . . . we had some fun times together over the summer. But I just want to focus on school right now, Teddy, you know I do. I just want to cool this off for a bit . . . OK?' I slow to a stop and smile at him. He *is* ridiculously hot. His dark floppy hair is slightly curled from the moisture in the air and his chiselled cheekbones are tinged pink with the cold. He's not shaved in a while so there's a bit of stubble on his face, making this conversation all the more difficult, because as I'm looking at him now I want nothing more than to pull the muddy Converse off, rip off his trackies and push him against the nearest tree.

He flicks his fringe and shrugs. 'That's cool. I get it.'

I know he doesn't. And I'm not even really sure myself, if I'm being totally honest. But he's fast becoming the distraction I don't need. I can feel myself falling – and that's not my style. I have these last two years at Illumen to get the marks I need to follow in my mum's footsteps and get into Oxbridge.

'You know what, Ivy? This is really shitty. I thought this was going to be *our* time. This is my last year, and I even made sure that I was a prefect too so that we could hang out together!'

'I didn't *ask* you to do that.' I really want to keep running. I can hear the tracker in my earpiece, the tinny voice telling me: *Last mile in fifteen minutes*. I'd forgotten to pause it on my phone. It's going to mess up all my stats; my training is important to me. School's important to me. If Teddy can't see that, then he's not the right person for me.

We've known each other since I started in Year Seven.

He was the year above, a nerdy little kid who loved gaming and always seemed to have the latest tech – but he grew into his looks and now he's painfully gorgeous.

Nothing happened between us until the summer after Year Ten, at one of the beach parties. A bit tipsy, he'd held my hand at sunset after an evening of catching each other's gaze, and he'd guided me down to the water where we drunkenly kissed for what felt like hours. It was electric immediately. You could almost hear the blood pumping through our bodies as we pressed against each other. I went from barely thinking about him to starting Year Eleven with him on my mind all day every day.

He blew up my phone all day every day too. Sometimes just with a joke, or a meme he'd found that he knew I'd like. Sometimes it was a selfie of him at his part-time job in the local Italian, smiling away, holding a handful of freshly made linguine.

But very quickly I made the decision to make it more of a physical thing than an emotional one. I didn't have time for a boyfriend even then, though I'd be lying if I said I didn't know he wanted more from our hook-ups. He's a good guy, so surely someone who has the time and the brain space for him will snap him up. I just can't be that person.

'I *do* like you, Ivy. More than I care to admit, standing here in the freezing cold at seven a.m. I've wrecked my sodding trainers too . . .' He leans in and cups my chin, his cold lips almost touching mine.

'I'm sure the mud will come out, Teddy,' I whisper against them.

'OK, OK, I understand. We can cool off, but I still want to be the only guy you creep on.' He laughs at his own stupid Ivy pun, the same one he's made for literally years, but my face doesn't change. He sighs. 'I'll leave you to your run. I have prefect duties to set up for.'

He leans forward, but I turn my face at the last second so that he kisses my cheek instead of my lips. I segue quickly into a jog so that he's left confused as to whether that was an accidental move or on purpose.

I like Teddy. It's just that I like my Plan even more. And I'm going to have to log a *lot* of miles if I'm going to forget about the podcast and Lola's death and get my focus back.

From behind, I hear him shout, 'You're trouble, Ivy Moore-Zhang . . .' and with that I run along the track faster than I've ever run before.

9

AUDREY

I see what Mrs Abbott meant when she said that today things were gonna get chaotic at Illumen Hall. I'd woken up, walked bleary-eyed to the communal shower, but had the shock of my life when I left the cubicle in just a towel and soaking wet hair to be greeted by some wide-eyed parents standing in the hallway, carrying boxes. I'd never sprinted so fast in my life, back to the sanctuary of my room.

I lean against the door, breathing heavily. Ivy has already left for the morning – she must be one of those early risers – and I'm glad to have a moment to myself. Today is gonna be different. Yesterday was a blip, an anomaly. This is the day that my life at Illumen Hall *really* gets started. We don't have many classes to begin with, so I think I might try and find this SCR that Theodore was talking about, and accidentally-not-so-accidentally bump into him. I intend to make a better second impression.

I take my time getting dressed. Considering we didn't have a uniform in my old high school, I never thought I'd wear something like this. But I like the feeling that I belong. To Illumen Hall. I throw on some bangles to bling up the look even more.

I blow-dry my hair, taking the time to curl it into perfect beach waves. I start applying my make-up when there's a knock on the door.

'Come in?' I say.

Mrs Parsons pops her head round the door. 'Oh, Audrey – there you are.'

I frown, my make-up brush still in hand. 'Am I supposed to be somewhere?'

'Did you not read your timetable? Breakfast is at seven thirty.'

'Oh, I'm not hungry.'

Mrs Parsons tuts at me. I'm really starting to dislike this woman.

'If you're here and moved in, you have to attend. Those are the rules.'

'What about Ivy?' I blurt out. 'She's not here.'

'Prefects have their own privileges, earned through hard work, and they have lots of additional responsibilities.' She looks down at her watch. 'If you head down now, you'll still make it. It'll be a great start to your day – it's not often you get to eat in the Great Hall!'

It takes everything I have to avoid a giant eyeroll. 'OK, I'll be down soon.' I only have one eye done, but it won't take me more than a couple of minutes to finish off the other side.

To my surprise, Mrs Parsons walks in and grabs something off the top of Ivy's dresser. A packet of make-up wipes. She hands it to me. 'You can even it out as we walk,' she says.

'You're kidding. Make-up is against the rules here too?'

She purses her lips. It doesn't look like she's joking at all. 'If it makes you late, then yes. So unless you're looking for your first demerit points already . . . ?'

Internally, I scream. I take a wipe from her, passive-aggressively yanking it so that she drops the pack and has to pick it up from the floor. I furiously scrub at my eye as I follow her. I walk past my phone, still encased in its glass prison. And the same old iPhone sits in Ivy's spot. I almost growl, I'm so annoyed.

Yet my bad mood is swept away by the sight of the Great Hall. It's like something from a Shakespearean film set – a long rectangular space with dark mahogany beams that criss-cross like the skeleton of a ship under a cream-coloured ceiling. Huge tapestries hang on the walls, depicting scenes right out of myths and legends. The tables are laden with breakfast goodies – pancakes and fruits, steaming trays filled with scrambled eggs and sausage. It feels like a cruise-ship buffet. I wonder if it's like this every morning, or if it's just been laid on for the benefit of the new students and their folks.

There are faces, accents and languages from all over the world here, chatting and congregating round the long wooden tables. I even think I hear a fellow American twang or two. The atmosphere is quite subdued – not the first-day-of-school chatter and excitement that I was expecting. People are huddled together in groups, exchanging gossip in hushed whispers.

They're not talking about you, not this time, I remind myself. I step into the room, holding my head up high.

'Audrey, over here!'

I swing towards the sound of my name and see Bonnie sitting with Araminta and a few other people at one of the long tables. I walk over and Bonnie scooches along the bench to make room for me.

Araminta takes the lead, doing the introductions with her charming smile. She points at a handsome guy with spiky black hair and a shining HS badge to match her own. 'This is Xander, our head boy, and next to him are Katie and Jane. They're both prefects.'

'Hey,' I say with a small wave. It feels kinda dorky, so I reach over to grab a croissant.

'Everyone, this is Audrey, our new girl from America!'

'Oh cool! What part of the States are you from?' Katie's curly red hair almost drops into her cereal as she leans forward.

'Watch out!' says Jane, sitting next to her. She catches a lock of Katie's hair before it becomes milk-soaked.

'Georgia,' I reply.

'Isn't that a country?' Xander asks.

'Is it?' I reply with a small frown.

'You have to excuse Xander – just because his parents are diplomats he's obsessed with geography,' interrupts Araminta. 'Audrey, how was your first night?'

'Oh, you know, it was OK. Kinda spooky with the wind battering the windows. Also, this place is huge. I'm never gonna learn my way around.'

'I'm surprised you didn't jump on the first bus out of this place,' mutters Jane.

'What do you mean?' I ask.

'You didn't listen?' She raises an eyebrow.

'Listen to what?'

Almost as one, the group leans back in their chairs and lets out a collective breath, exchanging surprised looks. I cringe, wondering what I could have done – or rather what I *didn't* do.

'Well, I for one am happy for you. And you shouldn't listen. It's just vile, nasty gossip anyway,' declares Araminta. 'Let's change the subject. You're in Helios House, right? What's your room number? That way we can send out a search party if you ever get lost!' She cackles at her joke.

'I'm in room seven.'

A shadow passes over Araminta's face, so quick I almost miss it. Then her eyes turn glassy with the welling of tears. It's not the response I expect. 'Oh, poor you!'

'What is it?' I ask in alarm.

'You have Lola's old room. Poor, poor Lola,' she says, more to herself than to me. *Oh, right.* I have to admire how perfectly she looks the picture of grief, with her hands clasped in her lap and a single tear rolling down her cheek.

'Minty, are you OK?' Bonnie asks, squeezing her shoulder.

'I'm still just so upset about what happened,' she replies. There's a squeak from Jane, and then she starts crying too. Is drama contagious here?

Araminta sniffles. 'I guess we can't avoid this subject after all. You know those flyers that fell during the power cut in assembly yesterday?'

'Yeah . . .' I reply.

'They led to a website with a link to a podcast all about Lola's accident. It's the worst thing, having her death dredged up like that. To think she should have been head girl right now, not me.'

'It's horrible,' says Jane, wrinkling her nose.

'Disgusting,' says Araminta, nodding in sympathy. 'It's full of lies anyway and I'm sure Mrs Abbott will be shutting down whoever did this as soon as possible.'

My stomach churns. I know I shouldn't ask, but I can't help feeling curious about what everyone in the school seems to be talking about. Even though it's exactly what I should be running away from. 'So . . . if it's not too fresh, does anyone mind telling me what happened?'

Looks are exchanged between all the people at the table, but the consensus seems to land on Araminta to take the lead. She breathes in deeply.

'Wow, I kind of forget that there are people in the world that might not have heard what happened to Lola Radcliffe.' She pauses as if searching for the right place to start. Everyone around the table is quiet. 'OK, so every year we have an end-of-term party down by the beach. It's an Illumen Hall tradition, one of the biggest nights of the year, to be honest, and it was all going really well. We had perfect weather, a bonfire, great music . . . But then at some point in the night there was a scream and we all rushed down to the waves and –' Araminta's voice cracks.

Katie-with-the-red-hair picks up the thread. 'Her body washed up on the beach. Just like that. The police did this huge investigation and I'm pretty sure they interviewed the entire school over the summer, but eventually they ruled that it had been an accident. But most people think she must have, you know . . . killed herself.'

'Even though there was no note,' interjects Jane. 'And Lola would *never* have done that.'

Katie nods. 'And then yesterday that creepy podcast dropped. This anonymous voice claiming that it wasn't an accident, or death by suicide. Instead, they think it was a –'

Araminta leaps to her feet, her hands now balled into fists. 'Katie, don't you dare say it!' Her voice rings out so loudly the entire hall goes quiet. Araminta doesn't look like she cares. All her focus is laser-like on Katie, who is cowering under the force of the taller girl's rage. 'Never speculate on stuff like that. Don't you know how offensive it is? Just because you weren't friends with her doesn't give you the right to make accusations.' She flounces out of the Great Hall, leaving a dozen gaping faces in her wake.

I stare over at Katie, who looks shell-shocked. I don't blame her. But then she says something so quietly I almost think I mishear. 'It's not like you were friends with her either, Minty,' she mutters.

Bonnie jumps up and runs after Araminta. Jane turns to Xander, who gives her shoulder a squeeze, and they leave together. Meanwhile, Katie looks over at me. 'You OK?'

I realize I'm trembling so much that croissant crumbs litter my lap. I put the pastry down and brush them off. 'I just don't know what to say because I didn't know her . . . Lola.'

'Hardly anyone here was super close to her – except maybe Jane and Heloise – but everyone pretends they were her best friend, you know? Especially . . .' She nods in Araminta's direction, then shrugs. 'It's sad, but people will move on. It happened months ago. That podcast is utter crap. No one wanted to *murder* Lola. It's just creating scandal where there isn't any. Let's change the subject. How's it been sharing a room with Wunder-Ivy?'

My throat has gone completely dry at that word, but Katie doesn't seem to notice. I swallow a few times, trying to behave like a normal person who hasn't just broken out into a cold sweat. 'Wunder-Ivy?' I repeat.

She laughs, covering her mouth with her hand. 'Oh my God, please don't repeat that. You probably haven't got to know her well enough yet, but that girl is good at *everything*. Seriously, it's scary. She's some sort of prodigy. Full scholarship every year. Cross-country champion. Music maestro. She's guaranteed to be head girl next year – well, she was.'

'What do you mean?'

Katie looks around, checking no one's close enough to hear us. 'Look, this is kind of deep Illumen Hall politics stuff so I get that you're not familiar with it. But normally there's one or two prefects appointed in the lower sixth who are sort of like . . . the chosen ones. You know, they get to shadow the current head students and normally they'd get their own rooms and stuff – special privileges. That was supposed to be Ivy this year. She was Lola's chosen replacement. But now Araminta's head girl. So Ivy's position is a little uncertain. Araminta might pick someone else. Like Bonnie.' She straightens up. 'So, tell me about your classes?'

I return the smile, grateful for this normal conversation. I go on to fill her in about my schedule, and in turn she lets me know which teachers I'll like and which to avoid.

Before I know it, the bell rings. 'What's your first class?' asks Katie as we stand up and make our way out of the Great Hall.

'History with Mr Willis.'

She whistles. 'Ooh, good luck being able to concentrate in his class! Look, word of advice?'

I nod and smile as she pauses just outside the doors. 'I know you're room-mates with Ivy, but you're a natural fit with our group. Stick with us. It'll make your life a lot easier.'

'That's fine by me. I don't think Ivy has much interest in being my friend.'

'Good. That settles it. Meet us in the SCR after class?'

She flounces away before I have a chance to ask, once again, what the *hell* is the SCR?

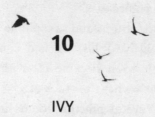

10

IVY

When I get back to school, I'm still on edge from my encounter with Teddy. I have an hour before I have to be on duty, so I quickly jump in the shower and then head downstairs into the basement of the building, where the music-practice rooms are.

Music is another escape – and a burden. Whatever I put my energy into, I have to be the best at it. I had a couple of sessions with a school therapist last year, when they worried about me burning out. But going a million miles an hour is my default speed. It doesn't take a psychology degree to figure out why.

I've always known that, if I want to get anywhere in life, I have to make it on my own. Music gave me a pathway to that – it's the reason I've got a full scholarship to Illumen Hall after all. My parents aren't in a position to help.

After Dad left, Mum enrolled me in every after-school activity possible and it's fair to say I've tried my hand at almost every musical instrument over the years. I guess throwing money she didn't have into my future was her way of coping and giving me the life she felt she failed at herself. She worked three jobs to fund my endless classes and tutoring, and reminded me constantly that nothing worth having comes easy.

Although the drums and saxophone never made it past lesson four or five (plus, we had complaints from our neighbours), it soon became clear that piano was my calling, so that's what I've stuck at.

There are several practice rooms in the basement of Illumen Hall, but my favourite has the Fazioli grand piano. It's an amazing instrument, polished to a gleaming black, not a single smudge visible on its surface. Whoever donated this piano to the school must have had some serious cash. Using just the very edge of my finger pads, I lift the heavy fallboard that covers the keys. I stretch my hands, the joints popping as I loosen them.

It takes only a moment for my fingers to adjust to the weight of the keys, to find their positions. Then my fingers are flying along the ivories, warming up with scales that would make my tutor, Miss Chigwell, proud.

I'm currently practising for my Grade Eight exam which I'll be taking in a couple of months. The first piece is Beethoven's *Presto alla Tedesca*. I feel like I've almost got it, but there's just one bit towards the end my hands fumble over every time and it's beginning to frustrate me. As I approach the part I'm struggling with, the alarm goes off on my phone – the one that means I'm supposed to be in class in thirty minutes – and I swear at myself for not realizing how long I've been sitting at the piano.

I close the lid gently and stand up, collecting myself. Then I place my palm on the lid. When I lift it up, the ghost of my hand still lies on the glimmering black surface before fading back into obscurity.

I hear soft applause coming from behind me and spin round to see Clover standing there, beaming.

'Ivy, *HONESTLY* . . . I can only ever dream of being able to play like you do.'

'One day you will, if you keep practising.' I grin as I try and swallow down my embarrassment. 'How long have you been standing there?'

'Only a couple of minutes. I just caught the end!'

'Oh, the bit I fucked up, you mean?'

'As you often say to me, "Don't be so hard on yourself – it will come eventually!" ' She erupts into a billowing laugh. I love that she finds herself so entertaining. Clover is just over five foot and very petite, with black skin, bleached curls and a quirky sense of style – but she's anything but fragile or delicate. She is feisty and bold and everything I wished I was when I was an awkward fifteen-year-old.

'What did you get up to over the summer anyway? I didn't hear from you much. I did see on Instagram that you spent a lot of time with . . . Spencer, was it?' I wink at her, knowing she'll hate me for bringing that up. 'Did I see you two together at some Extinction Rebellion event?'

'*Ivy!* Yes, we hung out, but it's not official. I kind of want to just focus on me for a bit. Do a bit of soul-searching, yanno? Especially after this Lola stuff. I feel a bit off balance. Things like that don't happen in Winferne Bay.' She pauses, watching me closely. 'How are you feeling about it all? You guys were close, right?' She sits down on the floor and crosses her legs.

'I mean, we weren't *close*-close, but we hung out a lot, especially last year. I feel a bit weird about the whole thing. I'm even in her room now . . .'

'Oh man, that's top-level weird. Sorry, Ivy, it must really suck.'

'Life goes on!' I force myself to shrug. 'Have you listened to that podcast?'

'Yeah, a bit of it. It's pretty predictable, but I do wonder if they have a point suggesting it could be murder. There are some definite gaps in the official story. What d'you think?'

'I think it's vile. I think the person posting it is bored and wants to stir things up while this is still fresh in everyone's minds.'

'I guess so.' Clover tugs at one of her curls, lost in thought. Then she springs back to life. 'Anyway, the real reason I came looking for you, not that I didn't want a catch-up obviously, is because Mrs Abbott wants you to go to her office during your first free period at eleven. How does that probing bitch even know your timetable?' She laughs again and I join in.

'She always has to know where I am at every waking moment of the day, apparently! I wonder what she wants?' My heart sinks. I hate that she has that power over me. Have I forgotten to help register the Helios students for their library passes? No. Was I supposed to be taking families on a tour I didn't know about?! *Urgh.*

'Anyway, I'll see you around, Ivy! Send for help if she puts you in the "chokey".' Clover heads out of the door with a wink.

My phone buzzes in my pocket. It's Teddy.

> Sorry for intruding on your run. I
> mean it though. I do like you,
> Ivy. I don't want this to come to
> an end. I feel like we had a good
> thing going. T x

I don't reply. I can't think about him right now. Besides, I have less than ten minutes to drop off my sheet music and grab my books before the first lesson of term starts.

I run up the stairs, pivoting round the banister as I approach the entrance to Helios House. But then I see something that stops me dead in my tracks.

Lola.

11

AUDREY

As I enter my first class of the day, I'm grateful to see Bonnie at a desk, an empty chair beside her, and glad that she's chosen a seat by the window. She waves me over. Looking out, I can see the grounds of the school where we walked yesterday.

'Wow, breakfast was kinda intense,' I say. 'Is Araminta OK?'

Bonnie sighs. 'Everyone's a bit on edge at the moment because of the podcast thing. But Araminta's fine. She's just under a ton of pressure. She's so strong and super cool normally.'

'I'll take your word for it.'

I take a moment to inspect the room. History is located in the most modern part of the school, which is ironic. The room is pleasingly bright. There are huge floor-to-ceiling windows that automatically tint to cut the glare of the sun and, if I crane my neck, I can see the ocean. It's not nearly as serene as the coastline I'm used to back home. There are no soft sand dunes here, with waving grasses and beautiful pastel houses with wide porches. It's all jagged cliffs down to a roiling sea, the waves crashing up against the shore despite it being a nice day. The sky is blue, but the sea still looks grey and menacing.

I scan the faces, but there's no Theodore. I wonder if he's in a different year from me? I bite my lip, slightly disappointed. Ivy's not here either.

Bonnie introduces me to a couple of other people in the classroom – Max, a cute black guy with bronze-framed glasses, and Rhonda, a brown girl with long black hair tied in an elaborate braid.

Luckily, my American accent is enough to break the ice with most people. I end up chatting to them about life in Georgia, and I gather an enraptured audience as I describe the turtles that hatch along the beaches on Tybee Island.

It makes my heart ache to talk about all the good things I had at home. For so long, my memories have been overshadowed by a dark cloud. I don't think I'll ever miss my life there, but I feel . . . nostalgic for the way things were. Still, the whisperings about this dead girl have brought up so many of the issues I've been trying to put behind me, and I've worked too hard with my therapist to regress.

Even yesterday, Lydia messaged me to say she still thinks I'm running away. I'm sure Brendan agrees, although we haven't talked – he said as much before I left. It was almost too perfect that my parents had always planned to move to the UK; I just had to go with them. But Lydia and Brendan are closer to the truth than I'd like – I *did* want to run far away from that house, the mile-long beach, the dripping Spanish moss and the woman with the creepy painted tarot cards whose every prediction seemed to come true. It was just my luck that I've ended up in the middle of a whole new drama.

I'm cut off from reminiscing by the sound of the door opening. I sit up straight in my chair and the crowd around me disperses. I hope that class life will lead to something a bit more like normality.

It's not the teacher who walks in though, but Ivy. *So she is in this class*. Her face is flushed, her skin slick with sweat. Her hair is immaculate though, and I swear she's wearing a little make-up – a touch of eyeliner flicked up at the corner. How does she get away with it? I feel like I need to watch her a little more carefully to learn the tricks to life at the school.

She doesn't make eye contact with anyone, but slips into a desk right in the front row.

Striding in behind her is the teacher, Mr Willis. Now *he* catches my attention. He's got a fluffy mess of hair, little round glasses and broad shoulders that fill out his faded plaid tweed blazer nicely. He barely looks older than us – he must be in his late twenties at most. I'm surprised – all the teachers I had in the US were so much older. Under the blazer, he's wearing a cream shirt and brown pants; if I didn't know any better, I'd have thought he was an actor playing the role of a teacher. Maybe this is gonna be the first time that I pay real attention in a history class.

'All right, Illumenites,' he says, dropping his books on the desk with a clatter. 'Are we ready to get straight down to some history? We don't need any orientation lark, do we?'

Some of the other students are buzzing, as if something more interesting has happened than just the teacher walking in and asking a simple question. A dozen hands go up around me. Have I missed something? I stare down at my laptop, the cursor blinking at me furiously.

Bonnie's hand is one of the ones straining towards the ceiling, and Mr Willis nods in her direction. 'Yes, Miss Lewis?'

'Sir, are you the teacher on the podcast?' she pipes up. I watch as Ivy's head whips round and she gives Bonnie such a vicious glare that even my skin feels like it's burning with the heat of it. Bonnie doesn't notice though, her eyes trained solely on Mr Willis. Ivy seems to collect herself and spins back to face the front, her reaction smoothed over so quickly I wonder if I imagined it.

Mr Willis leans against the whiteboard, his hands drumming along the metal edge where the pens sit. 'Good ear. Yes, I suppose there's no point hiding it – it is me.'

Another dozen hands go up, but he waves them away. 'I'm not going to answer anything else about it – I don't know any more than you do. All I can say is that, when a student passes away, it affects the teachers who knew them as much as the students. We're people too, you know,' he adds. His eyes have a far-off look to them, and they turn a little glassy, as if he might actually cry. Then he blinks hard. 'On the other hand, if you truly are interested in the podcast, may I suggest that delving into the school's history is a truly fascinating endeavour. It would be worth heading to the library, which has some incredible original editions and some primary-source material. If anyone would like to write me an essay on some of the history of Illumen Hall, I could bribe you with chocolate. Anyone? Anyone?'

Those words are enough to quieten everyone down. He claps his hands together, and his eyes pass over me for the first time. But then his attention flickers back. He looks down at a piece of paper on top of a book. 'Miss Wagner?'

I nod, jumping in surprise.

Even more surprising, he walks down the aisle and shakes my hand. 'Mr Willis. Pleasure. You're from the States?'

'Georgia,' I reply.

'Some great history in that part of the world – yes. Not all of it pleasant, but still fascinating. Maybe you can write me a report about it?'

'I, uh . . .'

'I'm only teasing. It's just my sense of humour. You'll get used to it. Right, class?'

There's a titter of laughter.

'You'll do fine,' he says. 'Although you might have to catch up on your eighteenth-century English history knowledge. I'm afraid we don't have a catchy hip-hop musical to help us remember. Do you think you'll need some extra attention, Miss Wagner?'

'From you? Sure,' I say with an exaggerated wink – and the class erupts into laughter. Mr Willis's face flushes pink – he clearly ain't used to American sass.

'All right, all right, settle down,' he says as he strides towards the front of the class.

I stare at the back of Ivy's head. She was the only one who didn't laugh as I made my quip. She didn't even turn round. She looks up at Mr Willis as he passes, and I swear that she bats her eyelashes at him. He pauses for a microsecond and they lock eyes.

Wow. Is there something between this Mr Willis and Ivy? Or is she just a favourite student?

I can't help thinking there's a bit more to it than just a shared love of history. Who knew such a small school could hold so much drama?

12

IVY

As Mr Willis lays out what we'll cover in history curriculum this term, I close my eyes for the faintest second. The image of what I saw this morning remains seared into my eyeballs.

Lola's portrait is hanging at the entrance to Helios House, looming over us every time we go back to our rooms. The oil painting is eerily lifelike, her eyes piercing through the canvas. She was painted in her school uniform, before the drastic haircut – so her shoulder-length blond hair curls neatly at her shoulders, her lips slightly parted as if she's about to speak. She's walking away from the canvas, her head turned back to us, her fingers stretching out and slightly curled, as if she's trying to lead us into the portrait with her.

But Lola won't lead anyone anywhere now. She's immortalized as an Illumen Hall student. Whatever she might have gone on to accomplish or achieve ... she's now frozen in time. Just another part of the school's long history.

It took forever to convince my feet to move again. I'd only had time to change, do the barest eyeliner flick and then rush to class.

'You OK?' Harriet leans over to whisper to me.

'Yeah. Lost track of time while I was practising.'

She grins. 'No surprise there.'

Mr Willis pauses in his lecture to look at us, and we fall quiet. I guess the one good thing about history this year is having him as my teacher. When he started at our school last year, there'd been a rush of students signing up for extra history tutoring with him. He'd once presented a BBC history show as a grad student and written a book about some obscure Scottish lord – he was basically the closest thing we had to famous. He was hot too – helped along by his kind of disoriented and slightly flustered air, as if he's constantly distracted. Hot and a bit geeky. You wouldn't find one student – male or female – who didn't agree with that statement. He seemed curiously unaware of the effect he had on us too, though he made a big announcement when he got engaged to his girlfriend last Christmas, even down to showing us the vintage ring he'd found. It was kind of tacky, to be honest. But I guess he felt the need to show he was taken.

I once watched him play rugby against some of the senior boys, a teachers versus students charity event. His rugby kit showed off a surprisingly muscular frame – normally hidden under some truly hideous suit jackets. It's a shame he hides away – what's the point in working out so hard if you're going to bury it under a mountain of tweed?

I played the piano in the school musical of *Billy Elliot* last year and Mr Willis was in charge of rehearsals on a Wednesday evening. We got on really well, often joking about the same things and discussing the crazy antics his flatmates had been getting up to. On those evenings, with him in jeans and tight grey T-shirts that hugged his toned torso, I saw him in a different light.

Now, standing before me at the front of the class, all stern and assertive, but still a bit bumbly, he's definitely a lot more professional. One bit of his fringe keeps flopping on to his forehead, and he sweeps it back up every couple of minutes. In that moment, I find myself daydreaming about running my hand through his hair . . . I've been so engrossed in my thoughts that, for a few moments, I've managed to forget about Lola and the podcast drama. But now my thoughts turn back to her.

Lola smiling as she takes her iced latte.

Lola carrying out her prefect duties with endless patience.

Lola dead on the beach, a strange magpie tattoo visible on the pale skin of her back –

No!

My pen flies from my hand, spinning across the room. Inside, I groan. First lesson back and I'm already messing up. I can't get control of my thoughts. Then there's Mrs Abbott to worry about. What could she possibly want from me? We've only been back a day. My mind feels like it's in overdrive, spinning faster and faster.

Just then, my racing train of thought is interrupted by a piercing scream. I spin round and see Audrey standing by the window, pointing at something outside. When she shrieks again, I feel like I'm back on that beach, a terrible wailing in my ears:

'THERE'S A BODY IN THE WATER!'

13

AUDREY

I rush out the door, only one objective in mind. To get to the girl I saw outside, the girl face down in the pond, her long white dress billowing across the surface of the water. I hear footsteps as the rest of the class dash out behind me. It's like my legs are moving even though my mind is shutting down and thinking, *No, no, no, not this, not again . . .*

Bonnie catches up with me, and she repeats the words, 'Holy shit!' over and over like some kind of mantra. I want to take her by the shoulders and tell her to shut up, but I'm unable to summon the words.

The sun on our faces is incongruously warm as we race to the pond. Mr Willis overtakes me with his phone out, ready to call an ambulance. *Can we save* this *girl?*

'Oh, thank God,' I hear Mr Willis say once he's reached the pond. He leans down, his hands on his knees, out of breath.

I can't even bear to look, but I gather from everyone's collective sigh of relief that there isn't actually a dead body there. Bonnie and I hug, my body trembling.

Ivy stands up on the stone wall that surrounds the pond. 'It's OK, people,' she says, her voice ringing out. 'It was just a sheet that had blown into the water. Nothing to worry about.'

'Ivy's right,' said Mr Willis. His right arm is soaking wet – he must have pulled the sheet out of the pond and on to the ground. The crowd clears enough for me to see the crumpled mess. Did I really think that was a girl? *But did you even look that closely? Or did your mind just jump to the worst possible conclusion?* I shudder.

For me to instantly freak out like that? Not a good sign.

Mr Willis looks down at his watch. 'Come on, back to the classroom. We've all had a bit of a scare, but it's OK.'

Bonnie grips my arm. 'I really thought there'd been another drowning.'

I don't reply. Darkness creeps at the edge of my vision. When I close my eyes, I see a girl, face down in water, but when I open them . . . it doesn't go away.

'Are you OK, Audrey?' Bonnie's looking at me, concern in her brown eyes. She tries to catch my eye, but I can't hold her gaze. I pull away from her.

'I can't stay here. I can't take this.'

'Oh my God, you're shaking.'

'I gotta go.'

'No, don't – no one blames you.'

'I'm going to my room.' I turn away from Bonnie, from the crowds, from the pond.

'No, you can't!' I hear Bonnie call after me. 'They don't let us into the dorm rooms during school hours. Audrey, wait!'

I don't care. I don't care about their stupid school rules. All I know is that I have to leave immediately. I feel bile rising in the back of my throat. I have to keep telling myself to breathe, as if my body doesn't remember its basic functions.

Somehow I manage to find my way back to my room, and even Mrs Parsons forgives my rule-breaking when she sees the state of me. I collapse on to my bed and dive under the covers. Something unexpectedly sharp digs into my stomach.

Reluctantly, I sit up, drawing the comforter around me like I'm wrapping myself up in a burrito. Tucked underneath my sheets is a small rectangular box, tied with a green ribbon. Did something arrive from one of my friends? I can't think who would be sending me gifts. And why would Mrs Parsons hide it like that? I'm nervous now that it's some sort of practical joke. I wouldn't put it past Ivy.

I sit down on the bed, toying with the ribbon, running the silk through my fingers. It's such a small box – it can't be anything horrible. And I need the distraction after the pond incident. I slide the lid off the box. Inside is a phone.

I frown and lift it out, spotting the note underneath.

I told you this might come in handy. Theodore

I breathe a deep sigh of relief, my anxiety easing, and the note brings a welcome smile to my face. I turn on the phone, happy that Theodore had the forethought to remove the Pokémon case. I clutch it to my chest as it boots up. *How ridiculous to have such overwhelming feelings of love for an electronic device!* I'll have to be careful to hide it from the prying eyes of Mrs Parsons.

As soon as the phone turns on, a message pops up.

> I preloaded my number, just in
> case you wanted to say thanks.

I chuckle at Theodore's boldness. Maybe the polite British guy is actually just a Hollywood stereotype.

> Well, in that case, thank you
> very much.

I flick through the rest of the phone, download the apps that I need and sign in, sending my friends back home a message about my new number.

Lydia replies almost straight away with a posed selfie in giant sunglasses and holding a giant Panera iced tea.

> GLAD TO HAVE YOU BACK, BABE.
> BEEN WORRIED ABOUT YOU.

I send her a photo of the greying English skies as a response. Back home, the heat must still be searing. Here? Not so much.

But there's something else I should do now that I have a working phone, and my heart rate has returned to normal.

I guess I have to listen to that damn podcast.

14

IVY

Two of the boys are flicking the sheet at one another and Mr Willis is telling them off. The panicked atmosphere has most definitely gone. With the tweed blazer off and one sleeve of his cream shirt rolled up to frame his bicep, his hot level just rose by a solid thirty per cent.

'Stop perving, Ivy!' Harriet slaps me on the arm playfully, pulling me out of my trance.

'If everyone could start making their way back inside, please?' Mr Willis bellows. I notice everyone starting to walk back except . . . *Where's Audrey?* The prefect and room-mate in me knows I should ask Mr Willis if I can go and check she's OK, but there's also the fact that I really don't want to. So I don't.

Harriet and I link arms as we follow the rest of the class. 'What's happening with you and Teddy these days?' She squeezes my arm with excitement at the thought of new gossip.

'Honestly . . . not a lot. I sort of . . . ended it.'

She gives me 'the look' – lowering her chin and raising an eyebrow. 'Classic Ivy. Gets too serious and you run a mile. Teddy's gorgeous – even this particularly fussy lesbian can see that!' She laughs.

'This is *not* classic Ivy. It wasn't getting serious. I just want to focus on school for these next two years and he's such a distraction.'

She gives me 'the look' again and I roll my eyes as we make our way back into the classroom and take our seats. We only have ten minutes left, so Mr Willis just puts on a YouTube video as everyone is so distracted and fidgety.

As the bell chimes and I zip up my bag, I notice that Mr Willis is looking at me. I wait until everyone else has left the classroom, waving Harriet off as she makes an obscenely suggestive gesture, then approach his desk.

'Hi, sir.'

'Ivy, nice to see you again this year! How's that piano coming along?' He smiles up at me politely and then gazes down at his phone.

'Same old.' I pause. 'That was a bit wild today, wasn't it? I feel like everything's so unsettled at the moment. Things just don't feel right for our first day back.'

He puts his mobile back in a drawer and gives me his full attention. 'I think you're right. We can already see the effect that podcast has had on a lot of the students. Poor Audrey thinking the sheet was a body! Everyone must be so on edge. How are you coping?' He places his hand on my arm and I look at it for a little longer than acceptable.

'It's hard, but every day gets a little easier.' I place my hand on top of his and I feel myself blushing.

The first Year Eight student in his next class comes bounding in and Mr Willis pulls his hand from my arm so quickly I almost get friction burn.

'Well, you keep your head up and try to stay focused.

You're a bright student, Ivy! Lola would have wanted you to do well.' Back in teacher mode, he welcomes his next class.

'Thanks.' I plaster a smile on my face and leave. I sigh. Maybe I imagined the connection Mr Willis and I had last year.

Now there's another task I can't put off any longer. I turn in the direction of the headteacher's office.

Mrs Abbott's office is like a giant fish tank just off the centre of the main building. The far wall is made of one-way glass, so she can always see out, but you can't see in, unless she adjusts the opacity herself. It looks so modern encased within the old walls that it sticks out like a sore thumb, though there is something quite magnificent about the contrast. I wait outside on her plush sofa until the light shines green. I push open the heavy glass door to see she's sitting at her desk with her glasses round her neck and a pen in her mouth.

'Ivy! Hello. A lower-sixth prefect now, huh?' She smiles, and I notice a spot of red lipstick on her teeth.

'That's right! Can you believe it?' I place my arms behind my back and link my hands, wondering if I should sit down.

'Well, of course. You're one of Illumen Hall's brightest students. What an exciting two years you have ahead of you. Sit, sit. Please . . .' She gestures at the chair in front of her desk. She leans forward in her chair and I catch a whiff of her morning coffee breath, shadowed by a hint of mint chewing gum. 'And things are all right with your new room-mate?'

'Yeah . . .'

'I know it's not what you were expecting for this year, but it's important that Audrey feels welcome.'

I keep a neutral smile on my face, but inwardly I cringe. Is that why she asked me here? Maybe she's caught wind of the fact that I haven't exactly been friendly to Miss Congeniality.

'So you're probably wondering why I've called you here? Don't worry – you aren't in trouble . . . this time!' she says cattily. 'I'd actually like to ask you a small favour, and I know you'd be the best person for this.'

I relax in my chair. So I'm not in trouble.

Mrs Abbott steeples her fingers. 'There's a podcast being produced about our school. I don't know if you've heard it . . .'

'I have,' I reply tentatively, trying to quiet the alarm bells ringing in my head. This is *not* the direction I thought the conversation was going, and I'm back on edge.

'Well, it's causing me a *lot* of hassle. I need to find out who's behind it. We've already run checks on laptops, school computers and have emailed parents, but we just haven't found anything significant. We don't want to have to take this to the authorities if it *is* a student . . . you know full well that we allow – in fact, encourage! – you all to produce media and exercise your creative freedoms. However, this podcast is particularly sensitive and we feel it's very . . . *detrimental* to the student population. I'm sure you understand the importance of this, Ivy?'

'Yes, of course. The podcast you're talking about, is it the one about Lola being murdered?'

Mrs Abbott reels back at my bluntness. 'Have a lot of students listened to it?' Her eyebrows knit together in concern.

'I think so, yes. The flyers that fell during assembly had the link on them. I know a lot of people visited the website last night . . . myself included.' I pause, waiting to see how Mrs Abbott reacts.

She nods, her expression grave. 'So you understand why we have to shut this down.'

'Yes, but what exactly do you want me to do, Mrs Abbott? I'm no detective.' I shift in my seat, wishing she'd asked just about anybody else for help.

'I realize that, but I'd like you to do your best to discover who's making this podcast. I know what students are like, especially here at Illumen Hall. Secrets don't stay secrets for very long. Someone will spill the beans eventually. You may not be a detective, but you're a popular student and I know you can keep an ear to the ground for me. Ask some pointed questions maybe?'

'I mean . . . I don't know . . .'

Mrs Abbott leans forward again, arching an eyebrow. 'If you do this for me, Ivy, I will ensure you get the best possible outcome for your future. I have lunch with an old friend who's a dean at an Oxford college coming up. It would be very easy for me to arrange a meeting between the two of you . . .' There's a long, awkward silence while I digest the fact that she's very clearly attempting to bribe me into becoming her spy. She doesn't break eye contact and suddenly I want more than anything to get out of here. I swallow.

'Consider it done.' I smile as sweetly as I can and stand up to signal the fact that I'm most definitely done with this conversation.

She looks relieved. 'Great. I knew I could count on you. Have a good day, Ivy!' She turns back to her computer and waves her hand over the top of it as I shut the door behind me.

I don't think I've ever seen the headmistress look so desperate in all my time here. And, if I pull this off, maybe my future will be a bit more secure too. But I have no idea where to start to find out the identity of 'Voice Unknown'. For all I know, it could be a student, a teacher, or some desperate journalist looking for a scoop.

But, now I think about it, if someone *is* trying to profit from Lola's death, then that makes me furious. And now that I have Mrs Abbott's endorsement – no, *encouragement* – I'm not going to stop at anything to find out who's behind it.

THE <u>WKL?</u> PODCAST TRANSCRIPT

EPISODE TWO

[Intro] Quiet sound that rises slowly, like quickening heartbeats.

                    VEE
Welcome to the second episode of WHO KILLED
LOLA?, a podcast where I, your Voice Unknown,
am attempting to uncover the truth of what
happened to Lola Radcliffe, the student who sadly
passed away at Illumen Hall's summer party.

Now, I know the launch of this podcast last week
caused quite the stir at Illumen Hall – so hello and
sorry to all the students and staff listening right
now – but the truth will out.

I bet most of you are wondering why I even started
this investigation. I can shine a little light on
that – someone sent me an anonymous note
saying that there was a witness who saw TWO
people up on the cliffs that night.

Someone who has reason to question the official version of what exactly happened to Lola.

An anonymous tip – doesn't sound very trustworthy, does it? So I did what any person would do: I went to the police. After all, they seemed pretty convinced that they'd figured it all out. And, if I was wrong, they could set me straight.

Now it was pretty hard getting to talk to Detective Constable Copeland and he wasn't particularly interested in speaking to a random person who wanted to remain anonymous. He dismissed me, obviously, and we only spoke for a few minutes. But what he had to say changed how I thought about Lola's death forever. Will it change your mind too? I've put in the audio unedited so you can judge for yourself.

The sound of a phone ringing.

DETECTIVE CONSTABLE COPELAND
Hello?

VEE
Hi, Detective Copeland? I was told you might speak to me about the death of Dolores Radcliffe?

DETECTIVE CONSTABLE COPELAND
I'm sorry, I don't have time for this now.

VEE

This is the fifth time I've tried to call – please, I only need five minutes.

DETECTIVE CONSTABLE COPELAND
[long pause]

Fine, five minutes. But that's all I have for you. We probably won't even need that. There isn't anything to discuss here. This was a cut-and-dried case in the end.

VEE

Just to let you know that I'm recording this – are you OK with that?

DETECTIVE CONSTABLE COPELAND

Whatever.

VEE

You believe that this is a cut-and-dried case, but did you find any evidence that Lola's death might be by suicide?

DETECTIVE CONSTABLE COPELAND

No, we didn't. She didn't leave a note that we could find, although that's not entirely unusual with the deaths of young people. It's why the coroner ruled 'death by misadventure' rather than suicide. It may have been a tragic accident. Those cliffs have claimed many lives.

VEE

So she was alone on the clifftop?

DETECTIVE CONSTABLE COPELAND

Yes. We found no evidence of any additional persons.

VEE

But what about the testimony of an eyewitness who claims to have seen a second person?

DETECTIVE CONSTABLE COPELAND

[irritated]

How did you find out about that?

VEE

I can't reveal that information. But this witness swears to the fact that there were two people on the clifftop that night.

DETECTIVE CONSTABLE COPELAND

We carefully went through all eyewitness statements, but categorically ruled out the presence of a second person.

If that's all you're basing your questions on, then I'm afraid it's a dead end. I'm sorry, but a young woman died and we don't consider it to be suspicious. Now, if you don't mind . . .

VEE

But wait – another question, if I may – did you
ever find Lola's phone?

DETECTIVE CONSTABLE COPELAND

What? No. The students told us that they didn't
bring phones to the party.

VEE

Yeah, but that doesn't mean they didn't OWN
them. Lola definitely had a phone. Didn't they find
it near the scene?

DETECTIVE CONSTABLE COPELAND
[sighs]

No, we didn't find a phone. At the scene or
anywhere else. But we did gain access to her cloud
and there wasn't anything of note that would
point to foul play. It was probably lost at sea when
she fell.

VEE

And what about the tattoo? Everyone who was
at the party has stories of seeing a huge tattoo
of a bird – maybe a magpie? – that stretched
across Lola's back. She didn't have that before.
She was a champion swimmer – we all would have
seen it. I've done a bit of research into all the
tattoo shops in the area and none of the artists
say they tattooed a magpie in the week prior to

Lola's death. Maybe the tattooist knows what
happened to her – or can give some insight into
her state of mind before she died? Did you look
into that?

DETECTIVE CONSTABLE COPELAND
[a dark chuckle]

VEE
I don't think this is very funny.

DETECTIVE CONSTABLE COPELAND
This is why private individuals shouldn't conduct
their own investigations. You've wasted an awful
lot of your own time.

VEE
What do you mean?

DETECTIVE CONSTABLE COPELAND
Well, you can cross one thing off your list. It wasn't
a tattoo at all.

VEE
[surprised]
It wasn't?

DETECTIVE CONSTABLE COPELAND
[serious now]
No. It was drawn on with marker pen. A Sharpie.

                        VEE
But why a magpie?

              DETECTIVE CONSTABLE COPELAND
Why do kids do anything? Look, this is a very sad
case and I'm sure you're all very upset. But it
wasn't a murder. True-crime shows and podcasts
have a lot to answer for. We left no stone unturned
in our investigation. Now, excuse me, I have
serious work to do.

Sound of the phone line clicking off.

                        VEE
Were you as shocked by that revelation as I was?
Not only did he confirm to me that there WAS
eyewitness testimony (even if he discounted it),
but now we know that Lola didn't have a tattoo
after all – but an intricate drawing made with
your average Sharpie.

You'd think I'd be disappointed to hear that – after
all, there's a much smaller pool of people who
could tattoo than wield a permanent marker, so
my suspect list is growing even longer.

But perhaps even more important than WHO
drew the magpie is the question I asked the
detective: WHY? What's the significance of the

magpie? As we all know, Lola's full name was Dolores. Dolores in Spanish means sorrow.

One for sorrow.

But maybe I'm getting distracted. Perhaps it's a question of who had the most to gain from Lola's death. Maybe it wasn't a premeditated murder, but a terrible accident – caused by someone in a jealous rage? Someone who instantly benefited from her death, and has now been putting on an absolutely outrageous display of grief, when they didn't even know the victim in question . . . ?

I've disguised the next passage to preserve the anonymity of my source.

UNKNOWN FEMALE VOICE
She always wanted that head-girl spot. When Lola was given it, she told me she'd do anything to take Lola's place.
[pause]
Anything.

VEE
And how long was that before the party?

UNKNOWN FEMALE VOICE
Just a few days.

But you know what's strange? No one saw her at the beginning of the party. I'd know because I'd been waiting for her to arrive.

                    VEE
But I thought the police had accounted for all the students' whereabouts?

              UNKNOWN FEMALE VOICE
                [suddenly nervous]
Oh, uh, I've said too much already. I'm sure she must have given a good alibi to the police or she'd be a suspect, right? I gotta go.
          [sound of heels running away]

                    VEE
Suspicious, right?

[Interlude] A low series of beats sound out the close of the episode.

And that's it for this episode of WHO KILLED LOLA? Tune in next time as I continue to unravel the mystery of what really happened to Dolores Radcliffe.

[End] Music plays, growing loud before fading out.

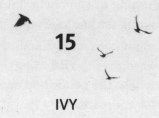

15

IVY

'Can I have a bite of that?' Harriet leans over the table and grabs my banana from my hand.

It's lunchtime and, as the sun's shining, we're sitting in our usual spot on the picnic benches near the swimming pool.

'You're such a savage, Harriet,' Max laughs.

Harriet, Max, Tom and I have a tradition of meeting on sunny days for lunch. The four of us might seem like an unlikely bunch of friends, but we each bring something to the group that makes it work. Max is a neuroscientist in the making, and Tom a gay, freckly surfer who thinks he's a stand-up comedian. Harriet and Tom are childhood friends, so when Tom arrived at Illumen a couple of years ago he automatically joined our group. If I'm honest, he'd be the first to go if push came to shove. He's harmless, but his incessant flirting can get extremely tiresome. Harriet mostly bosses him around, which is entertaining.

Max is from Toronto and moved here in Year Nine. He's probably the kindest, smartest guy I've ever met. He's also on the school hockey team, a sport which he picked up at lightning speed considering he'd never played it in Canada. Max was hugely into Harriet for a while until she explained why she'd just never be interested in him. We all laugh about it now.

'Did everyone hear the latest episode of the podcast yesterday?' Tom says, through a mouthful of crisps.

'Yeah, I listened to it this morning. How did Vee even manage to interview the detective? That's crazy!' Harriet exclaims.

'The whole thing feels pretty sketchy. Like a court case waiting to happen.' Max leans over and puts a hand on my arm. 'Have you got any closer to working out who's behind it, Ivy?'

Obviously, I told Max, Tom and Harriet about the conversation with Mrs Abbott. If they get wind of anything, they'll pass it on to me.

'Nothing, and it's been a week already. They're doing a great job at keeping it anonymous even from their sources. Whoever it is, is *too* good. Clearly someone with some knowledge of technology.' My stomach sinks. It's starting to feel like an impossible task – and on top of all my schoolwork too.

'OK, guys . . . fine. I think it's time I finally admit . . . it's me!' Tom jumps up on to the bench and stretches his arms out wide. Harriet grabs his arm and yanks him back down.

'Tom, you fucking idiot. Don't mess around like that. It's not funny. Also, when it comes to tech, you don't even know how to use TikTok. So it's clearly not you, mate.' Max chuckles and I force a smile.

'The cool kids don't use TikTok, Harriet . . .' He scowls back.

'In all seriousness, it's got to be someone with a good network. A popular student perhaps?' Max interjects.

'I don't know – a popular student feels too obvious. I was thinking it's someone who's flying under the radar . . . who'd avoid suspicion. A teacher maybe? Although I guess it would result in instant dismissal,' I add.

'Yeah, a very bad career move if you're found out. To be a teacher here you have to be next-level smart and the tests they make them do are supposed to be absolutely impossible.' Tom carries on munching his way through his crisp packet, so he's speaking with his mouth open. Gross.

'Are you talking about the podcast?' A voice I know all too well comes up behind me and I watch as Harriet's face lights up.

'Look who it is! Nice of you to join us. Take a seat!' Harriet slides up the bench, making room for Teddy to sit down opposite.

'No, this side of the bench is so much warmer,' says Tom with an exaggerated wink.

'Down, boy,' says Harriet with a laugh.

Teddy smiles at me as he sits next to Harriet and I smile back, an automatic reflex. Why does he have to be so freaking cute? It makes keeping away so much harder.

'We are indeed talking about the mysterious Voice Unknown,' says Max.

'It's got to be a journalist, right?' Teddy says.

I shrug. 'Most likely. That's the direction I've been leaning towards, but I still have literally no idea . . .'

'Guys, did you hear that someone in Year Ten says they

heard *screaming* down the hallway by Vega House the other night?' As Harriet talks, the hairs on the back of my neck stand up. 'Then someone else said they heard the music that was playing that night on the beach when her body was discovered. What song was it again?'

'Wasn't it that "Pumped Up Kicks" song?' says Max. 'I remember thinking how weird it was. It's so peppy, but it's actually about a teen shooting if you listen to the lyrics.'

'Oh God. That's the one! Yeah, someone said they heard that exact song echoing down the hallway to the dining room! Obviously, it's all bull. Ghosts and messages from beyond and all that. If Lola really was a ghost, pretty sure she wouldn't come back here . . .'

They all seem to be vibing off this morbidity, these ghosts, noises, memories of Lola . . . and my breathing is getting shallower. Then I feel a hand on my knee under the table and know immediately it's the firm, familiar grip of Teddy. I lace my fingers round his and squeeze. I know I shouldn't be encouraging this after our last talk, but I can't help it. This conversation is stressing me out and I can feel my throat closing up. In that moment, Teddy knew I needed reassurance, and without having to say anything he gave it to me.

'Anyway, guys, enough talk of death and ghosts. Harriet, how's Cassie?' Teddy interrupts while squeezing my hand back.

'She's fine. Says the college is pretty dull, but there's an old public toilet on the grounds that they all gather in to smoke . . . so I guess it's not all bad!' She cackles loudly. 'Guys, I really miss her. It was nice seeing her every day over the summer. Thank God for FaceTime though, eh? Plus, half-term can't come soon enough.'

Harriet and I have always spent our summers together, with me visiting her family home as much as possible to get out of our small London flat. But last summer was different. For a start, Lola died – and I pushed everyone away. Then Harriet met Cassie and fell head over heels in love. It was the first summer we weren't in each other's pockets. I was happy for her, but so wrapped up in my grief at the same time. I practically threw myself at Teddy as a welcome distraction. I darted between my mum's flat and his family's enormous countryside property, the differences between us never more stark than in the moment I'd step off the train platform and into one of his fancy cars.

Just then, I spot Clover making her way across the field towards the art building.

'Got to dash, guys. I need to speak to Clover about our duet this year!' I hop up from the table, throwing a peace sign in the air as I leave. 'Clover, wait for me!'

She turns round and stops. 'Hey, Ivy!'

'You're a hard one to get hold of during the week! I've got this book of sheet music for you. Have a look and see if the piece I marked sounds good.' I rip open my bag and flip through until I find it.

'Ah, thanks, Ivy! I've kind of been neglecting my practice recently, so probably should get on that.'

'How come? Found something new to protest about? Oh God, please don't tell me you want Ms Cranshaw to make more vegan meals. You know she absolutely ruins tofu.'

'No, nothing like that – just my coursework getting away from me already. How's your mission going, by the way?' she asks, tilting her head to one side.

'The podcast thing? No luck. Have you heard anything?' I had to bring Clover into the loop too. But she's like my little sister and the more eyes and ears I have, the better, right?

She pauses, pressing a finger to her bottom lip. 'Not exactly. Well . . .'

'Go on. Seriously, I have no leads so, if you have something, spill!'

'OK, it might be nothing. But everyone loved Lola, right? I mean, why go around spreading gossip?'

'Good point.'

'So what if it's someone who *doesn't* know Lola? Totally new to the school?'

'Like one of the Year Sevens?' I ask sceptically.

'Or not. I dunno. Probably a wild theory. I know the voice is all creepy and disguised, but I thought I heard a turn of phrase that was kind of . . . American.'

I frown. 'I hadn't thought of that.'

'Well, it was just a thought. Thanks again for the music. I'll let you know how I get on!' She puts up both her thumbs in that cute way of hers.

'No, wait a sec.'

My mind is running at a hundred miles an hour. There are loads of new kids in Year Seven of course, but there's no way an eleven-year-old could pull this off. However, there *are* a few other new students, and the most obvious one shares my room.

I think back to how pale she went at the first mention of Lola's death, and the drama she caused in history class for no reason at all. She's so secretive with her laptop – she's been hiding it under her duvet all week – and she was so cut up about her phone being taken away . . .

It makes total sense that she's hiding something. And, thanks to Clover, I think I know exactly what it is.

16

AUDREY

Hey, what are you up to?

My phone lights up with a message, and I can't help the smile that creeps on to my face when I see the name of the sender.

Theodore.

Oh, you know, hanging out at
the SCR.

Wow, like a real Illumenite!

Haha, I guess so. Only taken me
a week.

It had been Bonnie who finally told me that the SCR is the senior common room.

'Ohhh,' I said. 'Wait – what's a common room?'

Bonnie had laughed. 'Only the place you'll hang out the most in the whole school.'

She wasn't wrong. The common room is like an enormous

lounge, filled with old leather sofas and rich, patterned carpets. Students are relaxing everywhere, some playing what looks like pool at the back of the room. There's no TV, but some students gather round laptops, streaming movies in their free periods.

Today I'm sitting with Araminta and Bonnie on a pair of chestnut-brown leather sofas, an abandoned game of Cards Against Humanity on the low wooden coffee table in front of us. Araminta leans forward. 'So, who are you texting?'

'Oh, just some guy I met on my first day here. I haven't seen much of him around since then unfortunately.'

'Ooh, tell!'

'It's probably nothing. Some guy called Theodore? I don't know his last name.' I feel a blush rising in my cheeks.

Araminta's eyes widen and then she smiles. 'Oh sure, we know him, don't we, Bonnie?'

'Yeah . . .' she says with the slightest hint of hesitation.

'He's cute – but a bit too techy for me,' continues Araminta. 'I swear if he wasn't at school he'd be gaming all day. But I could see you guys together. You should totally go for it!'

'Oh, I don't know about that. Besides, I swore off guys for a while. Brendan and I broke up just before I came out here and it's still a little fresh. Wanna see a pic?'

'Do you even have to ask?'

I pull up an old picture of Brendan and me on the beach, his tanned arm lying across my shoulders as he pulls me close into his bare chest. He always had such muscular arms from swimming on the varsity team – and a great body in general. But there really was something about those arms. My cheeks are rosy in the photo (from a couple of beers we'd swilled), my eyes closed. I can almost smell the light coconut scent of suncream, feel the gentle breeze off the ocean as it tousles my hair . . . I look happy.

Then my gut twists as I see my old home in the background – the cream-coloured clapboard and white-pillar-framed wrap-around porch.

I put down the phone.

'Oh my God, he is so gorgeous,' says Araminta, grabbing it off the table and zooming in on Brendan's face. 'I wouldn't have been able to leave a guy like that behind! I swear they make them better in America.'

'I sincerely doubt that,' I say with a big eyeroll, stretching out to take my phone back.

'Don't you miss him loads?' Bonnie asks.

I shrug. 'Sometimes. But, most of the time, I'm glad I left. Otherwise how would I have met you guys?' I say, trying to inject some brightness into my tone, hoping they don't catch how artificial it is. 'This place is way more interesting than my old school anyway. Even your "common" room is fancy!'

'You're telling me. It could be cleaner though.' Araminta reaches up and runs a finger along the top of the mantelpiece, and wrinkles her nose at the dust. 'I might mention to Mrs Abbott that the feathers aren't doing their jobs very well.'

'Feathers?' I ask, frowning.

'Oh right! You wouldn't know. Just our little Illumen Hall word for the domestic staff here. It's like having our own language, honestly,' Araminta says with a laugh. There's a commotion from behind me, and she tuts.

I look back to see that Ivy has entered the common room, followed by a younger student carrying a bunch of folders.

'Hey, Ivy.' Araminta raises her voice so that she can be heard across the room. 'You know that Year Tens aren't allowed in the senior common room. Tell Clover to go back downstairs.'

To my surprise, Ivy strides straight over to us – looking directly at *me*. Clover follows in Ivy's wake, ignoring Araminta entirely.

'I don't know what you're playing at, Audrey, but I'm on to you. I know you're responsible,' Ivy says, her arms folded across her chest.

I frown. '*On to me?* I have no clue what you're talking about.'

'Oh right. So it's only a *coincidence* that this podcast started just as you arrived at the school? I know everyone in this place and *you're* the only one who "claims" not to have listened to it. So what's the plan? Trying to become internet-famous or something off the back of our tragedy?' The rest of the common room falls silent, everyone turning to face us.

I stand up, my body shaking with rage. 'You think *I* had something to do with this? I had no idea who this Lola person was before coming here, had no idea she'd died and I'm sorry, but there's no freakin' way I would have come to this school if I'd known. What about *you*? You're the one who's never in our room, who's always skulking about all over the school. Maybe it's *your* podcast and you're just trying to throw suspicion wherever you can!'

'That's ridiculous. Why would I want to create a podcast like that? I'm trying to figure out who's doing it so that it can be stopped. I just want everyone to forget about the whole thing!' The last words fly out of Ivy's mouth and she immediately looks like she wishes she'd never said them. Her lips clamp shut and tears spring up in her eyes.

She turns on her heel and storms out, Clover slowly inching her way out behind her.

'Holy crap, what just happened?' asks Bonnie.

Araminta stands up and puts her hand on my wrist. 'It's OK, Audrey. Ivy's clearly lost her mind.'

'I'm not responsible for that . . . that podcast thing,' I say, the words stuttering as my heart hammers in my chest.

'We know . . .' says Bonnie, but I can barely hear her.

All I can hear is screams.

'Do something!'

'Call nine one one!'

'DO SOMETHING!'

'You *were responsible.'*

'You *were responsible.'*

I squeeze my eyes tightly shut. Suddenly the wood-panelled walls feel like a prison too. I can't stay a moment longer. I need to get out.

17

IVY

Once I'm far away from the common room, I take a deep breath and lean back against the banister.

Fuck. What have I done?

It doesn't make me feel good knowing I accused Audrey of something so huge. But, after Clover planted the idea in my head, it's like I saw red. Even as the words were coming out of my mouth, I heard how ridiculous they were. Audrey spends more time on her nails than schoolwork and, despite our differences, she doesn't really seem like the spiteful type.

It's been a particularly weird start to the term for me, and I suppose Audrey has borne the brunt of that. But, even as I think about trying to build a bridge between us, I remember her instant alliance with Araminta, Katie and Bonnie. Araminta is all sweetness and light on the outside, but rotten to the core underneath. We're civil with one another, most of the time, but we've definitely clashed over the years. It worries me that Audrey has slipped right into her circle.

I look down at my watch and swear under my breath. Now I'm late for the Yearbook meeting, and I know Araminta won't be happy. Well, she'll just have to deal.

Straight after it's over, I'll find Audrey and apologize. It's the right thing to do.

I arrive at a small, slightly dank room beneath Polaris House, lit only by a very tiny square window near the rafters in the roof. It smells like stale mothballs. I spot Araminta, Katie and Jane talking quietly together around the table, and Harriet's on the other side, doodling on her notebook. To my surprise, Bonnie's there too. She isn't on the Yearbook Committee, so why is she here? Their hushed tones and hurried whispers come to a halt as I close the door behind me. Araminta locks eyes with me as I approach the table. 'Well, that was quite the outburst.'

I tuck my hair behind my ear. 'I know.' I try and sound bored. 'I'll apologize to Audrey as soon as we're done here.'

'What happened?' Harriet looks up from her notebook.

'I'll tell you later,' I mumble, sitting down next to her. There's a distinct chill that has nothing to do with this draughty old part of the building.

'We do need to talk about this bloody podcast though,' says Araminta. She seems really riled up. There's colour high in her cheeks, and her eyes are wide.

Here we go.

'What about it?' I ask, eyeing her up.

'It's just not *right* and, since I'm head girl, I want to make it my priority to get it shut down.' She nervously bites her nails like she's not eaten for weeks. 'Xander's against it too.'

'Where is our head boy by the way?' I ask, looking around.

'She's right,' Bonnie chimes in, cutting me off. 'How is this anonymous person getting away with it?'

I sigh. I *can't* let Araminta work out who's behind the podcast before I do. 'Look, I know we're all pissed off about it – me more than anyone – but it's all speculation at this point. The person is just going over old ground.' I pull out my notebook, pointedly laying it on the table. If this Yearbook meeting isn't going to happen, there are more important things I could be doing. Like finding Audrey to put my guilty conscience to rest. And then discovering the *real* person behind the podcast.

'Ivy, why aren't you more bothered by this?' It's disgusting to be talking about Lola's death so openly. I heard a group of Year Eights discussing the podcast yesterday and saying they think maybe another student was involved . . . They'll suspect one of us next!' Araminta's eyes dart round the room. Is she looking for reassurance, or does she genuinely worry about being a suspect?

I've known Minty for a long time. She's one of those people that seem to get away with doing the minimum effort – she always played second fiddle to Lola. She's never been top dog. Now that she is, she seems to be loving the attention. Still, it's pretty out of character for Araminta to be this bothered by the podcast. I'm actually surprised she's not begging to be a guest. She's totally the sort of person who thrives on school gossip. Actually, the fact that she's *not* a guest makes me wonder . . . maybe she's the Voice Unknown?

'Why are you so bothered, Minty?' I furrow my brows in confusion.

'I'm not bothered! I just . . . I don't know. It's not right that this anonymous person is dragging this up when they've no real evidence. That's what the police are for. We gave our statements. It was horrible that night.'

'Didn't you arrive late though?' Harriet pipes up, looking up from doodling a heart round Cassie's name, and it stops Araminta mid-rant.

'What?' she splutters.

Harriet shrugs. 'I mean – what about what was said in the podcast? About you not being there when . . . well, when the whole body-washing-up thing happened.'

'I was there!' Araminta says, her voice rising in pitch. Harriet and I exchange a look as Araminta continues. 'Lola would have hated this – all this gossiping about her. If she wanted to die, then we should just let her rest in peace . . .' Her arms flail and red blotches are starting to appear on her neck.

'Look, are we going to have this meeting or what?' I snap, interrupting her mid-flow. 'Some of us have things we need to do.'

'The Yearbook meeting is about recording school events, Ivy,' says Araminta, drawing herself up with authority – although it doesn't quite work with her still-flushed cheeks. 'If you don't think this podcast is an important part of that, then maybe you should leave.'

'Fine.' I grab my notebook and stuff it in my backpack, which I throw over my shoulder. 'The guys haven't bothered to come anyway. Maybe they knew something I don't. Let me know when this is actually going to be about the yearbook, OK?'

'Wait, Ivy . . .' Harriet calls after me.

But I can't take another second in that room. If this is what the rest of the school year is going to be like, I'm going to be in for a lot of trouble.

18

AUDREY

The bus seems to take forever to come and, not for the first time, I internally cuss my dad out for not giving me a car in the UK. I miss my beautiful blue BMW with its buttery soft leather seats and chrome-edged dash. Now I have to stand outside at the bus stop – which doesn't even have a shelter. Dark clouds are gathering above me. It would be just like this country to pour down with rain once again.

I hop from foot to foot, this time cursing myself for not bringing an umbrella. It's not exactly like I had a lot of time to plan an outfit – I was just desperate to get out of there – and so I threw on some running shoes and a hoodie over my leggings and grabbed my handbag. I'm not likely to see anyone from school in town, since we're technically not supposed to leave the grounds. But screw it. I just couldn't stay there any longer. All that talk about the girl who died was bringing up way too many painful memories. Being accused by Ivy of being behind that creepy-ass podcast, in front of everybody? That was the final straw.

And if they find out I've made a break for it . . . what are they gonna do, kick me out of school?

In fact, would that be such a bad thing? Why do I have to stay? I scramble for my phone to send a message to my dad that I want OUT. But then I remember that then I'd have to live in their awful new house and listen to my mom lecture me on whatever her Goop-inspired *craze-du-jour* is. Illumen Hall might actually be the lesser of two evils – if I can get a grip on this Lola situation. It might be time for me to learn a bit more about what happened.

The wind picks up, blowing my ponytail into my face. When the bus finally pulls up, I step aboard and the heavens open.

It's about a half-hour bus ride to town, so I take a deep breath, and then type *Lola Radcliffe* into Google on my phone.

Several news articles pop up immediately.

BOARDING SCHOOL STUDENT FOUND DEAD IN HALF
MOON COVE

SMALL COMMUNITY DEVASTATED BY DEATH OF
POPULAR STUDENT

BEWARE THE CLIFFS: CALLS FOR INCREASED BARRIERS
AFTER LOCAL TEENAGER FALLS

I'm soon lost in the story, and it's clear that the police are one hundred per cent convinced that it was an accident. Still, I'm not surprised the podcast has been such a hit. And it *is* a hit – even with only two episodes, social media is buzzing. It has a top-ten position in a bunch of true-crime charts, and there's a whole Reddit forum dedicated to the investigation. If I was the architect, I'd be pretty pleased with my performance.

But it must feel real twisted for the students who knew

her. I clear my history, not wanting any trace on my phone that I've researched her. I've had my binge – now I can forget all about it.

It's still raining by the time we get to the town of Winferne Bay. The bus lets me off – and again there's no shelter – but I've seen exactly what I wanted: a small branch of an anonymous, generic-brand coffee shop. I send a prayer of thanks up to the sky because, for a sinking moment, I thought there wouldn't be one and I'd have to huddle inside a fish-and-chip shop or something equally horrifying.

I'm drenched even by the short jog from the bus to the cafe, my bangs sticking to the side of my face. The bell above the door dings as I enter and a few curious eyes turn to look at me. I feel like a drowned rat.

There's a small queue, so I get in line. I breathe in the scent of coffee and disinfectant, glad to be somewhere a little familiar. I need a sugary coffee asap. If I could have it directly fed into my veins like an IV drip, that would be great.

'What can I get you?' asks the curly-haired woman behind the counter. Behind me, the bell rings again.

'The biggest pumpkin spice latte you got, extra whip,' I reply.

'Name?'

'Audrey.'

There's a prickle along the back of my neck, a feeling like someone is standing just a little too close for comfort. I take a big step to the side, and turn my head slightly to look at the culprit.

I blink. Right beside me might be the most handsome man I've ever seen. He looks vaguely familiar, but I'm sure I've never met him before. I would have remembered a guy with eyes like that – dazzling blue and wide, like a Colorado sky. I stare for just a moment too long, then spin sharply away, the colour rising in my cheeks.

I move further down the counter to wait for my order. I scout a chair in the corner, trying to distract myself from looking back at the man.

'Pumpkin spice, extra large, extra whipped cream for Audrey!' shouts the barista.

Suddenly my order sounds so childish. Why didn't I order, like, an Americano? Americano for the American. Maybe that would have been worse. I collect my drink and take a quick sip.

'Audrey Wagner?' comes a voice from behind me.

I hastily wipe my mouth, hoping there's no whipped cream on my lips. 'Oh, um, hi.'

The gorgeous man stares at me, and I can't help myself – I stare back. Then I give myself a small shake and remember who I am. *Not* someone to get bamboozled by a guy with stunning blue eyes. 'Wait a sec, how do you know my name?'

He gestures at the coffee cup, with my name scrawled on it in big black letters.

I narrow my eyes. 'That doesn't explain the last name.'

He places his hand on his chest. '*Mea culpa*. You got me. My sleuthing goes deeper than that. I saw the monogram on your bag, AW. Pair that with Audrey and the American accent ... I took a guess. I'm Patrick

Radcliffe.' He hands me a business card, which I take in surprise.

That last name. *Radcliffe.*

'My parents have had a few meetings with your father, so I've heard a lot about you. Never thought I'd run into you on my coffee break though. Random, isn't it?' He chuckles. 'Want to sit?'

I've been so stunned by the guy's posh, cut-glass accent that I haven't taken any notice of the people tutting at us, forced to go around us to get to the counter like we're boulders in a river. 'Sure,' I think I reply. I might have just opened my mouth like a fish. He takes my arm and guides me to a seat.

'You're a student at Illumen Hall.'

I snap out of my hot-guy-induced stupor. 'OK, now you're freakin' me out.' I stand up to leave.

'Sit down,' he says and, although it's a command, he says it so gently I find myself obeying.

'Like I said, I know your father. And I was at your recent assembly . . .'

He waits for me to join the dots, which I do seconds after he speaks. *Radcliffe.* His voice is familiar too, and I suddenly know why. He was featured on that horrible podcast.

He's Lola's brother.

'Oh my God, you're . . . um . . . oh. I'm so sorry for your loss.'

He's surprisingly dismissive, waving his hand in the air. 'Don't be sorry. I haven't lost her yet. Not until I've found out what happened to her.'

I take a long sip of my coffee, grimacing at the fact that it's definitely not as strong here as it is in the States. I *need* strong coffee right now. I came into town to try and escape from all the noise about Lola, and I've walked straight into it again. Straight into the eyes of Lola's hot older brother.

'Terrible, isn't it?' He gestures at my cup.

'Yeah, it's pretty bad.'

'There's no good coffee around here. I just bought a flat in this godforsaken town so I can be closer to the investigation, but I'm not really getting anywhere. It seems like no one wants to talk to me about it.'

'I'm sorry,' I reply, not sure what else to say.

'It's bloody frustrating because everyone knows me and my family. Our ancestor was one of the school founders.'

'Seriously?' *Holy crap.* As far as I know, my family is not that interesting. There might be some German in there somewhere, owing to the last name, but no important ancestors that I know of.

'Seriously,' he says, and I think he might be mocking my accent. 'So of course I was a student at Illumen Hall too. I wasn't as good a student as Lola, but our family has been attending the school for generations. Not that it's going to be around much longer,' he mutters. I frown and am about to ask why when the coffee-shop girl comes over and hands him his order. He takes it from her and throws down his espresso in one. Then he lowers his voice, forcing me to lean in closer to hear him – not that I mind too much. 'The one thing I know is that there's no way Lola killed herself or went walking alone on the cliffs at night, or whatever the police story is. And, if she didn't, that means that someone is out there who knows what happened to her. Maybe someone who's still a danger to students at the school.'

Is it just me or is my coffee suddenly scalding hot? I almost drop it. The temperature seems to have risen in the room. Am I sweating? I think I'm dripping on the table. Patrick doesn't seem to have noticed. 'It's actually a happy coincidence that I've met you. I've been thinking that I need help. Someone on the inside who can –'

I suddenly worry what he's about to ask me. 'What about the podcaster?' I interrupt.

His stare intensifies. 'That anonymous person? They tricked me into doing an interview with them. I want someone I can actually contact.'

I shake my head, trying to stop the rest of my body from shaking. A thought enters my head: *What if* he's *the Voice Unknown?* 'I didn't even know Lola. I'm new to the school. I . . . I wouldn't even know where to start.'

'Even better. You won't have any preconceived notions about who she was, and you'll have an excuse to ask questions. Lola was . . . complicated. But she would never have risked her own life. I firmly believe that.'

Now I stand up, and he doesn't stop me. 'I have to go. I can't help you. I have schoolwork to do. I shouldn't even be here; I'm technically not supposed to leave the grounds. But you'd know that already.'

'I'm sure the daughter of Walter Wagner doesn't have to obey the rules.'

But I barely hear him. I'm already out the door. I ditch my weak coffee in a nearby garbage can, breaking out almost into a run.

When I reach the bus stop, I check the timetable on my phone, but there's not gonna be another bus back to Illumen Hall for ages. There's a distinct chill in the air, and I have nothing to do but wander the streets of the small town until the bus comes. I dig my hands into my pockets. My fingers touch a sharp piece of card. I pull the offending paper out of my jacket.

It's Patrick's business card. **PRONTO ESTATES** is printed on the front, with his number on it and an elaborate logo of his initials, PR. I flip it over and see that he's written on the back:

Check out the Magpie Society.

It seems like the harder I try to run from this mystery, the harder it tries to find me.

19

IVY

My attempts to find Audrey are completely useless. How a freakishly tall, bright blond, very loud person can disappear inside these halls is a mystery, but no one seems to have seen her. There are too many places to hide here, too many rooms and corridors, small nooks and – of course – the vast expanse of grounds. I have my doubts that she'd have ventured outside in this weather, but you never know.

My apology will just have to wait. But, in the meantime, there's something else I could do, and it might be better than any sort of apology. I have to find out the *real* identity of Vee.

That's why I find myself lingering outside Mr Willis's classroom once again (at least I tell myself that's why). I can hear him through the door, bringing another history lesson to a close. When the bell rings and everyone filters out, I slide my way in and shut the door behind me.

'Oh, Ivy, didn't see you there!' He smiles up at me from his desk.

'How are you? How's everything?' I pull on the straps of my bag and make direct eye contact. His eyes glint as they take me in, and he glances down after holding my stare just a moment too long.

'Great, thank you, kind of you to ask,' he says, shuffling papers round the desk. 'Actually . . . I moved house last week, much to the disappointment of my two best friends. I do love them, but they were so messy . . .'

'If *only* I could have my own space! Would be the absolute dream.'

He shrugs. 'I had some of the best times living with my friends – however crazy they were. But it's not exactly going to be my own space. I'll be living with my . . .' Before he can finish his sentence, he reaches for his coffee mug – but ends up knocking it over all the papers on his desk. 'Oh shit!' he says. The flurry of movement causes a cloud of his aftershave to drift towards me. I recognize it immediately. Fresh sea fennel and musk.

'Oh, sorry for swearing, Ivy. I'm such an idiot!'

I give him a conspiratorial smile, and help to mop up the liquid with some tissues.

'So, um, I wanted to ask you something.'

'Please, go ahead. Anything for one of my best students.' He winks at me and I swear my heart melts a little.

'Well, have you looked much into the history of the school yourself, sir?'

He smiles. 'I've never known a student to be as keen to learn as you, Ivy! Does your brain ever stop?'

No, not really. My. Brain. Never. Stops.

I laugh, probably a little too overenthusiastically. 'I just enjoy our chats, I suppose . . .' The honesty of that statement hits me around the same time it hits Mr Willis.

He softens and leans back in his chair, placing his arms behind his head. 'Ah, that's kind! Well, this school does have a fascinating history. I particularly enjoy reading about the Victorian era, when young women like yourself were first permitted to come here. That was quite revolutionary in its time!' His eyes get this sort of dreamy, faraway look in them. Then he shakes his head as he seems to remember where we are – and who he's talking to.

I take a deep breath. 'The reason I ask is because . . . I'm trying to find out who's producing the podcast.' I wait, holding my breath for his reaction and response. His eyes widen and he leans forward in his chair.

'I see.' He rubs the gingery stubble on his face.

'And the most recent one mentioned magpies, and Lola's tattoo, and it got me thinking about our start-of-term tradition. I was wondering how to go about finding out how that started?'

'Hmm, that's interesting, Ivy. I hadn't thought about it myself. I suppose I'd try the school archives in the library first of all.'

'You were interviewed for the podcast, weren't you?' I jump in, while he's in a chatty mood.

'I was . . .' He trails off cautiously.

'Well, how did the person – Vee – get in contact with you? If you don't mind me asking . . .'

Mr Willis sighs, but, to my relief, he answers the question. 'Through email, first of all. I assumed it was a journalist investigating the story. Then they called me up and I did think it was a bit strange that they'd disguised their voice, but I wasn't really thinking straight . . .'

I narrow my eyes slightly. His words sound a bit forced.

'I really hope you can find out who's behind this,' he continues. 'Mrs Abbott had me in her office immediately after the snippet of my voice came on the first episode of that thing. I explained to her what I've just explained to you. I had no idea it would end up on a gossipy podcast that's making its way through the school! Honestly, I'm dreading they're going to air the full interview.'

'The email,' I jump in. 'Can you give it to me? I know you probably shouldn't, but I have a question I want to ask them and it seems like the easiest way to get in touch?'

He stares at me for a second, then turns to his computer and pulls up a browser window, his fingers flying across the keys. 'I'm afraid I can't *give* you it. But, if you were to accidentally stumble upon it, that's not my problem.' He smirks and pushes his chair back, moving to the far side of his desk to start up his projector.

Muscles, intellect and slight recklessness? *Nice*. I sneak round the desk and see the email he's pulled up. I quickly jot down winfernelocal.89@gmail.com into my phone and save it. No wonder he assumed they were a reporter. Clever move.

When I'm on the opposite side of the desk, he looks back at me. 'Be careful, Ivy. Don't get yourself in trouble. Whatever Mrs Abbott is offering you.'

I nod. 'I'll try and be careful, sir. See you around.'

My head is buzzing with the thought of having Vee's email address. It's my first real break. I head straight to the library. I want to send this email before starting third period.

Hello, Voice Unknown,

My name is Ivy Moore-Zhang. I'm an Illumen Hall student and was a close friend of Lola's. I think I have some information that might be of interest to you, concerning your investigation. You can contact me at this email, or my phone number is 07————.

Sincerely,

Ivy

I send it off immediately and stare blankly at the inbox. Almost instantly, I get a reply. No name, just the email address.

I know your game, Ms Moore-Zhang. I won't be needing any of your 'information'.

'WHAT?!' I shout, looking round the library. I get a shiver down my spine, and I wonder if Voice Unknown is watching me right now. I drum my fingers on the desk. There's got to be some vital information in this email. I refuse to have just found this lead and take absolutely nothing away from it. I drop Teddy a text.

I need your help with something.
You about?

Just in the common room. What
is it? You OK?

> Is there a way to get an IP
> address from an email?

Yeah, forward it to me.

I do as he asks immediately.

> HOLY SHIT. IS THIS THE
> PERSON RUNNING THE
> PODCAST?

Yeah! They just sent me this!

> Give me a minute. I'll try and
> grab it.

I sit, cradling my phone, like it's the most precious thing I've ever owned. My heart is in my throat and I can feel my temples throbbing. If Teddy can tell me where this email came from, I'll be one step closer. Minutes feel like hours and it's getting close to break being over. Just then, my phone buzzes.

> I've got the IP address. Whoever
> sent it did it from inside school.

20

AUDREY

When I finally get back to Illumen, it's a little after five in the afternoon. I feel quite proud of myself, having managed to sneak back in without drawing attention to myself. Taking the running gear was an inspired choice. It would have looked to anyone that I'd just popped out for a jog around the grounds.

I get back to the room in time to change for dinner. My stomach rumbles – I should've grabbed a muffin at the coffee shop. Maybe I would have done if it hadn't been for Patrick.

I check my 'fake' phone where there are a whole slew of notifications. Most of them are from Lydia. I feel a gnawing sense of guilt. I haven't really been that good at keeping in touch with her since classes started. Considering we used to be in contact basically 24/7, I'm not surprised she's feeling left out.

> Please text me back. Any
> updates on that cute Theodore
> guy? YOUR BFF WANTS TO
> KNOW.

I blast off a couple of quick replies, explaining about my busy afternoon – and that no, there are no updates on Theodore – but leaving out the sheet-in-the-pond-screaming-the-class-down detail. I don't know how Lydia would react to that. It would go one of two ways – she'd either be really worried about me, or else she'd insist on finally updating me about the incident back home. I don't want either thing to happen, so it's easier just to leave it out.

There aren't any messages from Brendan, but that's no surprise. We're broken up after all. Still, I'm a little hurt that he seems to have completely forgotten about me. I think about sending a quick selfie, just to remind him what he's missing –

There's a swift knock on the dorm-room door. 'Hello?' I call out, hurrying to bury my phone in my covers and rearrange my shirt. I pull the sheets straight hastily as the door opens and Mrs Parsons pops her head round.

'Ah, there you are, Audrey.'

'Hi.'

'I've had notification that you left the school grounds this afternoon, without permission.'

Heat rises in my cheeks. 'I went for a jog. That's allowed, isn't it?' When she continues to stare at me, I find another lie tripping off my tongue far too easily. 'I had an urgent call from my dad. He needed to meet with me.' But I know she isn't buying it.

'We called your parents to notify them. They weren't aware you needed to leave the school.'

I open my mouth, but Mrs Parsons continues to talk

over me. 'As I've mentioned before, at Illumen Hall we take our rules very seriously. We trust in the intelligence of our students. So we *trust* that you were intelligent enough to read and understand the rules the first time you were told about them. We don't give you three strikes here.'

'I'm sorry, but –'

'No need for apologies. Just don't do it again.'

'I won't.'

She smiles at me, but there's an edge to it. 'I know you won't. And, to make sure the lesson really sinks in, you're going to sit here and think about it all through dinner.' Then she slams the door shut. I sit stock-still, shell-shocked. But what snaps me out of it is the sound that follows.

The sound of a lock turning in the door.

'No!' I cry out, and launch myself at it. I yank at the handle, but it won't budge. That bitch has actually locked me in the room. I smack my hand against the door, hard. 'Hey! Lemme out!' I bang a few more times. 'You can't do this! This must be illegal!'

But she doesn't come back. I'm so angry that my entire body is shaking. Then there's a creaking noise behind me.

I spin around – my eyes scanning the room. My heart races with the adrenaline rush, and I wonder if I'm hearing things. But then I see it. One of the panels of wood lining the wall on Ivy's side of the room, just beneath her desk, has swung open. It's still moving ever so slightly, swaying back and forth. It must have been opened by the force of Mrs Parsons slamming the door.

For a moment, my back stays glued to the door. I don't wanna know what's in the hidden compartment. I want the main door to open, so I can go downstairs and eat dinner like a normal person.

I swallow, then walk over and prise it open wider. I have to crouch down a bit, but I can almost fit inside the compartment that sits behind the wall. It's small, cramped – and empty.

No, not completely empty. In the corner there's an envelope. In beautiful cursive writing on the front are the words:

To my beloved

I pick up the letter, hastily shut the compartment and run my hand over the wall. There's almost no evidence that the panel opens. I would never have known. I press down on it firmly, and it clicks open again.

Huh. I wonder if Ivy knows about this. I look down at the letter in my hand. *Is this Ivy's?* Somehow I doubt it. The handwriting doesn't look anything like what I've seen of Ivy's neat, all-caps-lock style. This is much more flowery. And the paper looks old. It's stained yellow at the corners and covered in a layer of dust.

Curiosity killed the cat, Audrey. Yet another mystery I don't want to be dragged into. I throw the letter into my desk drawer without opening it. Putting the letter out of my head, I sit on my bed, grabbing my laptop so that I can send an incensed email to my dad.

Dad, I can't take this any more. I'm quitting Illumen Hall. You can find me some other school, but I'm not staying here a moment longer.

If you have to know why, try this: http://whokilledlola.com.

Audrey

THE <u>WKL?</u> PODCAST TRANSCRIPT

EPISODE THREE

[Intro] Quiet, with low beats like a heartbeat. The chilling atmosphere builds.

> ### VOICE UNKNOWN
> Welcome to the third episode of WHO KILLED LOLA?, a podcast where I, your Voice Unknown, am attempting to uncover the truth of what happened to Lola Radcliffe.
>
> It's been a month since we launched. Need a recap? DC Copeland dropped the intriguing titbit that the magpie 'tattoo' on Lola's back was drawn with a Sharpie. And an interview with one of Lola's friends raised a lot of questions about the current head girl of the school.
>
> So what have I been investigating in the meantime? I've been down the rabbit hole when it comes to the history of magpies and our school. I can't wait to share what I found . . .

In an old yearbook from 1967, I found a reference in a leaver's note to 'the Magpie Society'. Is this some kind of secret organization in the school, and could it have had something to do with Lola's death?

To find out a bit more, I've come to Winferne Bay, a small town on the mainland, where Illumen Hall students can often be found at weekends. I'm here specifically to talk to Mrs Trawley – a local historian. She was a pupil of Illumen Hall, class of sixty-seven – her face is in that yearbook.

Mrs Trawley, welcome to the podcast.

MRS TRAWLEY
Thank you. I'm not sure I quite understand what a podcast is. Is this OK?
[sound of a finger interfering with a microphone.]

VEE
[laughs]
It's fine, Mrs Trawley. You're doing great. Now, you were once a student at Illumen Hall.

MRS TRAWLEY
Oh yes, a long, long time ago.

VEE

Oh, I'm sure it wasn't that long! But you've also worked as a local historian in the region.

MRS TRAWLEY

Yes, I'm somewhat of a busybody, I'm afraid, always with my nose in the town's business! But first, let me say I was so sorry to hear about that poor young girl. It shouldn't be something that happens in this kind of community.

VEE

I know.

MRS TRAWLEY

I knew her a little. She used to come into town and help me with my market stall. I wish she could have spoken to someone before she . . . it's so sad.

VEE

But this isn't the first time something like this has happened at the school, is it?

MRS TRAWLEY

No, it's not. When I was at the school, we used to avoid the Tower Wing because we believed that it might be haunted.

VEE

Haunted?

MRS TRAWLEY

Well, yes. After all, the story was particularly gruesome and fired up our teenage imaginations. Long before our time, a student died after falling from that tower.

VEE

Really? I've never heard that.

MRS TRAWLEY

It's not exactly the kind of thing that you'd put in a school brochure! At any rate, the Magpie Society quickly cleaned it up.

VEE

The Magpie Society?

MRS TRAWLEY

Why, yes. The Magpie Society is an Illumen Hall institution. No one quite knows when it was founded, but for many decades, if anything was happening at the school that threatened its reputation or the safety of its students, they stepped in to sort it all out.

VEE

Wow, that's fascinating. I knew about the tradition of leaving a shiny offering to the magpies so as not to offend them, but I thought it was just a quirk of the school. Who exactly is the Magpie Society?

MRS TRAWLEY

Well, that's part of it, isn't it, dear? Nobody knows. They just swoop in and change things.

VEE

Huh. Did you ever try and join?

MRS TRAWLEY

Join the Magpie Society? Why would I ever do that? I wouldn't even know where to begin. No. If it was a group of students, I never received an invitation.

VEE

Right, OK. Just one other question. Why is it called 'the Magpie Society'?

MRS TRAWLEY

Haven't you seen the magpies around the school grounds? They seem to protect the place. I suppose it comes from that. But I've never really thought about it. It was just part of the idioglossia of the school, the mythology – as integral as the Samhain party or even that creaking stair at the top of Helios House – do you know the one?

VEE

Yeah, I do. But no one at the school seems to have heard of this Magpie Society. Why is that, do you think?

MRS TRAWLEY

Maybe there's been no need for them . . .

VEE

Thank you for your time, Mrs Trawley.

MRS TRAWLEY

Thank you, dear.

[Interlude] Music plays.

VEE

So, as you can see, magpies have a strong association with our school. But, while it's absolutely fascinating, that still doesn't bring me any closer to figuring out how the magpies are connected to Lola's death.

My next interviewee is a very special one. Patrick Radcliffe, Lola's older brother, and former head student of Illumen Hall. Lola should have followed in his footsteps . . . but she never got the chance.

The Radcliffe family are practically Illumen Hall institutions in their own right. Lola's portrait joins five other portraits of the Radcliffe family that hang on the school walls. And Patrick is absolutely certain his sister would not have gone to the cliffs of her own accord.

[Interlude] Music plays.

> ### VEE
>
> Hello, Patrick.

> ### PATRICK
>
> Hello. And thank you for keeping the investigation into my sister's death open, rather than sweeping it under the carpet like the police.

> ### VEE
>
> They do seem in a rush to close the case.

> ### PATRICK
> [bitterly]
>
> You're telling me.

> ### VEE
>
> So, tell our audience about Lola.

> ### PATRICK
>
> Happily. Lola was the baby of the family, and she was our beloved. Her favourite thing was riding horses, and she'd applied for a place at Bournemouth University to study acting.

> ### VEE
>
> Oh yes – her best friend, Jessica, is at Bournemouth now, isn't she?

PATRICK

Yes. And Lola was such a brilliant actor – she shone on the stage and onscreen. She'd actually got a couple of commercials booked for the summer, did you know that? She wouldn't have thrown that away. I'm so tired of the police and their narrative. There's no evidence of her being unstable – no note, no journals, none of her friends thought anything was wrong. She had no history of mental illness. She was always so happy, like sunshine in a bottle. We can't understand it.

[sound of muffled crying]

VEE

Thank you for talking to me, Patrick, I can only imagine how hard this is for you and your family. And don't worry: I won't rest until there's justice.

The beats sound out the close of the episode.

And that's it for this episode of WHO KILLED LOLA? Tune in next time as I'll air an exclusive interview with Lola's very best friend … and what she has to say about the men in Lola's life will shock you.

[End] Music plays, growing loud before fading out.

21

IVY

'*I asked Mum about the Magpie Society and she actually said that she remembered it! She said the society caught old headmaster Gallagher when he was embezzling funds from the boarding fees.*'

'*That tattoo did not look like a Sharpie drawing. Do you think the police could be trying to throw Vee off the scent?*'

'*Can you believe Patrick agreed to an interview? OMG, I had such a crush on him back in the day.*'

'Can someone *please* talk about something other than that podcast! I can't hear myself think,' I snap at a group of Year Ten girls at the table beside me, who have been nattering non-stop.

One of the girls looks over at me, her eyes wide. 'Sorry, Ivy.'

'Don't worry, I'll move.' I slam my textbooks shut and gather them up.

It's been a few days since the third episode aired and talk of the podcast floats round the library like a bad smell. It's becoming such a distraction. In every lesson, a student raises their hand to ask the teacher a question about it, which is always met with some bullshit, wishy-washy response.

It's been another week – and now another episode – and I'm still no closer to finding out who is doing it. The email had been like a little carrot dangling in front of my face. I thought maybe, once we had the IP address, we could trace the email to the exact computer that had been used to send it. Then I could check the logins and . . . bingo! But apparently that was beyond the realms of even Teddy's encyclopaedic IT knowledge.

I find myself being suspicious of everyone. Someone will speak up in a lesson and I question whether their voice, disguised, could be Vee.

Now, instead of studying in the common room as I prefer, I'm in the library waiting for Mrs Ling, the librarian, to pull my request for the 1967 Yearbook from the archive. The one mentioned in the podcast.

The gossip is getting out of control. The other day I passed a Year Nine telling their friend that *Mrs Abbott* had pushed Lola off the cliff. I actually laughed out loud at that one. Well, before sending them to detention. As prefects, we've been instructed to squash any ridiculous rumours. *Not good for school spirit*, said our headmistress. People are gossiping like magpies, and misinformation is starting to spread like wildfire.

I'm beginning to feel overwhelmed. Not only am I still trying to figure out who's behind the podcast, but there are some intense mock exams I have to revise for. If I want to follow in my mum's footsteps and get into Oxbridge, I have to work my arse off this year. Doesn't look like I'm going to get that leg-up from Mrs Abbott after all.

'Over here,' says a voice. I look through the stacks and

see Harriet waving at me, and feel a rush of relief. Thank God – a normal human being. She's sitting in the corner of the library with Tom. Harriet passes me a boiled sweet from a small paper bag that she's had hidden down her tights. We call her Willy Wonka, as she always smuggles something sweet into lessons to pass around. Sweets are completely prohibited anywhere but our bedrooms, not that that stops her.

'I'm OK, thanks. I'm not sure I trust anything from your gusset . . .' I raise an eyebrow at her and push away the wrinkled paper bag. 'Where did you get those from anyway – 1934?'

'They're actually from the village post office. It's got a whole retro vibe going on, which you'd know if you ever left the grounds at the weekend. And what's wrong with my gusset?' She takes out a lemon sherbet and pops it smugly in her mouth.

Even though I wrinkle my nose in playful disgust, it's so refreshing not to be talking about the podcast. I turn my attention back to my literature coursework, but I can't concentrate. My eyes slide over the room and fall on the table opposite, where Araminta sits, surrounded by her posse.

She's wearing her usual disgruntled expression, but I can't quite pick up what they're all talking about, although I can make a pretty educated guess. I continue to watch from the corner of my eye and her arms start flapping and her voice gets louder. I overhear her saying: 'They're definitely implying that, Katie!' I mean, the podcast is not looking great for her, and her reaction isn't helping by being so shifty.

Ugh, I've been thinking about this now for ten minutes – and absolutely nothing from this page of my textbook has sunk in. I put in my earbuds to drown out the speculation and go back to my 'Historical Background and Poetry Forms' assessment. A few minutes later, Harriet leans over and pulls out one of the buds.

'Oi, you didn't tell me that Mrs Parsons locked Audrey in your room over dinner last week!' Clearly, Harriet has other ideas instead of studying this evening. 'I heard her telling Bonnie in class today.'

I pull out my other headphone. 'Oh yeah. Turns out, after I, you know, flipped my lid at her . . . she went off to the village. I guess she needed some air.'

'She doesn't yet have a handle on Illumen rules?'

'Nope.'

'Don't blame her. If they didn't have such good fish and chips, I'd swear this was a prison, not a school,' says Tom.

I roll my eyes. I know he loves it here as much as I do. But there's a gnawing of guilt in my stomach. I still haven't apologized to Audrey.

It was a bit hilarious that she got locked in our room though. I can't imagine that went down well with 'Daddy'. The night it happened, Mrs Parsons escorted me back to the room after dinner so she could unlock the room to let me back in and, as the door opened, we were both met with the most flustered, red-faced version of Audrey I think I'll ever see. Her hair looked wild, unlike her usual sleek golden locks, and her face was blotchy and swollen. She'd obviously been crying. As I lay in my bed that night, I could hear her frantically typing on her laptop like a woman possessed – I assume chatting to her friends back home. I don't ever really think about the fact she left them all behind. That must be hard. I kept opening my mouth to apologize, but the words never came out. She didn't seem that keen to talk to me either, and so it just never happened.

'Bet she went out of her mind!' Harriet laughs.

'Probably should have warned her, but we don't really speak that much.'

Harriet nods. 'Sucks to have to share your own room.'

'Tell me about it. I'm a prefect with none of the perks. Me and Audrey just kind of . . . exist in the same space. We don't really have lessons together either. We're pretty different people. She's really girly and fancies herself a bit, I think.'

'Ivy, just because someone takes longer to do their hair and make-up than you doesn't mean they fancy themselves. You should make friends with her. I heard her dad bought that giant house on the coast.'

'All right, just because your mum's a Rightmove addict. I don't pick my friends based on the size of their bank account, you know.'

'Only based on their ability to provide illegal sub-stances . . .' She shakes her bag of sweets at me. I roll my eyes at her, smiling, and put my headphones back in.

'Ivy?'

I look up to see Mrs Ling has approached, the yearbook in her hands.

'Is this what you were looking for? Sorry it took me so long; it was *not* shelved in the right place. I found it in our donation pile – can you believe that? Some people have no respect for books.'

I jump up and almost snatch it out of Mrs Ling's hands, who rolls her eyes and walks off, muttering.

'What's that?' Harriet says, a boiled sweet bulging out of her cheek.

'It's the yearbook mentioned in the last podcast. I don't know if this is the *exact* one that the voice mentioned as I suppose they could've got it from an old student, but I thought it'd be worth looking at . . .' A piece of paper falls from the middle of the book as I'm flicking through. I pick it up and unfold it.

It's sheet music, ripped from a book. A piano duet.

Oh no.

'What? What is it?' Harriet asks. She must see the colour draining from my cheeks because she's out of her chair and leaning over me to try and see what I'm looking at.

'Clover. Shit. I think Clover's behind the podcast.'

22

AUDREY

I swear I'm never gonna learn my way around this place.

The only thing I can compare it to is a gigantic corn maze. Every hallway seems to have the same style paintings, the same polished brown railings and tiled flooring. Bonnie tried to teach me to recognize the different tile patterns, or to notice the artwork – follow the winding river with the flaming trees to the girl carrying the basket of apples to get to math – but, like I said, they all look the same to me.

All I want to do is find a freakin' bathroom.

I know I'm miles from my room and Helios House – and it could be actual miles, by the way. This school needs its own Google Maps.

I'm about to give up and head back, retrace my steps until I find a hallway that I recognize, when I catch sight of a long blond ponytail disappearing round the corner.

'Araminta?' I cry out. She'll be able to tell me where to find a washroom.

She doesn't reply, so I pick up my pace, hurrying to catch up. I can hear a few voices, including Bonnie's.

'Hey, guys?'

I turn the corner just in time to see them disappearing

through a door with ornate gold lettering reading LADIES. I breathe a sigh of relief. Thank God for that.

I push through the door and enter a storm.

'What makes you think this is OK?' Araminta's voice is high-pitched and squeaky.

I frown. A group of girls are crowded into a single stall. 'Hey, what's going on?' I ask. No one answers me. So I ask again, louder, 'What's going on?' Then I hear a girl whimpering, and I shoot forward. 'What the fuck?'

Bonnie is the first one to pull back from the stall. She has an angry look on her face, which she wipes when she sees me. She moves her body so it blocks my view. 'Oh, Audrey. Don't worry about this – you wouldn't understand. This doesn't have anything to do with you.'

'What doesn't?' I'm too invested now. I step forward. There's a cry of pain, and Bonnie spins round to glare at whatever – or whoever – is in the stall. I feel a growing pressure on my chest, a rise of bile in my stomach. This reminds me too much of the shit that went down back home. I won't stand for it here. I won't sit by and watch as someone else gets hurt.

Araminta is so angry she's almost foaming at the mouth, her face red with rage. Not exactly dignified 'head student' behaviour.

I crane my neck and spot someone pushed back against the toilet. She's struggling, trying to break out of the stall. When one of the girls tries to hold her, she shouts, 'Get off me, bitch! I'm not doing anything wrong!'

'You're not going to deny it? Tell me you're going to stop!' shouts Araminta.

'We'll ruin you!' shouts another girl that I barely recognize – Heloise, I think.

I sneer in disgust. Screw making friends. Nothing's worth this.

I reach into the stall, pushing Bonnie aside and grabbing Araminta's arm. I pull her and, as she stumbles backwards, she takes some of the others with her. Finally, I recognize the girl. It's Clover, Ivy's fledgling.

I feel a part of me that I'd buried deep come roaring out. 'What the hell?'

'Audrey, she's the one who's behind the podcast,' shrieks Araminta. 'She's the Voice Unknown!'

I want to reach out and slap my former friend. But instead I stand my ground. My height means I tower over most of these girls. Araminta's the only one who's a match for me. Any chance I had of getting through this school year under the radar is disappearing beneath my rage.

'Leave that girl alone. I don't care what she's supposed to have done.' My voice is cool and calm, even though my heart is racing inside my chest. I feel like I'm outside of my own body. This is how I always wanted to react, but somehow, back home, I never had the courage to.

Now my body isn't betraying me for once and I'm grateful to it.

Araminta's head drops into her hands. Crocodile tears, my instincts shout at me. When she raises it again, her mascara is streaked down her cheeks, her eyes rimmed red. 'You don't understand. I overheard Ivy say she's the "Voice Unknown" while we were in the library. I'm not the bad guy here. It's her.'

Now that there's a bit of air around her, Clover speaks up again. 'I'm not the bad guy! I'm trying to find out the truth.'

'She's making everything up, broadcasting all over the airwaves! That's why she had to keep herself anonymous. She's going to ruin everything that Lola stood for. It's all LIES.' Araminta spits out the word viciously.

'Get away from her,' I say, holding her arms as she reels back to strike again.

'Look, I don't need rescuing,' Clover snaps at me as she jumps up. 'I don't care what you all think. I'm investigating everything and every*one* fairly. I stand by that. Now leave me alone.' She pushes past us all and out of the stall.

I let go of Araminta, taking a few steps backwards. She breaks down into sobs, her back sliding against the bathroom door until she hits the floor. The other girls gather round her, speaking softly now – so different from the barking bullies they'd been only a few seconds ago.

'It's all true,' Clover says from behind me.

Araminta lunges, taking me by surprise. She almost gets past me, but there's a shout from Clover and a rush of air at my back as the bathroom door flies open.

'What's going on here?'

I spin round to see Mrs Abbott – and Ivy by her side. Ivy's face is flushed, her nostrils flaring in anger.

Ivy catches my eye as she spots me holding Araminta back. She seems as surprised to see me as I am to see her. But for once we're not battling with each other – this time we're on the same side.

It's Mrs Abbott's voice that snaps me back to the

present. 'Girls. Come with me.' She gestures at Araminta and her group, who are all looking pale.

The headmistress turns to Clover. 'You too.'

Clover's head is down, but she nods.

For a moment, it's only me and Ivy left in the bathroom. I open my mouth to say something, but before any words come out she turns on her heel and leaves.

I'm left alone, the silence in the tiled bathroom somehow deafening. Adrenaline is still coursing through my veins; I feel like I've just run a marathon. I look in the mirror, shocked at how pale I am. The lack of sunshine is really getting to me, and there's a sheen of sweat on my brow.

But there's something else staring back at me. A steely-eyed determination – a strength.

And then I hear another voice in my head.

'*OK, so you stood up to them. But that doesn't change what happened to me.*'

23

IVY

As I'm sitting outside Mrs Abbott's office, I watch as the other students carry on with their day, shuffling past quickly in case they somehow get sucked into the drama. There are already whispers about the fight in the girls' toilets. News spreads fast in this school, and Araminta had hardly been discreet.

Clover has been in there for a good twenty minutes now. I wanted to wait to make sure she was OK first and foremost, but also because I have so many questions right now. I feel angry and slightly betrayed. How could she have done this? I know she's passionate and determined, but to produce that awful podcast? It's too much.

And she knew I'd been searching for the culprit when it was her all along! She'd completely thrown me off the scent. It wasn't until the sheet music dropped out of the yearbook that I realized she could be the one. Things had fallen into place then: the fact that the IP address of the email had been linked to the school meant it pretty much had to be a student, and the way Vee had referred to Patrick as a 'head student' instead of 'head boy' was so Clover. Still, I would have asked her privately, given her a chance to explain – but Araminta overheard me.

Rather than follow Minty, I'd gone straight to Mrs Abbott. If this was about the podcast, then she needed to handle it. It shocked me how quickly Mrs Abbott was able to find out exactly where Araminta and her merry gang were confronting Clover. A mixture of being able to track their whereabouts through their school passes, and the cameras that are all over the school. Orwell's Big Brother, eat your heart out. It would freak me out if I wasn't already so preoccupied by the events of the last hour.

I feel a pang of guilt that I didn't see what was happening under my very nose. This might not have happened had I been more vigilant and kept an eye on her like I usually do. She's still just a kid.

I hear the door click and turn to see Mrs Abbott walk Clover out. Clover's eyes are cast down, her arms crossed over her stomach. Mrs Abbott shuts the door behind us both – I suppose she has Araminta and her crew to deal with now.

'Let's walk,' I say to Clover, and I guide her down the stairs, in the direction of the back entrance to the school.

Once we're outside, still in silence, we wander far from prying eyes looking down at us from the windows. I take her to a moss-covered bench overlooking a small stream. The silence is broken by the trickling of the water. It's weirdly peaceful.

'So it *is* you? Vee, I mean.'

She stares at the water, still not able to look me in the eye.

'Clover, what the hell?' I say softly.

'Ivy, I'm sorry. Really I am. I know I should have at least

told *you* what I was doing. But I thought if I told *anyone* I'd be more likely to be found out.' She pulls both legs up on to the bench and puts her chin on her knees.

'What did Mrs Abbott say?'

'She told me that I narrowly missed expulsion and that I mustn't continue to make or upload the podcast from school. She can't stop me from doing it all together, but she can stop me from doing it on school property.' She shrugs. I suddenly realize that Clover is only sorry she got found out.

'But you're going to stop now, right? Recording it? Interviewing people? Meddling in people's grief?' I turn her towards me and look her right in the eye, so she knows I'm being serious. 'Clover, you're going to get into serious shit if you carry on. You know that, right? Lola's death is a very real and hard thing for a lot of people. People who are all dealing with this in the best way they know how, and your podcast is really rocking the boat.' I keep my hands placed firmly on her knees, not taking my eyes off hers. She finally looks at me.

'I can't promise that, Ivy. I'm sorry. I know you're just trying to look out for me, but I truly believe this story needs to be investigated. Like you said, Lola's death is very real and hard for people. What about the people who feel something else happened that night? Her family? Her brother? Something's off, Ivy. Surely you can see that for yourself? Surely you haven't been totally sucked into the police's bullshit?'

'It's not up to you to appoint yourself as private investigator in someone else's death! You're fifteen! This is far beyond a school-field protest or sticking up for what you believe is right. There are *real* people involved.' I let out a sigh and place my hands back in my lap. This girl is unstoppable. Yet something in me tells me I can't be mad at her, because she reminds me so much of me.

'Exactly. I'm only fifteen and look how far I've managed to get in the investigation! I've uncovered stuff that the police didn't bother getting into! How is that possible? Why?'

'So you really believe it? That there was more to Lola's death?'

'I do, Ivy. I'm convinced. And I'm being careful. But the podcast is so popular now – look at this!' She shows me the podcast app on her phone and the reviews she's accumulated. Hundreds of them. And not just students at Illumen Hall or locals, but people all over the world.

'It's had five thousand downloads already. People are really invested in this and believe that what I'm sharing is going to help. I'm not giving that up.' She leans back on the bench and fluffs her hair. 'Look, Ivy, honestly, I'm sorry I didn't tell you. I knew you were investigating. When you emailed me, I so nearly fessed up. In fact, I typed a reply, then chickened out. I still had some leads to follow up, and having the anonymity of Voice Unknown was so helpful.' Then her expression suddenly changes. 'Wait. Did Araminta know it was me . . . because of you?'

'I found a page from the sheet-music book I gave you in the yearbook you mentioned in the podcast. Araminta overheard me. I am sorry about that. I didn't mean to out you before we'd had a chance to talk.'

She sighs, and her shoulders drop.

'I guess everything's going to change now it's out in the open. Did you see that room-mate of yours? The American girl?'

'Audrey?'

'Yeah. She was in the bathroom, trying to white-saviour me from Araminta's angry mob.' Clover chuckles. 'All right of her to try though.'

'I didn't think she had it in her, to be honest,' I say.

Clover waggles her eyebrows. 'Yeah, you judged that girl the minute she walked into your room.'

'Guilty as charged,' I reply.

'I bet there's a story there, with her,' says Clover. Then her eyes light up with an idea. 'But hey, now that you know, maybe you can help me with *my* story?' She leans forward. 'I've been racking my brains, trying to get into the Upper Wing. I either need to borrow your key card, or can you go in there and get what I need for me?'

'Clover, no. I'm not helping you with this!'

'Fine. Don't then. You'll find out soon enough that there are more secrets in this school than you realize, Ivy, and you'll wish you'd listened to me.' With that, she picks up her backpack, swings it over her shoulder and storms off.

24

AUDREY

Since the news broke that *Clover* was behind the podcast, the gossip fires of the school have been raging. People can't stop talking about the bathroom incident either – Araminta's reputation has definitely taken a beating.

But the worst part for me is that Araminta and Bonnie aren't speaking to me. Theodore's ghosting me. I really have alienated everyone in the school.

I also had to endure a two-hour lecture over FaceTime from my dad – the first time he's bothered to call in a month – about how I'm *not* leaving the school, how I have to grow a backbone and stick it out, blah-blah.

So, with no friends, and the prospect of eighteen more months at the school on my own, I've taken to wandering the halls like some sort of ghost.

I go up the stairs back to Helios House slowly, dragging my feet with every step. But, when I get there, there's a man blocking the door, staring up at the portrait of Lola. I try to avoid looking at it as much as possible. I hate how lifelike it is. No wonder there have been stories of her image haunting people's dreams.

'Excuse me,' I say, and then stop when I see his face. It's

Patrick. His face looks drawn, his blue eyes clouded. My voice softens. 'Oh, hey. What are you doing here?'

He looks at me, and a small smile lifts his lips. He wipes his hand under his eyes. 'Audrey. Hi. I had a meeting with Mrs Abbott after the identity of the podcaster came to light. I wanted to talk to the girl . . . what's her name, Clover?'

'Yeah, that's right. I'm so sorry, that must be real hard for you.' I reach out and put my hand on his shoulder. It feels like the right thing to do.

'I gave her my blessing to continue though. Don't think Christine was too happy about that.' He laughs at my confusion. 'You know her as Mrs Abbott. But I figure the more people investigating, the better. I hope she has more luck than I've had.' He sighs, then looks back up at the painting.

'I'm sorry I refused to help before.'

'It's OK. It was a lot to ask of you, completely at random. I suppose I'm still just desperate to find out what happened and . . . why?'

I shrug. 'Sometimes awful things happen.'

'And sometimes awful things are done by awful people,' he replies, an edge to his voice.

'Very true.' My voice almost cracks, and I squeeze my eyes shut. This time I feel his hands on my shoulders. Before I know it, he's pulled me into a hug.

'I hoped I'd see you again while I was here. Thank you for trying. Thank you for listening,' he says. I open my mouth to say I haven't tried anything at all, but he strides away, down the stairs and back into the depths of the school.

I wrap my arms around myself where he held me, a tiny shiver running through my body. I wish there was something more I could do for him. He seems so lost. And Lola's death was by no means clear-cut. It's natural to want justice. Like what happened back home.

I start to feel a little sick.

Maybe Tyler got what he deserved, but who was the one who ended up leaving the goddamn country?

I close my eyes and lean back against the wall.

Is that why I can't let this go? Even though I'd vowed to myself that I didn't want to get involved with any drama in this school, here I am, wondering how I can help.

I think back to his business card, and the number I have saved on my phone. *Check out the Magpie Society.* But what do I know? I'd never even seen a magpie up close until I arrived here – and now I see them everywhere. They have a strange sort of plumage that looks black and white at first glance, but really has this kind of oily sheen that turns blueish-purple in different lights. It's sort of beautiful. They stalk the grounds, popping up whenever I go out to get some fresh air. And, of course, there's the magpie pond.

I never did go back with an offering. The thought makes me shiver. Maybe all this bad luck isn't a coincidence.

I take a deep breath, check for teachers (or lurking prefects) and then send a text message to Patrick.

> Nice to see you today. I hope
> Clover ends up a better detective
> than me.

I head to the common room, where there are a few people hanging out. I wave at Rhonda, one of the girls in my history class, but she's sitting next to Bonnie, who gives her a kick in the shins. Rhonda shrugs at me sheepishly, before looking back down at her book.

Fan-freakin'-tastic.

Only eighteen months left.

If they want to cut me out for standing up against a bully, then for all I care this place can burn to the ground.

25

AUDREY

With an overly loud sigh, I slump down in an armchair, making a show of opening up a textbook. The IB diploma work is intense, and I definitely haven't been devoting enough time to it. Certainly not like Ivy anyway. That girl seems to find extra hours in the day. Thankfully, before I can even bother to pretend to be interested in my English coursework, my phone buzzes against my leg. I look down at the screen. To my surprise, it's Theodore. I wonder what prompted him to get in touch. I haven't heard from him in ages – I assumed, like everyone else, he had me marked down as PARIAH.

> Hey! What are you up to?

>> Oh, just chilling out in the
>> common room. What about you?

> I'm docking Old Sheila.

I read the text and actually make a gagging sound. Autocorrect has a lot to answer for.

. . . What the hell? That's
disgusting.

I'm just about to hit the block button when a message comes through from Theodore.

MY BOAT. Old Sheila is the name
of my boat.

You have like a yacht or
something?

Something like that! Not in the
Abramovich kind of way – it's a
little sailing boat. I keep it
moored in a harbour near
school. I'm bringing her into the
dock right now. Hence . . .
docking. You should drop by some
time. I'd love to take you out.

Sounds cool. Not sure how good
I am on the water though.

I'd keep you safe.

By the time dinner rolls around, our flirty conversation hasn't let up for a second. I'm beginning to really like this guy, I can feel it. He's smart and considerate and somehow more mature than most of the guys back home. He's also a bit of a nerd, in a good way – and now I learn that he's into sailing too.

Oh God. He's probably exactly the kind of guy that my dad would want me to date. Ew. Gross. But that's just it: Theodore *isn't* gross. I'm thinking maybe I should ask him out. Our paths haven't crossed much since that first day, and it'd be nice to get to know him.

'Everything OK?'

I look up to see Araminta standing on the opposite side of the dining table. She's got a puzzled look on her face.

'Oh, all good. Lost in my own world,' I reply. I chew my lip, feeling awkward.

She sits down opposite me. 'Look, I'm really sorry about what you had to witness in the bathroom. It was really wrong of me and definitely *not* very head girl of me. I want you to know that I've apologized to Clover too.'

'OK,' I reply. I give her a small smile. I think she's waiting for more, but I don't have anything else to give. She stands up.

'Right. Well – see you around.'

'See you.' I appreciate that she's trying to reach out to me, but I feel too drained to make any more effort. I'm not the same people-pleaser I was back home. She's apologized, I've accepted, but I don't have to be her friend.

After dinner, I head back to the room. I assume Ivy will be there when I get back, so I walk extra slow. But, to my surprise, she's not. I flop down on to my bed just as my phone buzzes again.

What are you doing now?

Wild night. Heading to bed!

Haha, wow. So close and yet so
far away. I just got back from the
harbour.

Old Sheila doing all right?

I gave her a lick.

. . .

Of paint.

You're gross ☺

While I'm busy searching for a gif to send to Theo, a
text from Patrick flashes up on my screen.

How are you?

I stare at my phone, shocked that I'm hearing from him
again.

I'm good. How are you?

Listen, I had an idea. You're in
Helios House, aren't you?

Yeah . . .

Lola's room last year was
number 7. I don't know who's in
there now, but would you be
able to check it for me? Those
old rooms have tons of hiding
places – and Clover won't have
access since she's in a different
house.

Oh God. I don't know whether to tell Patrick that this is
the room I'm in now. Suddenly I think back to the envelope
I found in the cubby behind the wooden panel near Ivy's
desk. *What if* . . . My phone buzzes again.

She loved writing. Maybe she
hid a diary or something? Any
insight into why she might have
done this.

I can almost feel his grief radiating off the message.

I'll see what I can do.

Thank you. And the next coffee is
on me.

I wish, I think. Somehow I feel like getting involved
with Lola's hot older brother would be very bad news, no

matter how cute he is. But I walk over to my desk, where I hid the letter. I take it out, staring at the handwriting on the front. *Lola . . . is this you?* I wonder.

My finger hovers at the edge of the envelope flap, but just then the door opens. I stuff the letter back in my desk, shutting the drawer quickly.

When I turn around, Ivy's staring at me. 'Everything OK?' she asks, eyeing me suspiciously.

'Yeah, fine,' I reply. 'Just, um, finishing up some work.'

'Cool.' She empties her bag, placing her books neatly on her shelf, then changes for bed. Even though she's clearly exhausted, she's still organized. If we were friends, I'd be worried about her. She's the definition of burning the candle at both ends. No wonder she didn't want a room-mate as a witness to her intensity.

I'm about to reach out, but she shifts in the bed, turning her back to me.

Point taken. I turn out the light, and I can see a glow from her side of the room. She must be texting as well.

I find myself thinking of Theo, and our flirty conversation earlier. Right on cue, my phone vibrates with a text from him.

> I wish I was the one sharing a
> room with you, creeper.

It's so unexpected that I actually let out an inadvertent snort of shock.

'Everything all right over there?' Ivy asks.

'Yeah, sorry.' I pause. Is this my chance to break through

the wall between us? I sit up. 'Look, I'm not that used to British guys and maybe this is normal ... You have a boyfriend, right?'

Ivy sits up in bed too, dropping her phone face down. 'Sort of. Yeah.'

'OK, would you say that "creeper" is ... what's the phrase? Like, a term of endearment over here? Because it sounds like he thinks I'm some kind of a stalker or something when really it's him that's being weird ...' I'm rambling so much that I don't notice immediately that Ivy has gone very still.

'This guy called you "creeper"?' Her voice is dark.

I frown. 'Yeah ... is that bad? Sounds like it's really bad.'

'Can I see the message?'

'Oh, um, I guess.'

This is the closest we've come to having a proper conversation since I started at Illumen. I pad over to her bed and she shifts to make room for me. I show her my screen. She lets out a low bark of a laugh.

'What's up?' I ask, frowning. It's a weird message, but it's not particularly *funny*.

She turns her phone screen to me. I don't really understand, but I scan it anyway. The opening words are **Hey, creeper.** My fingers suddenly feel like ice. The name at the top is Teddy.

I feel sick. 'Oh God. Teddy is a nickname for Theodore, isn't it?'

'Yup. You guessed it. I'm pretty sure that message on your phone is meant for me.'

'Oh, that's gross,' I say, dropping my phone on the

mattress as if it's on fire. 'He's been talking to us both *at the same time*, while *knowing we were in the same room*, and then was stupid enough to send a message meant for you to me?!'

'Looks like it.'

'Damn, that's shady.' I pause. 'Oh God, Ivy, I'm so sorry. I had no idea that Theo ... Teddy was your boyfriend. *Nothing* has happened beyond this texting. I swear I never would have –'

She waves her hands in front of her face. 'Ugh, don't worry about it. Clearly you didn't know. He's a prick, obviously, and not only that but an idiot too. *I* should have known! I told him I wanted to cool things down and obviously *this* is his interpretation of it.'

She's being so strong in her response, but I can see a wobble in her lip and I wonder if it's affecting her more than she's letting on. Even if you're the strongest person in the world, and even if you were preparing to dump the guy, it would still sting to know that your boyfriend was texting another girl. And he dared to call *me* the creeper?

As if she's read my mind, Ivy explains. 'It has to do with my name. Ivy ... creeping Ivy ... creeper. It was one of those in-joke-type things I always kind of hated, but also ...' Her voice trails off.

'Also it was yours. Oh, Ivy, he's a bum.'

'A bum?' Ivy snorts, and it sets me off too. Before we know it, we're rolling around on her bed, giggling – then roaring – with laughter.

When we finally calm down – which seems to take forever, because we keep setting each other off with different words for crappy men – we're both breathing hard. Ivy gathers up some of the covers in her fist. 'We can't let him get away with this.'

'I'm game. What do you have in mind?'

There's a twinkle in her eye. 'I think I have just the thing.'

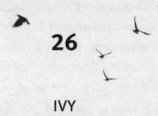

26

IVY

'Are we really doing this?'

Audrey's cheeks are flushed and, even though her legs are much longer than mine, she's struggling to keep up. We hopped on a bus down to the boat docks and now we're scouring the harbour looking for *Old Sheila*.

There's obviously a small part of me that feels jealous about Teddy and Audrey. But my pride is bruised more than my heart. *I* cooled it off with Teddy. *I* wanted this. Plus, Audrey is so not Teddy's type. Like . . . *at all*. She has no edge to her. In fact, I haven't seen Audrey be passionate about anything – except maybe the latest memes circulating the internet.

After discovering Teddy's deception, we lay in bed in the dark, cheeks aching from laughter. In that moment, we felt like friends.

'Do you really think this is gonna work?' Audrey asks me, jumping over a coil of rope on the slatted boards of the pier.

'Well, at least we'll find out if he really likes you,' I reply with a wink. 'I think he needs a dose of his own medicine. Saturdays are pretty boring around here in case you hadn't noticed. It's just a bit of light-hearted weekend tomfoolery.' I smile to reassure her.

'Who's Tom?' She stares back at me blankly.

'Oh, sorry, it's a British saying. Aha! Here we are. Knew it was around here somewhere.'

Audrey grabs my arm. 'Ivy . . .'

'What?'

'Thank you. For being so cool about this. I mean . . . Theo . . . Teddy is your "sort of" ex. This breaks a whole bunch of girl codes where I'm from. I don't know about here, but this would have gone very differently back home. I really didn't know you guys knew each other and . . .'

'Honestly, I don't care. Teddy and I were a summer fling. We aren't a proper couple – we never really were. He's a good guy really.'

'OK, well, I really appreciate it. I'd kinda get if you wanted to stab out my eye with the end of a stiletto though.'

'That's tomorrow's plan,' I say with a wicked grin. Thankfully, she grins back.

Fishing nets and crab pots litter the walkway and there are elderly fishermen pottering about, getting ready for a day out on the water or unloading their catches. Teddy's boat is a few metres away, sandwiched between two flashy yachts, making poor Old Sheila stick out like a sore thumb.

I can't help thinking of the first time I set foot on her. It was after we'd been forced to come back to Winferne Bay to give our police statements, so it was kind of a rough day. A group of us ended up drinking beers and playing card games until four a.m. It had been the perfect way to let off steam.

Old Sheila is pretty unique. Teddy's great-grandad was a fisherman and the boat was passed down to Teddy's dad, who put it into storage and never used it. But Teddy loves tinkering with things and it was only a matter of time before he was renovating her and making her all sparkly again. Her red-and-white painted exterior and little circular windows give her a proper homely feel.

'Right, got the camera?' I ask.

Audrey digs in her handbag for the instant camera we'd brought with us. 'Yep.'

'OK, you stay here behind this yacht and I'll go on board. Then wait a few seconds before coming in.'

As I walk up to his boat, I can hear Teddy inside, swearing at something. My stomach churns – he's really preparing the boat for a date with Audrey, just as they arranged after we discovered his treachery.

I clamber on to the boat, gripping tightly to the rope barriers. I tap on the nearest bench to signal my (or he'd think Audrey's) arrival.

'Oh, you're here!' shouts Teddy. 'Come through the side door. I'll just be a second.'

I don't answer him, but make my footsteps extra loud as I clamber down towards the door to the main cabin. I push it open slowly, hiding my face for as long as possible.

I almost scream, the sight that greets me is so absurd.

Teddy is lying on the bench in the cabin, dressed only in his boxer shorts, a pirate hat and an eyepatch. In his hand is a plastic sword, which he's using to protect his modesty. I gasp and throw my hands over my mouth.

'SHIT . . . Ivy!' He jumps up, his eyes wide and confused.

'Oh my God, Teddy. Weren't you expecting me?'

'Uh . . .'

'You invited me over last night! I didn't realize I was supposed to be in costume . . .'

'I . . . no? I don't think . . .' He looks around, then grabs his phone from the side table and panic-scrolls. At that very moment, Audrey appears in the door behind me with the camera and snaps a picture.

Teddy blinks.

'Or was it me you thought was coming?' she says as the camera begins to whir.

He looks from me to Audrey and back to me again.

'I'm very confused right now . . .' He blinks at Audrey. 'So you don't have a thing for pirates then?' He drops the plastic sword and pulls off the hat.

'Afraid not.'

'But *I* have a thing for blackmail,' I say, taking the Polaroid from the bottom of the camera and laughing as it develops into the goofiest photo of Teddy: the most ridiculous pirate I've ever seen. 'If you don't want this photo to become the front page of the yearbook, you're going to owe us big time.'

'*And* you won't play two girls off against each other, like you did with us, got it?'

'I promise. I swear. Ivy . . . Audrey . . .' He still looks shell-shocked.

I spin round and grab Audrey's arm. 'Come on, let's go while he thinks about what he's done.'

'*Old Sheila* stinks pretty bad anyway,' she says.

I turn back and stare at Teddy. 'Smells like a rat to me.'

27

AUDREY

'I still can't believe we got this picture! It's hilarious.' I stare at the Polaroid as we walk back along the coast from the harbour. Neither of us are in a rush to get back to school, and a long walk feels like a balm for our weary souls. The sun is shining and the sea sparkles, rising and falling with each one of its big ocean breaths.

'I know. We can get a lot of favours out of that,' Ivy laughs.

My hands are buried in my pockets, my fingers tingling with the cold. The bright October sunshine is deceptive; it looks like it should be warm, but the persistent wind brings a chill to every movement. My lungs burn with the effort of walking up and down the cliffs, each one a miniature mountain.

'Lola never thought he was good enough for me. She said he'd break my heart, but I never let myself get in that deep,' says Ivy.

'Did Teddy and Lola know each other well?' I ask when we reach the crest of one of the hills.

'A bit. They weren't super close or anything, but they were in the same year, started at Illumen at the same time,' she says. 'He wasn't actually at the party at the time her body was found.'

'He wasn't? I thought everyone went to it.'

'He was supposed to come. But I remember distinctly that I was looking all over for him. He keeps telling me he was stuck with his family and didn't arrive until after, but then his younger sister said he was out.' She shrugs. 'Hard to know what to believe.'

'Hmm,' I say, the wind stealing the words from my mouth. 'First Araminta, now Teddy . . .'

'It's not that I suspect him or anything,' Ivy adds. 'Like I said, he barely knew Lola. I just find it weird that I didn't know where he was . . .' Suddenly she stops and turns to face the ocean. 'Oh God. I hadn't realized we'd walked this far.'

'What do you mean?' I ask.

'This is where . . .' She trails off.

I look down at the chalky ground beneath my white sneakers. Even from here, well back from the edge, in the full light of day, it barely looks knitted together by the patches of grass. I wouldn't dare walk any closer to the edge than this. The cliff looks like it's perpetually about to crumble into the water, the jagged edge a testament to the places it's done just that.

But my body seems paradoxically drawn to the edge, as if wondering what it might be like to take a leap and jump. I don't, of course. In fact, I lean back, away from the edge. That's why my heart almost stops when Ivy takes a dangerous step forward.

'Ivy!' I shout.

'We used to take selfies here. Dare each other to get

closer. There are a couple of false edges too, so you could look as if you were in danger, but really there was a little ledge beneath you. Like trick photography.' She balances on one leg and puts a foot out over the edge, so that her shoe is hovering over nothing but thin air and water.

I reach forward and grab her sleeve, pulling her back. 'Don't joke around like that. It's not funny,' I say.

But Ivy's not laughing. A tear rolls down her cheek, which she hastily brushes away. Still, she grips my arm, and we stumble further away from the edge, then slump down on to the grass.

'I try not to let it affect me, but it's really hard,' she whispers.

'I know,' I say.

'But the more I think about it . . . if something really did happen to her, and it wasn't an accident, I'd want justice.'

'Oh, Ivy. I'd feel the same.'

We sit for a few moments in silence. Ivy tears up tufts of grass and tosses them into the wind, watching the blades get swept away into the sea.

'Did you know you can see Illumen Hall from the next bend?' she says.

'Really?'

'Yeah, come on. I'll show you.'

We walk a bit further, huddling into each other against the wind. 'Look. There,' she says.

I shield my eyes from the sun. The school seems so little from here as you can only see a small corner of it – most of the peninsula is hidden by cliffs. You could scan the horizon and not realize it was there at all.

'I think Lord Brathebone built it there on purpose. He chose that spot because it's so secluded. I think that's why I like it so much – it makes me feel safe.'

I try and look at the school through Ivy's eyes – as a warm, safe sanctuary, as opposed to the medieval stronghold it appears to me. It's not easy.

Once we get closer, the path becomes more clearly trodden, and there are more trees and wildflower bushes around us. My phone vibrates in my pocket – I've got a signal for the first time since we reached the clifftop. It's from Patrick.

> Any leads on her room or the
> diary? Please let me know. I'd
> really like it if we could meet
> again.

'Teddy?' Ivy asks me.

I shake my head. 'No . . .' I hesitate. I haven't told anyone about my encounter with the enigmatic Patrick Radcliffe. But maybe it's time to open up a bit. 'It's another guy.'

Ivy raises an eyebrow. 'Go on . . .'

'OK . . . so you know when I went into Winferne Bay.'

'And got caught and locked in our room?'

I wrinkle my nose. 'Yeah, that time. My God, do you remember everything?'

'I collect those shiny nuggets like a magpie.'

'I bet you do,' I mutter. 'OK, well, when I was in the coffee shop in town, I bumped into this guy. This *really hot* guy. He said his name was Patrick Radcliffe.'

Ivy's jaw drops. 'What, like . . . Lola's brother, Patrick?'

'That's the one.'

'What did he say to you?'

'He seemed normal at first, but then he got really worked up – I mean, he's obviously still grieving – and basically asked if I'd help him investigate. He kept talking about that podcast.'

'Holy shit.'

'Right? I mean, I said no, of course. But then I saw him again at school after we found out about Clover and I found myself wishing I could help. That was the night Teddy texted us both.'

'Oh.' Ivy's mouth is round with surprise, and it stays like that for a second as she connects the dots. 'I'd actually been thinking about going to the library to research the Magpie Society. Because of something Clover said to me.'

We pass through the school gates, and the meandering path towards the school feels like it lasts a lifetime. I haven't walked this far in a long time; every muscle is aching. Still, I don't really want it to end. Having this time with Ivy has been . . . exactly what I've been missing since coming here.

A real friend.

I don't want the spell to break.

'I've got to do my piano practice, but see you at dinner?' Ivy says, already walking away.

'See you,' I say. Because of course she doesn't feel the same way. She already has her friends – and her music, her studies and her running. She doesn't need me.

28

AUDREY

Here are those old chemistry IB tests you asked for, milady.

Anything else I can help with?

I stare at the email a few times, then nudge Ivy, who's sitting next to me. 'Man, having a guy like Teddy at your beck and call is pretty sweet.'

'You two *still* won't tell me what you did to our poor, sweet Theodore to have him running all over school on errands for you,' says Harriet.

'Afraid that's between me and Audrey,' Ivy says with a wink to me. It feels strange to have our own little secret. *Good* strange. Harriet looks a bit more put out though, and she exaggerates her pout.

'He's like our own grown-up fledgling – except far more useful,' Ivy continues.

'I still don't get this whole fledgling thing. Clover is yours, right?' I ask her.

'Fledglings are often students who'll eventually become prefects. It's a mentorship thing. Although I think Clover's blown her chances of that now . . .'

'A bit like how you were supposed to be next in line for head girl by being the only prefect in our year?'

'What do you mean "supposed to be"?' Ivy shoots me a dark look.

'Well . . .' I glance over at the table where Araminta, Katie and Xander are sitting, giving me and Ivy the cold shoulder. Bonnie's there too. She might not be a prefect, but she sure is getting a lot more mentoring than Ivy right now.

'Bonnie will never get the spot,' Ivy says brusquely, flicking over the page of her textbook.

'Hey, you'd know more than me.' I'm slowly learning the intricacies of the school, but I'll always be an outsider. At least now I have a friend who's *really* on the inside. Things have been so much better between me and Ivy since the boatyard incident last week. We literally caught Teddy at his most ridiculous, and he's been treating us both like queens ever since.

It's pretty easy to ignore the flutter of butterflies I get every time I see a message or email from him. Most of the time.

'Incoming,' Ivy mutters. At first, I don't get it. But then I see Araminta approaching our table and I sit up a little straighter.

'Hi.'

'Minty,' I say, smiling with all my teeth.

'Just wanted to remind you about our Samhain party on the last Saturday of half-term. It's going to be a big one.'

'Oh great,' I say. 'I'll be there.'

'You'll need to dress in appropriate colours – but I'm sure Ivy can help fill you in. You still good to help with the decorations, Ivy?'

'Of course,' she says, without looking up from her textbook.

'Great. I mean, you'll be here all half-term anyway as usual? So I'll expect you to have made a head start.'

Ivy's shoulders tighten. 'Your expectation is my command.'

'And, Harriet, are you still OK to put together a playlist?'

'As long as we have a better sound system than last year. It was so tinny it completely threw off my jams.' Harriet mimes scratching at a disc on a turntable.

Araminta rolls her eyes. 'Well, if you want to check it out before half-term, you'd better come with me now.'

'Do I have to?' Harriet says with a sigh. But she gets up from the table anyway. 'Catch you later.' She waves to Ivy and me, before sauntering off with Araminta.

It takes a good few moments after Araminta leaves before Ivy's shoulders finally relax. I lean across. 'So you're gonna be staying at school over half-term?'

'Yeah. I always do. It's hectic enough for my mum at home with my sister, without me piling in there too. Plus, they feed me here so Mum doesn't have to worry about that, and I like my alone time so . . .' Ivy bites the end of her pen and shrugs.

'Oh.' I shift uncomfortably. I've never had to think about whether or not my family could *feed* me. Hell, I thought nothing of ordering takeout if I didn't like whatever our chef, Reyna, was cooking. I don't think my mom ever set foot in the kitchen – except to grab her favourite smoothie out of the fridge.

I wince.

'What is it?' she asks.

'Well. It looks like I'm gonna be staying here over half-term too.'

Ivy arches an eyebrow. 'Really?'

'Yeah. My mom booked this trip for Dad and my brother to some yoga retreat in Ibiza or something.'

'And you don't want to join them? Sounds like heaven to me.'

'Uh, a week listening to my mom recite mantras and force-feeding me kombucha? Sounds like hell to me. Honestly, she goes through these cycles all the time where she decides she needs a "detox" and then she drags the whole family into it. At least this year I have a legitimate excuse to stay somewhere else for a while. They won't let me stay by myself in their brand-new house.'

My eyes search Ivy's face for a reaction, but she isn't giving much away. She taps at her temple with the end of her pen, then – thankfully – she smiles. 'That's OK – there's plenty of places to hide away in this school when no one's here. I'm sure we won't get in each other's way.'

I let out a long breath. 'Cool.'

We pause for a moment. But the moment doesn't last very long. There's a huge commotion and Clover rushes in. Her glasses are askew, her school tie unravelling around her neck.

Ivy immediately sits up in her chair. 'Clover?'

'Who did it?' Clover's voice is several octaves higher than normal, and her fists are balled up at her sides.

Ivy is the first one to rush over to her, but Clover takes several steps back so that she can radiate her rage throughout the entire common room.

'One of you did it! One of you's trying to stop me! Well, let me tell you, you won't. You won't stop me at all!'

Ivy manages to grab her arm and pull her in. Once she's enclosed in Ivy's arms, Clover bursts into tears. Ivy manages to steer her over to our table and sits her down. Clover's sobs slowly begin to subside, but the girl looks absolutely distraught. I exchange a confused look with Ivy. What could have caused this?

'They . . . they messed up everything in my bedroom. Like ripped up all my research notes, burned my SD cards, broke my microphone, everything.'

'What? You're kidding!' I exclaim.

'That is messed up,' says Ivy as she strokes Clover's hand.

'I don't know what they thought they'd find. Did they really think I was stupid enough to leave any evidence in my room? Like, honestly. When things started hotting up around here, I shipped all that stuff back home asap. I'm going there anyway for half-term and that's where I'll record my next podcast. And, trust me, that next one?' Clover's eyes flash. 'If people think I've lit a fire now, things are really going to go up in flames next week. But, Ivy . . . I have to show you something else.'

'What could be worse than that?'

Clover doesn't answer. Instead, she gratefully takes the tissue that Ivy has dug out of her schoolbag and wipes her face. Then she reaches into her pocket and pulls out a crumpled piece of paper.

On it are the words:

STOP LOOKING OR YOU'LL BE NEXT

29

AUDREY

Now that it's half-term, the halls echo as I wander around the school. I never realized how much of a buzz several hundred students could make until most of them have left. I have to pull my cardigan even tighter around my body, warding off a distinct chill. I don't think the school enjoys it when the students aren't there. It seems to be holding its breath. Suspended.

I've started to feel I can recognize its moods. Illumen Hall is no longer a stranger to me, and I finally know my way around. It was a tad depressing listening to other people discuss their exciting plans for the break, but I'd much rather stay here and get to know the school than be on some holiday with a family I really dislike.

My phone pings. My real phone – which I get to have for the whole week, free from the prying eyes of that witch Mrs Parsons. It feels redundant now, cracked screen and all.

Be there asap.

On my way

Thank God for Ivy. Another phrase I couldn't have

envisaged thinking at the start of the semester! But, since the Clover reveal and our walk along the cliffs, the energy between me and Ivy has definitely shifted. Everything that was tense is now so much looser, as if the elastic band has snapped, but no one got hurt. The way she handled the Teddy situation was hilarious, but somehow she's even managed to preserve their friendship.

Teddy's cute, but I don't wanna get involved with a guy like that. He seems to be a little *too* comfortable with having girls over to his boat. I'm starting to think even Ivy was way too good for him – and he probably knows it.

For the first time in my five weeks at the school, I feel at home and I'm able to enjoy my surroundings. Like the library. I'd never really appreciated it before, but it looks as if it's been plucked from a Victorian novel. There's an air of abandonment about it, but at the same time this feeling that, if you knew the special password, you could discover a million mysteries buried within. There are ladders that give access to some of the higher shelves, which are forbidden to everyone except sixth-formers (like us) or the librarian and teachers.

When Ivy arrives, she looks flushed from her afternoon jog. She'd tried to convince me to join her, but I swiftly declined. I might be in school, but it's still my vacation.

'So, where should we start?' I ask.

When Clover showed us the threatening note, I'd never seen Ivy look so angry. As soon as Clover was safely off school grounds and back home, Ivy told me she wanted to do some investigating of her own. And I agreed. Despite all my intentions, I was invested now.

'Let's go to the Upper Wing,' she says.

I frown. 'The what?'

'Think of it a bit like the rare books bit in the British Library . . . or maybe the restricted section in Hogwarts.' She grins.

I fake a look of alarm. 'Nothing's gonna bite me or set me on fire, is it?'

'Shouldn't do. This is just for books they don't want the younger students to get their sticky fingers on. Some of these editions should probably be locked up in a museum or something. Or at least they might go for a few quid on eBay. Sometimes, not gonna lie, I've been tempted when times have been tough.'

I laugh, but stop when I see the expression on Ivy's face. 'Wait, seriously?'

'I could get a hundred quid for some of the first editions in here!' Then she shrugs. 'I *am* joking. But only because I love this place so much. And Mum would go bonkers if she found out.'

'Is it just your mom and sister at home?'

'Yeah.' She lowers her head so that her hair falls across her face. I'm about to say that she doesn't have to tell me anything if she doesn't want to, but she continues. 'Dad left us when I was three years old, and we lived in a tiny bedsit until I was nine. He came back into the picture sometimes, but was never a permanent feature.'

'I'm sorry,' I mumble. I'm not sure what a bedsit is, but I can guess.

'My mum worked three jobs to keep a roof over our heads, make sure we could eat and fund all my activities –

until I got to Illumen Hall, of course. I barely saw her. I learned how to use the rice cooker when I was five.'

'What about your grandparents?'

She shakes her head. 'I never knew my mum's parents. They moved here from China when my mum was small, but unfortunately they died before I was born. My dad's side kept their distance too. Then my sister Violet came along a few years after me – and it got even worse. Honestly, it sounds stupid, but I feel like school saved me.'

She looks up, her expression distant. 'Even at primary school, I realized, once I walked through those doors, that despite my hand-me-down clothes and charity-shop books, I could be whoever I wanted . . . and what I wanted was to be the *best*. I put all I had into being good at everything. Maths. English. Sports. Science. And Mum poured the little money she had into helping me.

'That's how I landed a full scholarship here. Full term and board – not only easing the pressure on my mum, but giving me the leg-up that I needed. Honestly, I want to earn enough money to buy Mum a proper house one day. She deserves to live comfortably. If I work hard enough, I can be as good as the other leaders and politicians and medics that have graduated from Illumen.'

'That's a lot of pressure to put on yourself.'

Ivy shrugs. 'Perhaps, but I love it here.'

I smile. 'You do seem to thrive. I'm sure your mom's really proud of you.'

Ivy clears her throat, like she's just realized how much she's poured out to me. 'And what about you? Big plans for life after IH?'

Now it's my turn to shrug. 'I don't exactly feel at home in the UK yet. But there's not much for me in the States, not any more. Maybe I'll take one of those – what do you call them . . . gap years?' I glance over at Ivy, who's staring at me. 'Let's make a pact, you and me. February half-term, if we're both stuck here, we'll go somewhere cool like . . . Paris! I'll get Dad to pay,' I add hastily.

Ivy pauses and I wonder if I've taken it a bit too far. 'Venice?' she suggests.

'Deal!'

She laughs. 'Let's get down to business. Clover thought there might be something about the Magpie Society in this part of the library, only she doesn't have access.'

I think for a second. 'I did a bit of googling about magpies. They're pretty freaky birds.'

'One for sorrow, two for joy,' sing-songs Ivy.

'What's that?'

'You've never heard the rhyme?'

I shake my head.

'Let me see . . .' Ivy closes her eyes and I swear the temperature in the room seems to drop by a couple of degrees. She lowers her voice to a whisper.

> 'One for sorrow,
> Two for joy,
> Three for a girl, four for a boy,
> Five for silver, six for gold,
> Seven for a secret never to be told.'

A chill runs down my spine. 'Wow – is that like a

nursery rhyme or something? Oh!' I smack my forehead. 'I didn't get it before. The Voice Unknown – sorry, *Clover* – mentioned that "one for sorrow" thing, didn't she?'

'It's an old poem, I think. I have no idea where it came from. Maybe we can look it up?'

'What, like on Google?' Instinctively, I take out my phone.

'Well . . . no. I mean, you might get *some* answers. But we're trying to figure out about the Magpie Society here at Illumen Hall, right? And I don't think Google will know about that.'

I type in *One for sorrow + Illumen Hall* just in case but, as Ivy predicted, it brings up zero results.

Why do I always feel so stupid in her presence? I casually slip my phone back in my pocket.

'Let's look up magpies in the Upper Wing catalogue. Even though I feel that might be too obvious as well,' Ivy says.

We head to one of the iPads, which is embedded in a wooden cabinet. It's just like this school to have a mix of old-world furniture and the latest technology. There are even little GPS tags embedded in most of the books, so they can be tracked and to make sure they don't leave the school grounds.

'Wait!' A light flashes in Ivy's eyes. 'The Corvid Scholarship! Magpies are from the *Corvidae* family of birds. Maybe there's something there?'

'How the heck did you know that?'

Ivy blushes. 'Oh, my brain is a mishmash of stuff. Mr

Tavistock used to quiz me on the classification of the different birds and animals that live in the grounds.'

'Seriously?' I say, one eyebrow raised almost into my hairline. 'The weird groundskeeper guy?'

'Don't believe everything Bonnie tells you,' she replies. 'Plus, I find it fascinating, OK?' Her enthusiasm is infectious, and I immediately feel like we're on the path to something. We type *Corvid* into the search, and an old non-fiction text called *The Corvid Mysteries* pops up. Sounds promising. We note down its location and head to the marked bookcase. When we find the book, it's ancient-looking, thick, with dull, gold, peeling lettering. There's the outline of a bird – presumably a crow – on the spine. Ivy and I exchange a look. We take it down from the shelf with almost gentle reverence, and gasp as we see that the pages themselves are edged in bright gold.

We flip through to the front page. My jaw drops when I see a pencil inscription.

The first step is over the edge.

And underneath is a rough sketch of a magpie.

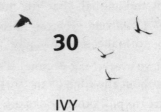

30

IVY

My mouth drops open and I glance at Audrey, who is staring, wide-eyed. Although the magpie sketch looks slightly different from the one that was drawn on Lola's back, it's definitely too similar to be a coincidence. This drawing is small and delicate, yet the pencil lines are rough and repeated, making the magpie look dishevelled – almost sinister. Its beak is wide open, wings outstretched.

But the words above it are even creepier.

'*The first step is over the edge.*' Audrey's voice trembles. 'Ivy. This . . . this is *really* freaky. Over what edge? Oh my God.' She grabs my arm and her eyes search my face. 'Do you think this has anything to do with Lola? The edge of the cliff?'

An image flashes through my brain of Lola, her hair twisting in the wind, staring out into the roiling darkness of the ocean beyond the cliff, of her moving forward to take that final step . . .

I shake my head. 'I don't know. How could it be and – more importantly – *why*? It would be a ridiculously small secret society if they're telling everyone who wants to join to walk off a cliff.'

Audrey chuckles at my dark joke, but I think it's more

out of nerves. I continue. 'Maybe we're overthinking it.' I close the book and run my hands over it, tracing my fingers along the spine and the edges of the cover, hoping for something to make sense. Maybe part of the cover lifts off?

'OK, what about the edge of the shelf?' Audrey kneels down and starts to pull other books off.

I put *The Corvid Mysteries* down on the floor and help. Maybe there's something carved into the underside of the shelf. I turn on my phone's torch and crane my neck to look. I'm glad we're pretty much alone in the school at the moment because, if anyone saw us, they'd think we'd lost our minds.

After an hour, we're both splayed out on the library floor, surrounded by a shamble of books. We're no closer to finding the next step – if there even is one.

'Maybe we're being punked,' Audrey says. She shifts so that she's lying down beside me, our heads propped up on an uncomfortable pillow of books. 'There's got to be something we're missing. I mean, that book looks ancient! What's to say the next step wasn't moved years ago?'

I sigh, and pick up *The Corvid Mysteries* again. I open it up to the inscription and stare at it, willing it to reveal its secrets. But the book imparts nothing but a dry, dusty smell. Audrey's probably right. Whatever sign there might have been, it's long gone now.

I fan the pages across my face, trying to cool down. 'Did it suddenly get really hot in here or is it just me?'

Almost instantly, Audrey sits up, grabs the book from my hand and inhales sharply. 'What's this?'

I sit up, a frown on my face as Audrey turns the book over in her hands. She then bends the pages over at a slight angle. 'It looks like . . . what the heck? A painting?'

'What are you talking about?' But just then I spot exactly what she did. At a glance, the edges of the pages are just gilt, but, as Audrey pushes on the cover so that the fore-edges form a waterfall, something that looks like a painting emerges. When shut, it disappears again. She spreads the pages at just the right angle to reveal the painting in its entirety.

'There! Hold it there!' I say.

'Oh my God. The first step is over the edge. Over the edge of the book?'

'Must be. In fact, I think I've seen this somewhere before . . .' I say. Audrey holds the pages still, and I stare at the somehow familiar scene of an old Victorian outbuilding, surrounded by billowing blossom trees. I click my tongue against the roof of my mouth. 'I know exactly where I've seen this. It's a miniature version of one of the paintings on the gallery wall in the corridor leading from the dining hall. The one next to the horses and hounds. They're all painted by former students!'

'The next step?' Audrey asks.

'It's got to be,' I say, and I can't hide my excitement.

'What do you think this is? A trail leading to the Magpie Society?'

'No idea. But we have to check it out, don't you think?'

'Absolutely. I feel like Robert Langdon.' Audrey goes to put the book in her bag, but I stop her.

'If you take it, we'll set off an alarm.' I feel impressed at whoever planned this – it's kind of genius. No one could move the book from the library without alerting someone. I know that, in the really olden days, books had actually been *chained* to the shelves. This first piece of the puzzle must have been here for ages.

'OK, let's take a photo instead,' Audrey says, balancing the angle of the painting while trying to take a photo with her phone at the same time. Once we've managed it, we put the book back and hurriedly toss the others back on to the shelves too, albeit a little haphazardly. Mrs Ling will throw a fit when she sees them, but we're pumped too full of adrenaline to care.

We rush down to the dining hall, not slowing until we reach the stone-tiled corridor with the gallery wall.

'God, there are so many paintings . . . I can't say I'm gonna be much help here. I've not paid much attention to the artwork these last few weeks!' Audrey stares up at the vast gallery before us filled with maybe a hundred paintings in varying sizes, and of varying ages. I've spent many a moment staring up at them while queuing to enter the dining hall. Some of my favourite pieces of artwork are among these paintings.

'There! Five down and seven in from the right – that's the same, isn't it?' I point up to the painting, with the same blossom trees and outbuilding. We pull up the photo on Audrey's phone to compare – and it's definitely the same. It's encased in an intricate golden carved frame that gleams without a speck of dust or spot of tarnish on its surface.

'Yeah, I see it!' Her eyes scan the picture. 'Um . . . what now?'

Audrey's right, of course. We've discovered a secret painting on the fore-edge of an old book that matches a painting on the school wall, but what does that have to do with the Magpie Society?

'Hold on – give me a boost.'

'What?' Audrey stares at me.

I place both my hands on the ancient iron radiator against the wall, and lift my foot up. Then Audrey gets it. She grabs my shoe and lifts me up. Once I find my balance, I help her up too. When we're both perched precariously on the radiator, we take another look at the painting. Instantly, I spot a tiny drawing of a magpie in the corner.

'There!' I cry out triumphantly.

Audrey looks at the image on her phone. 'That magpie wasn't on the fore-edge painting.'

We stare at each other, and then back at the painting.

'Ivy . . . the bird up there . . . its wing is bent, like it's pointing out in front of it. Kind of an unnatural pose for a bird, I'd say? Unless your British birds are different from the ones we have in Georgia . . .'

We both turn to look where the bird seems to be pointing. Opposite the gallery wall is a horizontal row of small, square windows. This corridor is in one of the oldest parts of the school so the windows have small iron bars on them. One of these windows sits directly opposite the painting.

I jump down from the radiator and walk slowly up to the window, pulling myself up on to the sill. Outside, I can see the familiar view of the grounds with its clusters of trees and Mr Tavistock's little stone cottage in the distance.

Audrey pulls herself up beside me.

'There! It's the same outhouse,' she cries out, pointing at a building half hidden by the trees. She holds up her phone to compare. 'Holy crap. That's weird.' She looks at me in alarm and my skin prickles with goosebumps.

I blink, looking from the phone to the window several times. 'I think you're right. I can't believe I didn't see it! I guess there must have been an orchard there before, but it's all been ploughed up. I run round that area all the time! I suppose it's one of those things that, unless you're looking out of this exact window, it wouldn't have the same aspect – so how else would you recognize it?'

Audrey slumps down on the window sill, her legs dangling. 'Ivy, do we really think a bird in a painting is giving us directions to some rotting building on campus grounds? We're not Sherlock and Watson. Maybe we're just overthinking this?' She crosses her arms over her stomach. 'I'm kinda hungry. Shall we just grab something to eat?'

I stare at her. 'You're really considering giving up now? After all this?'

She bites her bottom lip.

'Well, rotting building or not, this can't just be a coincidence. *I'm* going inside.' I pull my tote bag up over my shoulder, jump down off the sill and storm off down the hallway.

'Fine, I'll come! It's starting to get dark and I don't like to think of you out there on your own. But I want you to know: this shit creeps me right out. If there are bats in there, I'm gone!'

31

IVY

Once we're outside, I kind of wish we'd thought to grab our coats. There's a real chill in the air, but I suppress my shivers for Audrey's sake. She could turn back at any moment, and I don't want to spook her. I appreciate her presence – and I wouldn't have spotted that edge painting if it wasn't for her. A second pair of eyes is so useful.

She links her arm in mine and smiles at me as we pick our way across the grounds. I can't believe how close we've become, and so quickly. I'd really hated her guts to begin with. And then today, I *spilled* my guts all over the library floor, and she listened, really listened, in a way that even Harriet has trouble with sometimes. I can't remember the last time Harriet asked me about my family.

I turn back to look at the school, making sure that we're not being followed. I think then about the CCTV and the fact I hadn't checked if there was a camera here. I look back, squinting. I don't see one, but I can't be certain.

We pick up our pace slightly, sticking to the long shadows of the treeline. The outbuilding is even more ruined and crumbling than it looked from the window – I'm shocked it hasn't been pulled down for safety reasons. To reach the door we have to hack our way through thick weeds, brambles and stinging nettles, which is a lot harder than I anticipated, especially in the dusky evening light. I feel a little guilty for dragging Audrey into this as I watch her battle through the foliage with her freshly manicured nails.

'Oh my God! WHAT IS THIS? WHY IS IT STINGING ME?' she screeches, holding up a handful of green weed.

I cringe. 'That's *Urtica dioica*. Otherwise known as a stinging nettle. That's going to hurt like a bitch . . .'

Audrey shrieks again and drops the handful of nettles. She rubs her hands together in pain. 'Ugh, we have that at home but not on our school grounds! I hope it's not like poison ivy.'

'No, it's not as bad as that! Don't worry. Look, we're almost at the door.' I crouch down under the last bramble. I try and turn the old iron ring door handle, but it breaks off in my hand. 'Crap.' I show it to Audrey and she laughs.

'Shall we just head back? We'll never get in now!' She sounds relieved.

'No, I'll get it open.' I pull out a penknife from my tote bag and flick the latch. The old door creaks and opens towards us. Audrey gives me a nervous glance and I pull her through the last bit of foliage so she's crouching next to me in front of the slightly open door.

Inside, I can see blue evening light pouring in through an old cracked window and cobwebs are layered from wall to wall like Halloween bunting. There's nothing on the mud-covered floor, but moss is growing out of every stone where mortar once was.

'It stinks! Is something dead in there?' Audrey covers her nose and looks in over my shoulder.

'It's the smell of damp, not death.' I step inside, feeling an overwhelming sense of disappointment. There's nothing but a few crumpled bags of crisps, some squashed cans of Coke and a little heap of cigarette butts. A pile of rotten, slatted wood pallets are stacked up in one corner.

'At least we checked it out, Ivy. Just looks like a place that students used to hang out in, probably cutting class or something.'

She's right. I let out a sigh and turn back towards her. 'Yeah, I suppose so. I don't know what I expected. Sorry for dragging you out here to . . . Hang on . . .' Just as I'm about to go back out through the door, I spot something on one of the old stone slabs on the floor, near the pallets. Her torch illuminated it for just the briefest second. 'Point your light back there.'

She frowns. 'Is that . . . a feather?' Audrey tiptoes closer, kneeling down to look more closely at the slab by the light of her phone.

'I think so!' I brush the stone lightly with my fingers, cleaning dirt from an etching. It's definitely a feather, although the edges are worn and faded. I tilt my head to one side, knitting my eyebrows. Then I run my fingertips over the edge of the stone, which is slightly loose. In fact, I'm able to lift it up ever so slightly. 'Let's get these pallets out of the way.'

'I'm not touching those!' squeals Audrey. 'Something could be living under there.'

'Come on.' I kick one of the pallets aside and it almost

falls apart. 'Don't you think it's kind of suspicious that these pallets are just randomly here?'

'Er, no . . . this whole place is a dump.'

'I think someone put them there deliberately to hide . . . whatever this is.'

'Ew, I knew I shouldn't have worn my Paige jeans.' To her credit, Audrey gets down and helps me move the pallets away, wincing as her hands are steadily covered in mouldy slime. It's not pleasant for me either, but I have a feeling the result will be worth it.

'Help me lift this,' I say. Audrey crouches down and inches her fingers round her half of the stone, and then together we heave.

'It's a trapdoor,' I say, marvelling at the ingenuity.

'It *was*,' Audrey replies. 'Wherever it led, it doesn't go there now.'

She's right. There are some boards buried deep in the ground at uneven levels that look like they might once have been a staircase, but the tunnel – or whatever it was – is blocked by earth and dirt. It's impossible for us to get any further. I don't know whether to feel disappointed or elated. 'You know what this means though?'

'What?'

'There *was* a Magpie Society. All those steps lead here. Maybe this was a hideout or a meeting place or something.'

'A long time ago.'

'Maybe, but it was here.' I lean forward and shake one of the old planks, and to my surprise it comes loose, revealing a shallow cavity.

'Is there anything in there?' Audrey asks. She jams the

phone closer so the light goes all the way back into the hole and instantly we spot something. 'What is it? I'm not putting my arm in there, Ivy! You grab it!'

I put my arm into the gap and pull out what looks like an old journal, wrapped in plastic. The cover is so thick with dust that I can't see anything. Using the cuff of my sleeve, I wipe it down. Underneath the layers of dirt and dust is a scribble of pen – no, it's a *magpie*. Beneath the magpie drawing, I can just about make out the words ILLUMEN HALL: 1897 debossed into the old, dusty, red leather case.

I carefully unwrap it from the plastic and open the first page. Audrey squeals excitedly. 'It looks like a yearbook! A super-old one at that.'

She's right. As I flick through each page, I'm met with the black-and-white faces of students in old school photographs.

'Wait, stop!' Audrey says. I look down and almost drop the book in shock.

In the middle of the rows and rows of students' faces, unmistakable even in the gloom, is the picture of a girl who looks exactly like Lola.

32

IVY

Although the photos aren't very clear, the likeness is uncanny.

'Is that *Lola*?' Audrey asks. 'Surely not?'

We look at one another in shock, and then back at the photo.

'No, it can't be. This yearbook is from 1897 . . .' I turn the book over and look at the cover again to be sure. Then I flick back to the photo. 'And this girl's name is Lily Ellory. Look at this.'

Underneath her photo is a handwritten scrawl. When I show Audrey, her hand flies to her mouth. It's eerily quiet between us. The only noise is the evening birdsong and the distant crashing of waves against the cliffs.

'Can you read that?' As Audrey holds the phone light over the writing, I notice her hand is shaking slightly.

'I can't quite make it out – her writing's so small and scribbly.' I squint at the page. 'The year I almost died,' I read aloud. 'I owe all my . . . things? Thanks? THANKS – I owe all my thanks to the . . . magpies.'

'This *must* be something to do with the Magpie Society!' At that moment, Audrey's phone battery dies, leaving us sitting in semi-darkness among cobwebs and cold stone.

'Oh crap.' Audrey grabs my arm.

'Let's go.' I shove the book into my bag and replace the slab with the etching. Just as we close the door behind us, we hear a deep voice and see torchlight flicker nearby.

'Oi! Someone there?' It's Mr Tavistock. If he catches us, he will lose it.

Audrey drops to the ground like she's in the army and we've come under fire.

'Let's crawl around back,' she whispers as she starts shuffling along the ground as close to the building as possible so as not to get stuck in the foliage. Together we reach the back of the outhouse and wait until the coast is clear. But, just as we're about to leg it back across the field, we come face to face with him. We scream in unison as he appears in front of us, his features accentuated by the moonlight.

'You shouldn't be out here.' His voice is low and angry. I've never heard him use that tone with me before.

'Sorry, we were just watching the bats. It's part of our research for . . . er . . . science,' Audrey chips in quickly.

'Yeah, we're learning about migration,' I add.

'Well, Jesus, watch them from somewhere else. That building could have fallen down on you both any second! It's old and crumbling. Don't go back in there.' He clutches his hand to his chest like he's waiting for his heart to stop thumping.

'You're right – we won't go back in. Sorry, Mr T!' I smile at him as we turn to walk back to the school.

'You won't catch many bats around this time of year; they're flying south or hibernating. You might spot some in my cottage garden if you hurry – there's this huge, beautiful beech tree they roosted in over the summer. I can make you a cup of tea too.'

Audrey looks at me with alarm and shakes her head.

'That'd be great!' I say enthusiastically.

Audrey pulls me back and whispers, 'Not a good idea. I've heard strange things about this gardener guy.'

'Trust me, Audrey, he's completely harmless. Plus, he might have some info about the Magpie Society. He's been at the school longer than anyone.'

She sighs as we follow him back to his cottage.

'OK, fine, but I do have one very important question before we go any further.' Audrey looks at me, her face full of concern. 'How do I stop my hands from stinging so bad?'

She rubs them together frantically as I laugh. 'We need to find you a dock leaf to rub on them . . .'

She looks back at me, half smiling. 'What the hell is a dock leaf?'

'This.' I bend down and pluck a broad, ruffled, dark green leaf from a plant on the ground.

Audrey stares at it with scepticism, then snatches it from my hand. 'You know, half the time I'm not sure whether to trust you, Ivy Moore-Zhang.'

'Just a little further, girls,' says Mr Tavistock as he points down a path overhung with long, wispy branches.

'When have I ever led you astray?' I reply with a grin.

'You haven't. But each path looks spookier than the last – and I'm not sure I like where this is going.'

33

AUDREY

When we arrive, I'm pleasantly surprised. Mr Tavistock's cottage looks like it could have been plucked from a fairy-tale picture book. The bricks are worn and mismatched in size and colour, but somehow they seem to work together perfectly. A thatched roof overhangs the entrance, and vines crawl up a trellis. Under the moonlight, it looks positively quaint. Now this is more like the vision of England I'd had before I arrived.

Inside, it's warm and cosy. It's sparsely decorated, with a threadbare rug on the floor and a battered leather armchair that I'm sure must have come from one of the old common rooms. Everything's very neatly arranged and immaculately tidy.

'Tea? I just put the kettle on before I heard the commotion you girls were making outside.'

'Sure,' I say hesitantly.

'Yes, please,' says Ivy. 'But let me make it. You sit down.'

Mr Tavistock smiles gratefully and settles into his leather armchair. I perch on a footstool as Ivy heads into the kitchen. Almost on cue, a loud whistle sounds from the stove-top kettle. I can see Ivy pottering around in there, choosing teacups from the cupboard above the sink, grabbing milk and sugar and arranging it all on a tray. She even finds cookies to put on a little plate. It's like she's right at home. I stare at her. But then my eyes drift around the room. There are lots of old black-and-white photographs of the school, at different stages of development. I even spot the canteen being built, the huge glass structure just a pile of steel beams in one photograph. It's like a time capsule.

Ivy comes back into the living room with the tray and Mr Tavistock pokes the fire with a metal rod.

As I settle into the comforting warmth of the room, I'm wondering why I ever believed the stories about Mr Tavistock being creepy. He looks tired but friendly, and he's clearly very attached to the school. Ivy rearranges his cushions so that he's comfortable, then kneels down at the low wooden table and pours the tea.

After his first sip, Mr Tavistock turns to us – as if the Earl Grey blend has boosted the sharpness in his eyes and woken his mind. There's a twinkle there that was missing before. 'So, what have you girls really been up to? Don't tell me that bat story again – I know better than that.'

'Yeah, that was a bit of a stretch. Actually . . . we were studying this.' Ivy whips out the yearbook from her bag. I immediately raise my eyebrows at her. Should she really be discussing that with him?

'Where did you get that?'

'We found it in the library,' Ivy says. 'And there was a picture of that outbuilding in it, so we thought we'd check it out – since it looks so different.'

Ah, so she's not going to tell the truth about *everything*.

Ivy continues. 'Do you know what that outbuilding was used for?'

'Oh, it's been abandoned for a long time. I think it used to be a cottage for another gardener, but it was condemned after a small fire and then left to crumble.'

'We're also trying to find out who this woman was . . .' I open the page with the Lola lookalike.

Mr Tavistock studies the photograph for so long, I almost think he's fallen asleep. But then he closes the book and places it gently down on his lap. 'Oh yes, I know the story of Lily Ellory. She was the first female pupil to attend Illumen Hall.'

'Really?' Ivy asks. 'That's so interesting.'

'Yes, it would have taken a lot of courage for her to come to the school at that time.'

'And what about the little note? Do you know what that means . . . about the magpies?'

He shakes his head. 'I don't know a thing about that, I'm afraid.'

'Oh,' I say.

'That's a shame,' says Ivy, almost at the same time and our shoulders slump simultaneously. Every time we think there's a lead, it slips through our fingers.

'But Ellory. Yes. Ellory . . . There's a few interesting stories there.'

'The likeness to Lola really is amazing,' Ivy says in a half-whisper. 'Was she related to the Radcliffes at all?'

He shrugs. 'I don't know. If you're interested in learning more about her, I think Lily Ellory's granddaughter still lives in the village. Be worth asking around the market to find her.'

'Great, we will,' I say more brightly.

'Just remember that curiosity can be a tricky companion, a bit like Shadow here,' he says. His black cat, lithe and strong, springs up into his lap when Mr Tavistock says his name. 'It might lead you down paths that were covered up for a reason.'

There's a thud at the rear of the cottage, through the kitchen. Ivy and I spin round.

A hulking presence bends through the low back door, blocking out the light. He stamps his feet on the mat, then calls out, 'Any supper left, Granddad?' His gruff voice seems to shake the foundations of the little cottage.

He takes a few steps forward, so his face comes into the light of the living room. Or what part of his face that isn't obscured by either a scruffy beard or the hairiest eyebrows I've ever seen. He's way too tall for the tiny cottage, and he has to bend down even lower to get under the beam because his hair is piled up in a messy topknot.

Ivy scrambles to her feet, almost knocking over one of the teacups. 'We've taken up too much of your time, Mr T. We're going to be late for our dinner anyway.'

'What's Ms Cranshaw cooked up for you tonight? Something special for the remainers?'

'I hope so.'

'What I wouldn't do for a slice of her steak-and-kidney pie right now,' Mr Tavistock says, licking his lips.

I resist the urge to shudder. What is it with British folk and offal? I take my cue from Ivy though, and stand up too. I thought she might grill Mr Tavistock some more, but now she seems real keen to leave. I sneak a sideways glance at the guy whose presence neither Mr Tavistock nor Ivy seem to be acknowledging.

'Just don't let me catch you near that outbuilding again, you hear?'

'Loud and clear. Come on, Audrey.'

'Thanks for the tea,' I say with a small wave.

We slip out through the front door, and Ivy breathes a sigh of relief.

It lasts only a millisecond as a grubby hand, with dirt under the fingernails, reaches out to grab her. I let out a shout, then snatch her other arm so she's caught between us. The guy steps outside.

'I thought I told you to stay away from my grandfather,' he says.

'Let go of me, Ed. He invited us in for tea. Relax.' She shakes him off, then storms across the field. There's nothing else to do but follow. I look back at Ed, who's watching us leave.

'What the hell was that about?' I ask as soon as I catch up with her.

'Ed's a little possessive of his granddad. Just forget it.'

I'm curious, but Ivy's mouth snaps shut and I don't want to push.

As we head back, we spook a bunch of birds, who fly up into the sky with a few indignant squawks. It's too dark to tell what sort they are, but I can take a good guess.

'You don't think Mr Tavistock will know where that book really came from? What if he tells someone we have it?' I nervously bite my fingers.

'Nah, he hasn't a clue. We need to find Lily Ellory's

granddaughter though. We should go into Winferne tomorrow.'

'Good plan.'

We both fall silent as we come to terms with our eventful day.

'I wonder how Lily almost died?' I ask. 'And who saved her? Because I highly doubt a group of actual magpies rescued her, however clever they might be.'

'I don't know. It's a real mystery. The sooner we figure this out, the sooner Clover can stop her podcast. And, if this Magpie Society did have something to do with Lily Ellory *and* then with Lola's murder, it's up to us to figure out what they did. And why.'

34

IVY

As morning breaks and the autumn sun starts pouring on to the polished wooden floorboards, I'm woken by the cackling of magpies outside our window. The little birds I'd been leaving food out for are disturbing my sleep.

I can't help but feel that we're running out of time. Half-term will fly by and, when school starts again, we won't be able to investigate nearly as easily. Maybe Clover has hyped us up, but it feels like there's a lot more to Lola's death than meets the eye. I want justice for her and, if this society has anything to do with it, then I want to figure it out.

Audrey stirs as her alarm starts shrieking beside her head. 'Did yesterday really happen? Or have I just woken up from the weirdest dream?'

'I'm afraid your hands will tell you the answer to that.' I pull back the duvet and jump up, slipping on my dressing gown.

Audrey groans as she looks down at her hands and sighs at the speckled rash that's still very much there. 'Are we heading out into town to try and find Lily Ellory's granddaughter today?' she asks, rubbing them together.

'I think we should. I thought we could find Mrs Trawley –

the woman who spoke to Clover on the podcast. She sounded like she might have loads of information.'

'Good idea.'

'We can go via the canteen to grab breakfast before signing out.'

'I'm kinda freaked out by all this, Ivy – not gonna lie. Are we really cut out for investigating? It sounds like this Magpie Society thing is probably real – what if the whole thing gets really dangerous? If I get booted out of IH, it's highly likely my dad will actually disown me and I'll be homeless in the middle of nowhere in the UK.'

I chuckle, but Audrey has a point. It could be dangerous. Lola's dead and Clover's life has been threatened. This is a real and very serious situation we're sticking our noses into. I have no idea what could happen or how to handle it, but if I set my mind to something I have to give it one hundred per cent. And I'd rather do that with Audrey helping me. We have to trust each other.

'Honestly? I can't promise you we won't find ourselves in over our heads, but I'm into this now, Audrey, and I know you're invested too. We may as well be invested together. Two heads are better than one and we can't stop now! Call me crazy, but I just have this feeling that we're about to uncover something massive.' I pull my clothes out of the wardrobe and head to the bathroom to shower and change.

'OK, fine,' Audrey calls. 'But I'm wearing my cheap jeans today!'

We devour our freshly baked croissants on the bus and make our way to Winferne Bay's Saturday market. Every week locals set up stalls to sell fruit and veg, plants and flowers, pottery, cakes and, if you're lucky, you might catch a rarely seen Mr Hogan selling his gourmet dog biscuits and hand-made wooden spoons. It's all very cute and kitsch, but I usually avoid it unless I'm craving a freshly made doughnut. It's all a little twee for me.

'So Mrs Trawley runs this stall for – what was it? Vintage mirrors?'

'Over there,' says Audrey. It's not hard to spot: it's a sunny day and we're almost blinded by the refractions coming out at all angles.

'Hi there – excuse me – are you Mrs Trawley?' I ask. As we approach her table, she beams up from her little plastic chair. She's painting tiny gold daisies on an antique bronze hand mirror.

'I am indeed! But call me Maggie, please. What can I do for you girls?'

Although very old and wrinkled, she has a softness about her. Her face is warm and her eyes are bright. She wears silver rings on every finger and each fingernail has been carefully painted blood-red. Her long grey hair is tumbling down over one shoulder and she's wearing a black silk headscarf that's tied in a bow at the side. She must be in her late seventies, early eighties.

'We're actually here to ask you about a woman called Lily Ellory, if you can spare a few minutes?' Audrey dives straight in and I raise my eyebrows in surprise. Considering how hesitant she was to come out this morning and hunt for answers, she's now taking the lead. Mrs Trawley puts down her mirror and looks around.

'Is this for a recording, dear?' She smiles back at us.

'No, we're not recording anything; we're just a couple of enquiring minds,' I say. 'You also mentioned the Magpie Society on the *WKL?* podcast and, even though I've been at the school for nearly six years now, I'd never heard of it. Obviously, we have our little tradition of making an offering to the magpies at the start of the year, but we had no idea it meant something more. And then we found this –'

'While doing research for an assignment,' Audrey jumps in.

I nod and pull the yearbook from my bag. I hold it carefully while flicking through to find the right page. 'We were wondering if you recognize this person? We heard her granddaughter lives in Winferne.' Mrs Trawley holds my wrist as she focuses on the image.

'Of course I recognize her. She's *my* grandmother actually. She was what . . . sixteen here?' She takes her hand off my wrist and tucks a strand of hair behind her ear.

'*Your* grandmother? That's amazing!' Audrey looks at me, her eyes wide with surprise that we found her so easily. 'Are you related to the Radcliffes?'

The woman frowns. 'No. What do you mean by that?'

'Oh, it's just that . . .' Audrey looks to me for backup.

'This picture looks so much like a girl called Lola Radcliffe. She went to our school and died at the start of the summer.'

Mrs Trawley nods sadly. 'It does look like her. I'd never noticed that before. So you're Illumen Hall girls?'

'We are. Do you know what Lily means here about thanking the magpies?'

'Where did you say you found this again?' Mrs Trawley takes the book out of my hand and traces her fingers over the cover. 'This is very old. Very special, I should imagine.'

'We found it in the school archives. They have hundreds of them, not all in such good condition though.' I hope that the warmth of my smile brings her back to Audrey's previous question.

'Are you sure you were supposed to have removed it from the archive?'

'We got special permission. Because of our project?'

'Your project. I see.' Every mirror on her stall seems to reflect her disbelief.

Mrs Trawley sighs. 'Lily was a remarkable woman, but I can't say she had the easiest time at Illumen Hall. She was one of the only girls attending at that time, maybe even the first. It was a boys-only school then, you see. And there was a group of them that bullied her relentlessly. Except, with no cameras and no such thing as school counsellors, the bullying could go totally unnoticed. Goodness me, even the teachers whipped you and beat you back in the day. But this was different. Those boys would burn her with matches in her sleep, stuff her pillows with dead rats and slice her arms with scissors – horrible stuff.'

Audrey gasps and claps her hand over her mouth. My stomach turns.

'She was absolutely tortured by them, but never told a soul. She was a very timid girl, you see, didn't want to be any trouble, just wanted to do well. It was a different time back then, but Lily was smart and bright. Illumen Hall had opened its doors to her, but some of the boys didn't like it because they felt threatened. They didn't believe a girl like Lily should be there.'

'So what happened? She said something saved her life?'

Mrs Trawley traces the wording underneath the photograph with her finger. 'I'm getting there. So one day, as you can imagine, a boy went too far. He pushed her into the lake next to the school and ran off. He didn't realize poor Lily couldn't swim. Next thing she knows, she's lying on the ground and she's alive. All she ever said was that "the magpies" saved her.'

'As in . . . the birds?' Audrey nervously chews at her nail.

Mrs Trawley shakes her head, smiling. 'No, dear, not the birds. There was a group of people who called themselves the Magpies – and they were dedicated to preserving the integrity of the school. Although magpies are wonderful birds, aren't they? So *common* you might not notice them if they weren't so smart. Anyway, this group of people took Lily under their wing, protecting her from the bullies, and eventually more young women were encouraged to board there and pursue their educational dreams. It wasn't long before Illumen Hall became one of the safest places for girls to learn alongside boys.' She picks up an antique mirror and fiddles with her headscarf, smiling at her own reflection as if we aren't there.

'That's an incredible story, Mrs Trawley – sorry, Maggie. So that particular group of people – the "magpies"?

They must be dead now. Were they part of, I don't know . . . a bigger movement?'

She puts down the mirror and waves to an old man strolling past. 'Well, my dear, there were Magpies before them, and Magpies after them. Even when I was at school, the Magpies were a sort of legend. Everyone knew of them. Some said they were ghosts, guardian angels, loved ones who had passed away . . . There were less fanciful rumours too, mind!' She laughed. 'Some suggested it was a group of teachers with a conscience. But nobody ever saw them or knew where they met. While I was a student, the Magpies exposed a headteacher who had been embezzling large amounts of the school's boarding fees. The school was about to be wrapped in scandal, but the Magpies swooped in, caught him in the act, made him pay back the money and fired him before any of the parents or press got a whiff.'

'That's wild!' I can almost hear Audrey's brain next to me creaking with this information overload.

'We would always leave a penny for the magpies in the pond. To keep us safe,' Mrs Trawley says.

'We still do that now,' I say softly. I keep catching sight of my reflection from every angle in the mirrors. I don't like it.

'So . . . do we think there's still a group of these "Magpies" around now?' Audrey looks like a kid in a sweetshop, her face completely lit up.

'Like I told that voice, if nobody's mentioned them . . . maybe they're no longer needed?' She laughs to herself and dips her paintbrush back in the gold paint. 'But, if I were looking for a Magpie, I suppose I'd check where only those with feathers could go.'

I'm suddenly aware I've let Audrey do most of the talking, which is not like me at all. I don't know if it's the scenario, Mrs Trawley or the constant stream of people passing behind us, but everything feels a little chaotic and loud, and prickly heat is rising on my neck.

'Still, if the Magpie Society *is* back, then it's for good reason,' Mrs Trawley continues. 'Don't you see, my dear? That's what they're there for. We don't question the whys or wherefores. When they're needed, they rise up again.' She leans forward and touches me on the chin. 'It's students like you that benefit the most. You'll not want to disturb them. Let the Magpie Society do its work.'

'Mrs Trawley – do you think ... could the Magpie Society have been connected to Lola's death?' Audrey asks.

Mrs Trawley grabs the edge of her stall so forcefully the mirrors shake and jingle. She shuts her eyes but, when she speaks again, her voice is as cold as ice. 'I'm sure they had nothing to do with that.'

'So the drawing on Lola's back?' I ask.

Now she opens them again, and her piercing blue eyes bore into mine. 'I can't explain it. Maybe someone was creating a distraction. Something to misdirect questioning eyes ...'

A shudder runs through my body. Does she know more about the Magpie Society than she's letting on?

'Such a shame, Lola's death. A real shame.' She shakes her head and returns to painting her daisies.

I exchange a look with Audrey. 'I think we'd better be going,' she says abruptly. I follow her lead.

'Oh, I'm sorry I couldn't be more help, dears,' Mrs Trawley

says, her tone all sugary-sweet again. 'And do tell Mrs Abbott to pop by some time. I'd love to see her. I need to ask her about some very unpleasant rumours concerning the school. Well, it's been lovely to meet you, Ivy and Audrey.'

We all shake hands, smile nicely and make our way back through the rows of stalls.

'Well . . . that was interesting, right?' I turn to Audrey who's suddenly looking a little pale.

'Ivy . . .'

'Yeah?'

'She . . . she knew our names. She just said, "lovely to meet you, Ivy and Audrey".'

My stomach drops. 'Oh my God. She did, didn't she?'

'Have you met her before? How would she know that?'

I rack my brains for anything that may have meant our paths have crossed, but there's nothing.

We look at each other in horrified silence. 'No. There's absolutely no way she should know our names.'

35

AUDREY

'I still think that was messed up,' I say, once we're safely away from the market.

Ivy doesn't reply. She shivers and wraps her coat round her a little tighter.

'You OK?' I ask as we walk back towards the bus stop.

'I'm just going through everything we've learned about the Magpie Society. I'm kind of fascinated. A benevolent secret society operating behind the scenes at school? Trying to prevent bullying and corruption and . . . what else?'

'Well, whatever they are, it didn't sound like Lola would have come under the category of corrupt – or a danger to the school or anything. And she wasn't a bully, right?'

'Not that I know of. Everyone loved her.'

'So it doesn't really seem that relevant to the investigation.'

'But you have to admit it's incredible. I wonder what else the Magpie Society has done over the years. And did you hear what Mrs Trawley said about going "where only those with feathers could go"? I wonder if that means we should try and get into the staff quarters . . .'

'I think I might be done digging,' I confess. 'I'm pretty freaked out.'

'Seriously? After hearing all that, you're not just a little bit hooked?'

I shake my head. 'No way. The more I know, the less I want to know. Man, school is complicated enough without adding, like, murders and secret societies and cover-ups into the mix. And now you want to sneak around where the staff go? How would we even do that?'

Ivy's eyes twinkle. 'I have an idea. If I can pull it off so we definitely wouldn't get in trouble, would you be up for it?'

'Maybe,' I say.

'I love this kind of stuff. It's amazing that I've been at the school for nearly six years and I've never heard a single mention of the Magpie Society.'

'I guess Illumen Hall is a place that hides its secrets well.'

Abruptly, Ivy stops dead, then darts sideways into a convenience store. 'What the . . . ?' I say with a start, before following her. 'Um, what the hell?'

'Oh, just thought I'd get some mints . . .'

I furrow my brow, then head back outside.

'No, Audrey, don't –' Ivy calls after me.

And then I see him. I probably wouldn't have recognized him out of context, in his casual clothes, but it's unmistakably Mr Willis.

I walk back into the grocery store with a much sneakier look on my face. 'Something going on with you guys?'

Now it's Ivy's turn to frown. 'What, me and Mr Willis? No way. It's just awkward, right? I mean, who wants to see a teacher outside school . . . ?'

'Clearly not you. Or at least not when there are other

people around,' I add, and Ivy gives me a small shove. I glance down at my phone. 'Come on, we can't hang around here or we'll miss the bus and then we'll be stuck in town for another hour.'

'Yeah, you're right. I'm being a baby.' Ivy can't help but run her fingers through her hair, I notice, as she marches out in front of me.

'Should we go say hi?' I ask her, hurrying to catch up.

'I don't think that'd be a good idea.'

'Why not?'

But at that moment a woman in a burgundy peacoat storms across the street just in front of us.

'Carly, wait!' Mr Willis follows her. He clearly hasn't seen us. Ivy and I come to an awkward stop as we watch the two of them. Mr Willis grabs the woman's arm.

'Don't touch me!' she screams.

'You're causing a scene,' he says.

'I'm causing a scene?! If you hadn't been so stupid, then we wouldn't be in this position at all.'

'This . . . is . . . now . . . officially awkward,' I say to Ivy. The woman and Mr Willis are obviously in the middle of some massive argument. 'Maybe we should turn around?'

But it's too late. The woman has continued to stride away and it's Mr Willis who's turned – and seen us. A momentary look of despair crosses his face, but then he puts on this almost sheepish grin.

'Sorry you girls had to see that,' he says.

'Trouble in paradise?' Ivy says.

'It'll be all right. Carly can be fiery. I'd better go after her.'

'You do that,' says Ivy darkly and we watch as he jogs

away. 'Well, that didn't seem like a healthy relationship,' she continues, still staring after them.

I nudge her. 'Ivy, we've missed the bus. How about, instead of hanging around town, we call a cab and head back to my parents' house? It'll definitely be better with you there. Might be cool to kill some time? And we'll have the place to ourselves.'

'Will your parents be OK with that?' she asks.

'Like I care.'

Ivy smiles. 'See Casa Wagner? Why not? Lead the way.'

'Do you think Winferne Bay has Uber?' I joke. But, when I look down at my phone, I see something that's no laughing matter.

There's a new podcast.

THE <u>WKL?</u> PODCAST TRANSCRIPT

EPISODE FOUR

[Intro] Music plays, building suspense with pulses that sound like a heartbeat.

CLOVER

Welcome to episode four of WHO KILLED LOLA?, where I am unravelling the mystery piece by piece. You might notice that I sound a little different now. Well, that's because my identity has been revealed. My name is Clover Mirth, and I'm a student at Illumen Hall. Yep, a proper insider.

I'm glad my secret is out though. Because, as I get deeper and deeper into this investigation, it's clear there are plenty of questions still to be answered about Lola's death. And it shouldn't be wrapped in shadow and mystery. There's enough of that around already.

Abiding by the rules, I'm recording this from home. It's the Illumen Hall half-term, but don't think that means I've been relaxing. If anything, my investigation has stepped up a notch.

Last episode I revealed even more about the secrets of our school, and spoke to Lola's brother, who convinced me more than ever that she wouldn't have taken – or even risked – her own life.

But that's still a lot of speculation. I know many of you out there are interested in cold, hard facts. Well, all you had to do was wait for this episode.

Let me summarize. I have found two major flaws in the police's argument:

The first is that we have eyewitness testimony that someone was up there on the cliff with Lola.

The second is that now we know the tattoo wasn't a tattoo at all ... It was a drawing. But still not something that she could have done herself. So who is the mystery artist? And does our first suspect have an alibi?

Right now, though, I'm going to pivot in a slightly different direction. I didn't want to fall into the trap of only investigating one person and becoming too tunnel-visioned in my research.

The old cliché is that the culprit is often a partner or a family member. So have they been looked at closely yet? For the most part, Lola's family can be eliminated as they have strong alibis – living miles away from the beach at the time of her death. So what about a partner? Lola was into guys as far as we know, and she didn't seem to have a long-term boyfriend at the time of her death.

It's hard to believe that a girl like Lola wouldn't have a whole slew of suitors just dying to go out with her. I was lucky enough to convince her best friend, Jessica Parkins, who is now a student at the University of Bournemouth, to give me an interview, although my voice was still disguised at that point.

[Interlude] Music plays.

CLOVER

Hi, Jessica, thanks for talking to me.

JESSICA

Oh, um, hi.

CLOVER

So you were Lola's best friend.

JESSICA

Yeah. We'd been friends since primary school,
and we went to Illumen together, of course. She
was the best friend I could ever have. I miss her so
much.

CLOVER

Of course, I understand that. Can you tell me a bit
about her?

JESSICA

What can I say? She was so kind, so generous –
she really cared, you know? But she never
wanted anyone to see her as weak, especially
towards the end.

CLOVER

Towards the end? What do you mean? Some
papers have mentioned that maybe she was
suffering from some mental —

JESSICA

[jumps in]

She was getting a bit more anxious as uni was
approaching, but we all were! No . . . that's not
what I meant. She was under a lot of pressure
from her parents. Have you met her family?
They're intense. They expected a lot from her.
She wanted to be more of her own person. That's
why she changed her hairstyle. She wanted

something different, to form her own identity, I guess.

CLOVER

What about a boyfriend? Did she have one?

JESSICA

No one official, I'm pretty sure. She would have told me. There were loads of guys who were interested though. At school, she'd dated Alex Winters – but he was with Heloise the entire time at the party. And it wasn't like their break-up was particularly dramatic. She'd kind of given up on guys at Illumen, I think. I did mention one thing to the police, though I'm not sure how much they followed it up. She mentioned to me once that she was kind of into this older guy. She wouldn't tell me who it was. But, when she told me to go to the party on my own, I assumed it was because she went to meet him beforehand. I don't know.

[she starts to cry]

I wish I'd made sure we came to the party together, like we always did. It seemed like bad luck to break with tradition. We shouldn't have done it.

CLOVER

You can't blame yourself ... No one knew what was about to happen.

JESSICA

[through sobs]

I just can't understand it. She had plans. Dreams. She wouldn't have done this. I know it.

CLOVER

But do you think someone would want her dead?

JESSICA

[long pause]

Of course not. But she was so wild and carefree, you know? She was a light. A beacon. But lights attract bad things as well as good. And she loved danger. But she also loved cutesy things, like shells. She had this pair of shell earrings that she wore all the time. I asked the family if I could have them as a kind of . . . memory of her. They were a matching set, you know? I have the necklace. We found them in this cute charity shop in Brighton.

CLOVER

Oh, that's so cool. Did you get to keep them?

JESSICA

They never found them. They weren't among her belongings. Maybe she was wearing them when she died. They'll be at the bottom of the sea now.

I suppose that's where they belong. The shells, I mean. Not Lola.

[Interval] Music plays.

CLOVER

As soon as I finished this interview, I knew I had to work harder to figure out who this 'older man' was. Was it a consensual relationship, a crush gone wrong, or something more sinister?

Let me tell you, friends, I'm close to figuring it out. But, worse than that, I really think that this person might not be finished.

How far will they go to keep the truth covered up? And with another Illumen Hall party on the horizon – the Samhain gathering – who knows what could happen?

[Interlude] Ominous music plays.

In the next episode of WHO KILLED LOLA? I'll reveal exactly what I've found out about this 'older man'. And the shocking truth is that he's still out there . . .

[End] The music slowly grows louder, before fading out.

36

AUDREY

The house is even bigger than I remember it. I'd still been in a daze during that first viewing, at the beginning of August. Or maybe it's because I'm seeing it through Ivy's eyes. When we arrived in England, I didn't realize how ostentatious it is to approach a house through a road lined with trees that leads to a vast circular drive with three cars sitting out front. The house itself is an ultra-modern, glass-and-sandstone monstrosity, not classy-looking like Illumen Hall, or some of the other beautiful period homes I'd seen around the coast. No, my parents just had to go with something brash.

In typical American style, it's also completely dressed for Halloween, with pumpkins and cobwebs everywhere. That would have been my mom's doing before they went away. It's like she can't function without her little traditions, which include changing the sofa cushions and decor every season without fail, even if there are no visitors to appreciate it. I used to like the changes, thinking that it helped to mark the time. It seems so gaudy now.

I'm glad I won't have to introduce her to Ivy. It might ruin all the goodwill between us.

Ivy stares out the car window, not really looking at the

house. She seems a bit lost in her own world, which I guess isn't surprising after we listened to the latest podcast episode in the cab. I hope it wasn't a mistake bringing her here. She probably thinks it's over the top.

When we get to the house, I type the code into the pad by the front door and it clicks open. 'Hello?' I ask. My voice echoes up into the vaulted space. There's no answer. I turn back to Ivy. 'Yup, we're alone.'

'Great,' she says, shifting her bag further up her shoulder. 'Wow, this place is something else. Lucky you're so far back from the road – you wouldn't get any privacy with all that glass.'

'I know. Not exactly my taste, but . . .' I shrug.

'It's amazing. I could never imagine living in a place like this. I can see now why you didn't mind leaving the States!'

'Oh, this is nothing like our house in Georgia. Now that was really something.'

'What does your dad do again?'

'He's in property investment. Not like flipping houses, but big developments and stuff. He jets off around the world, spends months away, and then comes back home with lots of money. He doesn't really talk about what he does.'

'Or maybe you're not that interested.'

I shoot her a look. 'Hey.'

'Well?'

'I guess that might be true.' There's a crash from somewhere in the house, and I open my eyes in alarm. Then I hear a loud voice I definitely recognize. 'Uh, maybe we're not alone. I'll go see what's up. Make yourself comfortable. Kitchen's through there if you want something to drink.'

'Sure, thanks.'

I'd know that angry tone anywhere. My dad. He's in one of his rages, so I can only imagine that something really terrible has happened at work.

Sometimes, back in Georgia, I'd wished that Dad would show some of that same passion for us – just to prove that he cared – rather than the cool detachment with which he normally looked at us.

'Look, I don't give a damn that they've got investment coming in "a few months". We've given them months to get themselves together, and they haven't budged. Besides, I've had a direct report that conflicts with what they've been telling us about the safety of the building . . .'

'Dad?' I would knock, but there's no door. His office is in an all-glass wing at the far end of the house, looking out over a vast expanse of green fields. I wonder if Dad even looks at them, or if he's constantly staring at his computer or yelling at people on the phone.

He seems to have bulked up a bit since moving to the UK – which is ironic, since what Brits seem to say about Americans is that we have giant portion sizes. But he barely used to eat at home. Maybe leaving Georgia and its ghosts behind was good for the whole family – not just me. Or maybe not having me around all the time really has been good for his health.

He's tall, like me – it's where I get it from – with silvering hair that somehow suits him. I'm used to women – young, old, single, married – swooning over him, and he doesn't do much to discourage that. I've long suspected he isn't loyal to my mom, especially with all the business trips and months away onsite.

I don't look up to either of them as role models for my life. Still, of my two parents, I get more warmth from my dad than my mom. He waves me in. 'Look, I can't talk right now. My daughter just came home, and I'd rather talk to her than listen to more of this bullshit. Just get it done.'

And then he clicks off the call and turns to me with his charismatic smile. 'Deedee, honey! You're back! I thought you were gonna stay at the school over your fall break.'

'They call it half-term here, Dad.'

'Well, come on over and give your old man a hug. I haven't seen you in weeks.'

I'm so surprised that I do walk over and give him a hug. He wraps me in his arms and I see they have a sheen of bronze from the Spanish sun. I look up at him. 'I brought a friend over, if that's OK?'

'Of course, honey.'

'Business not going well? What happened to Ibiza?'

'Nothing to worry about at all, just had to cut my trip a little short. Duty calls. But how about you? Tell me more about life at that school of yours. The place still falling to pieces?'

I shrug. Typical of Dad to be more worried about the state of the building than my schoolwork. 'I'm settling in OK, I guess. Got some mock exams coming up soon.'

'You've brought a friend to visit though, so things must be going better than last time I spoke to you!'

'Yeah . . .'

'Aren't you glad you didn't quit now?'

I shrug.

'Had any thoughts about where you might wanna go to college?'

'God, no!' I reply instantly.

He chuckles. 'Good to know you haven't changed too much. I actually had a shock looking at my bank account this month – I have money in there now you're not asking for it every week!'

'Whatever, Dad,' I say. But it's true. Illumen Hall has pretty much cured my shopping addiction. Cold turkey. The place is virtually impossible to get packages delivered to. 'How about you tell me a bit more about the project you're working on?'

'What's with the sudden interest in my work? You'll find it dull.' As he speaks, he moves me by the shoulders out of his office. 'But a man's gotta do it to pay for his daughter's pricey school fees. Now we didn't have *that* in Georgia.'

I open my mouth, but nothing comes out. My parents still treat me like I'm the fragile human I was back home, but my time at Illumen Hall is changing me. I can feel it. Standing up to those bullies. My growing friendship with Ivy. I'm stronger and I like it.

But, rather than bite back, I take a deep breath. It's no surprise that my parents don't confide in me. I'll just have to show them that I'm not the girl I used to be.

'Now, how long are you and your friend staying? Because I have some business associates coming over . . .'

'Oh, we'll leave in a bit. I just wanted to show Ivy the house. Did Mom come home too?'

'Oh no, she decided to extend her yoga retreat a little longer. Apparently, she's loving it out there.'

I'm sure she is, I think bitterly.

'And Jason has met some new surfing buddies so he's just gonna hang out for a few more weeks.'

'Some life.'

'Now, now, your brother has been through a lot too. He'll go back to school when he's ready.'

'Sure, Dad.'

'OK, I'd like to meet this friend of yours!'

Ivy is busying herself making tea. I cough loudly to signal our arrival and, when she looks up, her eyes widen in surprise.

'Dad, this is Ivy. She's my room-mate at Illumen.'

'Good to meet you,' he says, stepping forward and pulling her into a big hug. The look of confusion on her face makes me burst out laughing. 'Hope our Deedee hasn't been too difficult to live with. I know she can be a slob.'

'Dad!'

Ivy laughs. 'No, she's fine.'

'Must be picking up those good habits from you then. Right, girls, I must get back to business. Take your time, but be outta here by –'

'Don't worry, we won't be long.' I cut him off quickly.

'Good.' He kisses the top of my head, then strolls back towards his office.

'So . . . that's the famous Mr Wagner.'

'I don't know about famous . . .'

Ivy shrugs. 'He doesn't seem so bad.'

I take a sip of my tea and don't respond. We drink in companionable silence. She doesn't ask me anything more about my dad, and I'm grateful. She's one of the first friends I've ever had who doesn't feel the need to fill every second with conversation. Once upon a time, I would've hated that. Now I appreciate it.

I breathe out a long sigh. 'So, tell me more about this party next Saturday?'

Ivy's eyes light up. 'Oh, it's a great event – one of our annual traditions.' Then she looks pensive. 'And . . . the first big party since Lola – you know. That'll probably make it even more important. Araminta's organizing it. That girl better not do a bad job.'

'What is Samhain though?' I cringe as I totally mangle the pronunciation. 'Never heard of it until I got to Illumen.'

'It's "Sah-wen", not "Sam-Hayne". It's an ancient celebration of the turning of the seasons – I think it can trace its origin back to the time of the Druids. It's now often associated with the Wiccan religion – and because it falls so close to Halloween they're often confused, but one has nothing really to do with the other.'

'Oh,' I say, slightly disappointed. 'So no dressing up in costume?'

'Did I say that?' she says with a wicked grin. 'Not costumes per se, but definitely nice clothes. It doesn't have any religious significance for us at Illumen these days, but it definitely does around the world.'

I reach over and grab Ivy's hand. 'I've just had the best idea. Come with me!'

37

IVY

Audrey leads me to her bedroom and I crane my neck, taking in the stark white walls. It feels cold, almost sterile. It's clear she's spent hardly any time in it, and I'm guessing she didn't choose the interior design or furniture. It's everything I *don't* assume her to be. There's no Audrey here. Not like our room back at Illumen, with her yellow duvet cover and the wall behind her bed covered in old vinyl covers and clippings from magazines. Her usual Audrey mess isn't scattered on the desk space – there's no sense of her here at all.

The bed is a king-size, sheets perfectly ironed and tucked in neatly. A beautiful white velvet blanket is draped artfully over one corner. A glass wardrobe spans an entire wall and a quote on one of the doors reads 'Live, Love, Laugh' in elaborate cursive writing. It makes me die a little inside. Audrey opens one of the wardrobe doors by pressing the side of the glass and it slides open to reveal her colour-coordinated library of clothes. It's like nothing I've ever seen before and I feel a pang of jealousy. None of them are my style, but I wonder what it would be like to live a life like this. Audrey must never have to worry about anything.

'So, what sort of vibe did you say the Samhain party

was?' She pulls out a beautiful floor-length sequined dress that catches the sunlight that's coming through the window and bounces small specks of mottled light round her room.

'Not *that* vibe,' I laugh, even though she'd look absolutely incredible in that dress. 'Do you have anything black? I think most people wear dark colours, something vampy and a bit autumnal?' I look out of her bedroom window and see two gardeners pruning the most beautiful little flower garden below. From Mr Tavistock's wealth of shared knowledge, I think they look like chrysanthemums, but I can't be sure from up here.

'How do you have so much . . . stuff?' I say without really thinking.

'Clothes, you mean?' Audrey laughs. 'When you have a dad who likes it better when you hang out with his credit card, you can end up with a lot of shit you don't necessarily need.' She laughs again, but it feels forced. She starts folding dresses haphazardly into a little suitcase. I wonder if it's her mum who keeps her room so immaculate, or maybe they have a housekeeper? I wouldn't be surprised.

Audrey pulls the suitcase off the bed and claps her hands together. 'Right, this should be enough options! I admit, I didn't expect to be able to wear these at a stuffy English boarding school. Shall we get going? I'll call a cab.'

'Sure.'

I let her lead the way back out of her room, following a few steps behind.

The taxi pulls up and Audrey and I bundle into the back seat, the suitcase wedged in between us.

Just as we exit her driveway, a red Audi TT pulls in. I

catch a brief glimpse of the woman behind the wheel. Of her neatly coiffed blond bob and oversized sunglasses . . .

We both turn to each other, blinking rapidly as if we can't believe what we've just seen.

Audrey breaks the silence. 'Oh my God. Was that Mrs Abbott?'

'I'm not sure I like where this plan is going,' says Audrey as we hurry across the courtyard towards Illumen Hall's front gates. It's dark out now, the lights down the driveway casting strange shadows along our path.

'Trust me.'

'I've heard that one before,' mutters Audrey, wrapping a scarf round her neck.

We pass by a large Tudor cottage, with a red car parked out front. 'Looks like Mrs Abbott has returned from her afternoon . . . adventure. Let's move a little faster. I'd rather she didn't ask us any questions.'

Audrey picks up her pace, and we jog to get out of view of the cottage windows. 'I wonder why she was at my house? Maybe I'm in trouble.'

'Can't you ask your dad?'

'Honestly, I think he'd rather I stay out of his business.'

'Fair enough.'

A figure steps out of the shadows. Audrey shrieks and grabs my arm. I can't help but laugh. 'Chill! We don't want Mrs Abbott calling security. It's only Teddy.'

'Well, how was I to know that?' Audrey clutches her chest, breathing deep.

Teddy is dressed casually in a hoodie and jeans, so I

admit he looks a bit menacing. But then he flashes us his trademark grin and we all relax. 'Hey, you two,' he says. 'So, what's *so* urgent that you dragged me off my boat at the start of half-term to come back to school?'

I smile. 'Since you *still* owe us for being a slimy, two-texting moron, we wanted to ask one more favour of you.' I pause for dramatic effect. 'We need you to give us full access round the school.' I whip out both mine and Audrey's key cards and flash my teeth at him.

'Oh? What makes you think I'm capable of that?' When he smirks, he gets this little dimple in his left cheek, which gives me the powerful urge to kiss him. I suppress it.

'Come on, I've seen you come out from the tech rooms often enough, and only senior teachers and staff are allowed down there.'

'Maybe I just happen to know the right people,' he says.

'Right. And *we* know *you*.'

He hesitates for a moment. 'Why do you need it?'

Audrey opens her mouth to speak, but I stop her with a glare. 'None of your business,' I say to him.

He chuckles. 'Fine. But, if I do this, will you both please drop this whole thing?'

'Maybe,' I reply, folding my arms.

He tuts, but thankfully relents. 'Come on then.'

He strides off in the direction of the Tower Wing. 'I've never been in this part of the school,' Audrey says as we approach.

'Yeah, most of us try to avoid it if we can.' It's always had quite a creepy vibe in my opinion. I've seen old black-and-white photographs of it where it looks like it had an elegant wisteria vine that spiralled up the outside – I imagine that would've been quite beautiful. But now it's dead, and only the twisted, gnarled branches remain.

'It's not so bad,' says Teddy. 'This way.'

He swipes us through the door but, instead of taking us up the tower, Teddy guides us down the circular staircase, into the basement. It's late, and we shouldn't be out of our rooms, but I know that Mrs Parsons won't be checking the dorm rooms for another hour so we still have plenty of time.

The basement is where all the electrical boxes, fuses, servers and media towers are kept – essentially the entire brain of the school. There's a little office down here too, housing three technicians during the day, who keep on top of it all and spy on what students are looking at on their laptops. As we start walking down, we can hear the low hum of electricity surrounding us.

'Won't they see that your card was used to get us in here?' Audrey asks as we enter the office with a clear sign: STAFF ONLY. She looks a little nervous. Three very organized desks sit together in a line, with computer monitors covering every available space. One wall is entirely filled with screens flashing up the CCTV from every possible angle and corner of the school.

'No, I know how to erase that from the log.' Teddy strides in with confidence and turns on the lights. 'They used to have one technician on a night shift, but the most he was ever needed for in his entire six years of employment was to rescue a baby fox from the tennis net.' Teddy sits at one of the desks and I follow suit. Audrey hovers near the door.

'Honestly, Audrey, you can relax. I've been coming here after hours for years.'

She bites her fingernails, a habit of hers I've noticed when she gets particularly nervous. *Why bother spending so much time painting them just to go and eat them?* This girl needs to learn to live a little.

Teddy taps the brand name on the top of one of the servers: GRANT. 'My family basically installed this whole set-up. No way Illumen Hall would have had the funds for this state-of-the-art stuff if it weren't for my dad. The technicians all know me and they don't care if I come down here during lunches and breaktimes. It's like work experience. Bring them first choice of the sandwiches from the canteen and just sit and pick their brains.'

'Like how to give us full access on our key cards . . . ?' I prompt.

He nods. 'I shouldn't, but . . .' He takes the cards and types their serial numbers into the computer. 'And why exactly do the two of you need full access anyway?'

'We can't tell you that,' I say, snatching my card back.

'Of course you can't.' He laughs. 'Just don't get *me* in trouble, OK?'

'Will the technicians be able to see we have full access?' I study the card, then look up and notice that our full profiles are on display on the monitor. Name, age, photo, student house, year group, guardian contact details and the areas to which we have access, which now reads AAA.

'Not if I do this . . .' Teddy taps in a few more codes, clicks the mouse and we see it change to 'Limited Access, Lower Sixth, Helios.' He does the same on Audrey's profile. She looks like a deer caught in headlights in her ID photo – and not to mention soaking wet. It must have been taken on her first day.

'Done.' Teddy jumps up from the computer and switches off the monitor. I point to the wall of CCTV screens. 'Do we need to do anything about this?' We'd made our way here carefully, avoiding the cameras, but I cast my eyes over the different screens to check there isn't one that could give us away.

'There are plenty outside, but I know how to avoid those.'

I can't help wondering how Teddy knows just the right way to dodge the cameras. Why on earth would he need to sneak around like that?

As we make our way back up the stairs with our AAA key cards safely in our pockets, Teddy turns to face us.

'I mean it, ladies – be careful with these. You need to really think about when, how and why you're using them.' He's dead serious now.

'We will, Teddy, and thanks for this!' Audrey smiles sweetly at him.

Teddy smiles back. 'So listen, I was going to ask –'

I look down at my watch. 'Shit, we'd better get back before Mrs Parsons checks our room.'

Audrey's eyes open wide. 'I can't afford another strike with her.'

I grab Audrey's hand, pulling her away from Teddy before he can finish his question. 'See you next Saturday!' I say.

We don't wait around to hear his reply.

38

IVY

'Audrey. Audrey, wake up!' My God, that girl can sleep for England.

'What is it?' says Audrey, her eyes still squeezed shut. 'Where's the fire?'

'Come on. We're going to miss breakfast.'

'Can't you go for a run?' Reluctantly, she opens one eye.

I sigh. 'Done.'

'Piano?'

'No way, not this early in the morning. Come *on*, lazy arse.' I drag the covers off Audrey and throw a towel at her head. She groans.

'You're seriously irritating, you know that?'

'Yeah, but I'll make it worth your while. I asked the cook to bake *pains au chocolat*. You like them, don't you? And they're so much better if they're warm . . .'

'Fine.' Audrey grabs the towel and growls her way to the bathroom. When she emerges again, she looks a lot more alive – but she still glares at me. 'So, where are these legendary pastries?'

We head downstairs to the canteen, where one of the cooks, Sandy, is waiting as promised with the fresh, warm goods. Audrey and I grab our share, then sit down at one of the dining tables.

'So, what's the plan for today?' Audrey asks. 'I'm kinda exhausted. Maybe we can just chill out and watch a movie in the common room or something?'

'No way – not now we've got these special cards. We have to check out the feathers.'

'You really think there's something to that?'

'Well, think about the domestic staff – the kitchen, IT, the groundsmen – here at Illumen Hall. These are the people who keep this school ticking over.'

'What's that got to do with the magpies?'

'Well, what I'm saying is, what if *these* are the people that have more information about the Magpie Society? What if they *are* the Magpie Society?' I look for any trace of agreement in Audrey's face. It doesn't come. I sigh. 'I know it seems like a pretty loose connection but look: we've got these AAA key cards now. The feathers are really busy today, deep-cleaning the common rooms. Let's check out the utility areas to see if there's any other information.'

'I guess?'

'Come on.' I stand up and grab her hand.

As the canteen is deserted, we rush over to a door marked STAFF ONLY. I swipe my key, and then push through. Audrey follows close behind.

'Wow, they really save the decor for the students, huh?'

I know what she means. As soon as we pass through into the staff quarters, the walls are an unadorned cream colour, with harsh fluorescent lighting. 'Yeah, seriously. In the oldest part of the building, that used to be a manor house, the "servants' quarters" are even bigger than the main house.'

'That's wild.'

The corridor leads to a utility-type room brimming with washing. Sheets hang from every bit of the ceiling and walls. All you can hear is the rumbling of the washing machines and tumble dryers. It's a little disorientating.

'Wow. We sure go through a lot of laundry in this place.'

'Hold on . . . don't you find this a bit odd? That there are completely dry sheets hanging everywhere, yet rows of tumble dryers?'

'So?'

'So . . . why would they need to hang any sheets up to dry when there are enough tumble dryers to get them done?' Why do I feel like it's a distraction, a cover-up? Am I seeing patterns that aren't there?

But then I look closer. 'These sheets aren't fresh. They smell a bit . . . old. Sure-fire sign they haven't been freshly hung.'

I turn to see Audrey sniffing the sheets. She wrinkles her nose. 'I don't really get why they'd have sheets hung up here permanently though. To always make it look like they're busy? To show exactly what the room is used for?' She searches through them, pulling at different sheet corners. I do the same, searching for . . . we don't know what.

'Oh my God, look at this!' I gasp.

Audrey rushes over as I pull a sheet back to reveal – a rich oak pannelled wall, decorated with elaborate carvings.

'Whoa! There are so many hidden treasures in this school. You'd never see anything like this back home.' Audrey traces the raised carvings on the wooden panels.

'Look here.' She points at a panel with a bird carved into it. It looks distinctly like a magpie. It *can't* be a coincidence.

I push it. Nothing. I try and prise it open with my fingernail. Again, it doesn't budge.

'Maybe it's not a door?' Audrey says, sounding deflated.

'I just – I feel like this panel is sticking out more.' I carry on pulling it and pushing it, until eventually I manage to swing it and it rotates inwards, revealing a small passageway. It's long and dark and I can't see anything inside.

'Oh my God!' Audrey claps her hands. 'Where does that go?' She peers over my shoulder into the dark corridor.

'I have no idea. I thought I could draw a map of this school from memory, but I didn't know this even existed. Maybe it leads to a bomb shelter – like from the Second World War?' I fumble my hand on the inside of the door, but can't feel a light switch.

'Are we sure we wanna go in here? What if we can't get back out? This school must have a floor plan like the Winchester Mystery House. Nothing makes any sense.' Audrey hesitates, but still falls into step behind me.

'We'll be fine,' I say with more confidence than I feel. 'Stay close behind me. We can use our phones for light. You fully charged this time?'

'Oh yeah, not gonna make *that* mistake again!'

I feel along the walls with one hand and shine my phone light out in front of me with the other. The corridor is very tight and the floorboards below us are old and dusty with rusty nails sticking out at odd angles. I take a step forward and feel a creak. I look down and realize I'm standing on a rotten floorboard, half crumbled away.

Then in the next moment I'm falling.

39

AUDREY

I scream as the floor crumbles beneath Ivy's feet. But she throws her arms out and I'm able to grab her under her armpits. I lift her back up on to solid ground, and we both collapse into a fit of adrenaline-fuelled giggles.

'What is this place?' I ask. 'Do you think it is one of those World War Two shelters that you talked about?'

'I dunno. This looks like it might be even older than that.' Ivy is clearly intrigued. 'Look at this – it's some kind of old graffiti.' She touches a scrawl of letters: *JB*. 'Maybe it's a priest-hole. I know there were some of those in this part of the school.' I must look confused, because she goes on, 'In Elizabethan times, they persecuted Catholic priests because they thought there was a plot to overthrow Queen Elizabeth I, so people used to hide them down these little hidden passageways to protect them.'

'Oh God, that's horrible.'

'Some of the holes were too small and the priests suffocated,' Ivy replies. 'A lot of old buildings claim to be haunted because of it.'

'Stop it, you're freakin' me out!'

'Ha, sorry. I used to love all the gory bits of history, but I guess it is kind of morbid.'

'You're telling me.' I duck to fit as the passageway narrows. Not for the first time, I curse my height. 'Man, the priests must have been tiny if they were supposed to fit in here. What part of the school are we even in?'

Ivy stops in her stooped-over position and looks around. 'You know, I'm actually not sure. Maybe we should go back the way we came?'

I take a deep breath. 'We've come this far. I wanna see where this leads. Maybe we'll find out a bit about how the Magpie Society operates?'

Ivy stares at me for a second, then nods. 'Just testing you,' she says with a small smile.

We crawl through the priest-hole, which leads eventually to an open space – there are beams crossing underfoot, and we have to be careful to walk on the joists – the last thing we want is to fall through the floor like Ivy nearly did. Our shoes leave footprints in the thick layer of dust. If the Magpie Society ever operated here, they haven't been around in a very long time.

'It's kinda wild that all this history is buried here at the school. I'm surprised it's not a museum or something.'

'Yeah. A lot of buildings in the UK are protected for their history, but – like that weird woman in town said – Illumen Hall has its own rules. I'm pretty sure they can build whatever they want here.'

'Maybe that's why the Magpie Society was created,' I muse. 'Like, it would only take one bad decision, one careless person, to wipe all this away.'

'You might be right about that.'

'Can you hear that?' I say. I put my hand on Ivy's arm. There's a low rumble of water against rock, and the distant caw of a seagull.

Ivy pauses. 'Is that . . . the sea?'

'Wow. Sounds so loud up here – without anyone else around.'

'Look!' Ivy jumps along the joists now, and I follow more cautiously. She's found the scrawled mark of a bird etched into the wood. 'Could be a magpie,' she says.

'Let's keep going,' I reply. The joists shift into dirt and earth, almost as if we've left the building's foundations and entered a tunnel in the grounds. We follow the sound of the waves crashing far below us. I really hope that the ground is solid – I picture the cliff crumbling and us being swept into that cold, grey, terrifying ocean. But I force myself to stop catastrophizing and focus on the part that feels exciting.

It gets darker, the walls closing in on us, and we use the crappy flashlights on our cellphones to light the passage-way in front of us.

'Look!' I point up to a small wooden plaque. 'Another magpie.'

'And another door over there!' Ivy exclaims.

The further we walk down this passage, the more entrances appear, seemingly from all parts of the school. I think back to the panel that swung open in our room. I wonder . . .

'This must be how the Magpie Society used to meet up,' Ivy says.

'Wow, this is so cool. Like discovering a portal to another world.'

We try some of the other doors, shaking handles and shoving up against ones that appear to be stuck, but most of them are boarded up properly – or locked – and of course we have no chance of getting a key.

Only one door budges and, as soon as it swings open, the smell of the ocean rushes in. Ivy and I turn to each other, then, without needing to say a word, we both pass through the door and along the passage.

40

AUDREY

The further we walk, the louder the sound of the sea grows, and the tunnel leads us to a yawning cavern – and daylight. Seagulls screech just outside, and we can hear waves crashing against rock. It's surprisingly warm in here, but the air smells salty. It must be a cave in the cliffs.

Ivy stops abruptly, and I bump into her back. It takes a moment for us to register what we see inside the cave. A sleeping bag is stuffed in the corner, stinking of damp, a mouldy pillow next to it. There are discarded fast-food wrappers and drinks cartons everywhere.

'Oh my God,' I say, gripping Ivy's shoulders. 'Someone *lives* here.'

'*Used* to live here,' Ivy replies. She kicks the sleeping bag with her foot, and – it might be my imagination – I'm pretty sure it moves. *Ew.* I try not to think about what critters might be lurking under all that garbage. 'Doesn't look like they've been here in a while.'

'We need to tell someone about this,' I say. 'I mean, it can't be safe here if someone can hide out in the school grounds. It could be anyone.'

'Hmm, I don't know.'

'Seriously?'

'Honestly, what would be the point?' says Ivy. 'Whoever it was has obviously not been here in ages. Do we really want all the students finding out about everything that's hidden underneath the school? Surely Mrs Abbott knows already.'

'About this?' I gesture to the remnants of human life.

'No, probably not about that,' Ivy concedes. 'But still.'

'OK,' I reply reluctantly. 'Wow, look at all this stuff.' I keep my voice to a whisper, even though I'm pretty sure we're alone. Now that I'm over the shock of seeing the sleeping bag, I notice little 'shelves' of rock along the cave walls. On them are bits of seaglass, turquoise and aquamarine, with soft, rounded edges smoothed from years of being tumbled by the pounding waves.

Ivy walks over and picks one up, rubbing it with her fingers. 'Whoever used to live here must have been a bit of a beachcomber. You can find all sorts of stuff if you walk along the shore.'

I run my fingers across the treasures. There are fossils here too, and bits of garbage-turned-beautiful – a child's tin lunchbox filled with odd bits of metal: the pull tabs from soda cans, old screws, coins and even a coil of hardened driftwood. Something glints, catching the light. It's a single silver earring, with little dangling shells. 'Hey, doesn't this look familiar to you?' I pick it up gently out of the lunchbox.

Ivy comes over, then gasps. 'Oh my God. That was Lola's.'

I drop the earring as if it was a stinging nettle. I feel the burn of it on my fingers. 'Shit! And now my fingerprints are all over it . . .'

'Fingerprints? What are you talking about? Whoever lived here must have found it washed up on the beach.'

'That *could* be it. Or what if this person had something to do with Lola's death?'

'What, and just before pushing her off the cliff they asked her to kindly remove one of her earrings?' Ivy snaps.

I pause, chewing my bottom lip. 'OK, that does sound a little far-fetched. So, do you think this has anything to do with the mysterious Magpie Society?'

Ivy shakes her head. 'I don't think so. I mean, if the society has been around for centuries, since the school began, why would they be hanging out in a cave? I think we just stumbled across someone's temporary home.'

'Every time we get close, it just slips through our fingers, huh?'

'Oh, Audrey, you're shivering.'

I hadn't even noticed. But, now that she points it out, I realize that I do feel cold.

'Let's go back,' she continues. 'And don't worry. I'll tell Mr Tavistock. He'll come down here and board up the entrance. That way, whoever was living here won't be able to come back.'

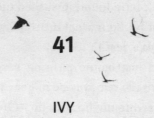

41

IVY

Practising the piano is the only thing keeping me distracted from this weird pressure that seems to be building up inside me. I feel almost manic as I sit at the piano now, hammering too hard on the keys. Each one makes a dull clicking sound beneath the beautiful tone of the music.

I'm starting to feel like I've become way too distracted with all this Magpie Society stuff when I should be focusing on my schoolwork. Get back to the Ivy Plan. We have our AS mocks coming up, rehearsals for the Christmas concert will be starting, and I don't feel anywhere near as prepared as I should. I can picture the disappointment on my mum's face if she ever found out what I've been up to instead of focusing on my work and my music. Thank God we don't touch base enough for me to have to lie to her.

Right now, something's telling me that if I can play this piece of music perfectly from start to finish, everything will be OK.

Half-term is almost over and students are already beginning to pile back into school – so as not to miss the big party. The corridors are filling up and the common room and library are buzzing. I think about the time we wasted chasing pointless leads all week. Lola, her earring, the unknown corridors, the magpies, the fact that someone has been basically squatting on school grounds . . . I swear as my finger slips and I mess up. I start again from the top.

Anyway, it's not going to be as easy sneaking around now that the staff are coming back. Mrs Abbott will be more eagle-eyed than she already is with me because I'm sure she'll notice I've been slacking. Maybe we need to stop the whole thing. What is even the *point* –

I forget to press the damper pedal and the notes land clumsily on top of each other. 'FUCK!' I slam my hands down on the keys and put my head in my hands.

'Ivy?' I turn and see a confused-looking Mr Willis staring back at me from the doorway.

My face burns. 'Sorry, I was just . . . I keep messing up.' I pull myself together, sitting up straight and taking a deep breath.

'It's OK. I bet that can get frustrating! It sounded wonderful to me, but I can barely play "Chopsticks".' He comes over and leans on the piano, then obviously decides it looks awkward and straightens up again. 'Listen . . . I don't suppose you've seen Clover about? Has she signed back in?'

I shake my head and then frown. A red rash seems to be creeping up from underneath Mr Willis's collar. He looks younger than ever dressed in light jeans and a white T-shirt – since term hasn't officially started, there's no need for formal attire. I wonder if he and his fiancée have recovered from their fight. I kind of hope not. I force myself to focus. 'No, I don't know. Sorry! I'm guessing it's urgent – do you want me to try and get hold of her for you?' I shut the piano lid and turn to face him. His face lights up.

'That'd be great. I really need to ask her a question about her upcoming podcast episode and our interview.'

'OK.' I pull out my phone and text Clover. 'She seems to really believe it all.' I don't tell him that I believe it now too.

'That's what I'm worried about,' he says.

I keep my expression neutral as I compose my text.

> Mr Willis wants to see you, stat.
> He seems quite panicked. Are
> you back yet? X

I look at Mr Willis and smile. 'I've texted her and told her you're looking for her, but she's not online. I can let you know if I hear from her if you're hanging around for a bit?'

'Thanks, Ivy, I really appreciate your help. I'll be in the staffroom for a couple of hours.'

'Are you . . . OK, sir? You look a little flushed.'

'I'm fine, I'm fine. Just have to get this sorted.' And with that he heads out.

That's when I get a reply from Clover.

> DON'T TELL HIM I'M BACK YET.
> It's because I'm late with my
> coursework.

My fingers drum the top of the piano. Something about that entire interaction felt very off. Mr Willis seemed really uneasy. And why would Clover lie to me about having coursework due?

I text her one more time.

Where are you??

What could Mr Willis know about the upcoming podcast that we don't? A cold feeling settles in the pit of my stomach. *What if he wants the next episode stopped for his own reasons?*

In a mad panic, I text Audrey.

Meet me in our room asap. X

42

AUDREY

When I walk into the SCR, I almost jump with shock: it's completely rammed. When did all these people arrive? I'd been so used to having this place to just Ivy and me that it's weird to see everyone back again.

'Audrey, over here!' Araminta is sitting with a bunch of her friends. She waves, and hesitantly I make my way over.

'Hey,' I reply. 'Um, have a good half-term? Katie? Bonnie?'

Katie shrugs. 'Didn't do much. Just chilled out at home really.'

'I went to the Cotswolds. Honestly, my parents are psycho,' says Bonnie. 'Glad to be back.'

'How about you, Audrey? Was it miserable staying here?' Katie asks.

But Araminta jumps in before I have a chance to answer. 'Look, we were just talking about something important and you should be involved. Even though what I did to Clover was wrong, what she's doing to us isn't right either.' She addresses the wider group now, who murmur their agreement.

I frown. 'What do you mean?'

'What, apart from the malicious and terrible lies she's

spread about me? Well, it's obvious from her last podcast over half-term – did you listen?'

I nod cautiously.

'Well, she said that something bad was going to happen at the Samhain party. She is *clearly* trying to get back at me. It's just cruel.'

I must look confused, because Araminta rolls her eyes. 'Don't you see? *I'm* the one organizing the Samhain party. She's trying to scare people into thinking something awful's going to happen. She wants to ruin my first big event as head girl! Well, I'm not going to let her.'

'And you shouldn't!' says Bonnie.

'This is going to be the biggest and best Samhain party the school has ever seen,' says Katie.

I can't believe I didn't realize how far up Araminta's ass they all are.

'Oh, Audrey, you're going to love it,' says Araminta, all warmth now. It's kinda freaky how this chick can switch from hot to cold and back again.

'What if Clover *does* know something?' I ask.

There's a pause.

'No way,' says Araminta, the ice back in her voice. 'I think she's full of shit. And, if she knew anything real, why wouldn't she just come out and say it rather than forcing everyone to listen to those horrible podcasts and dragging out this "investigation"? I, for one, am not going to listen to them any more. Who's with me?'

'I am,' jumps in Bonnie. One by one, the rest of the group agrees.

'I dunno,' I reply. 'Me and Ivy . . .'

'Oh, what, you guys are best friends now?' says Araminta.

'Yeah. We've actually been doing some of our own investigating,' I blurt out.

'And?'

Oh God. I should've kept my big mouth shut. 'Well, just that there might be something to this Magpie Society thing.'

'Oooh, I love the idea that a secret society operated at the school. Or maybe there *is* one operating? Though, if I was a member, I wouldn't go around shouting about it!' Araminta throws her head back and laughs. She's definitely mocking me. It's not always easy for me to figure out the British sense of humour, but I'm fairly certain about this one.

Just then, Teddy walks into the common room, and my stomach flips. He makes a beeline for our table.

'Hi, Teddy,' says Araminta, tossing back her hair.

'Hey, all. Audrey, actually, I was looking for you. Can we talk?'

'Um . . . I guess?'

Araminta's eyebrows shoot up, and there's a chorus of *oooh*s from the crowd. 'You and Ivy so close that you're sharing a boyfriend now?'

'Grow up, Araminta,' I snap back at her. 'See you guys,' I say to the rest of the group.

'Don't forget your Samhain outfit!' Araminta says cheerily to my back. Ice and fire, that girl. I wonder if she has a *killer* instinct too?

We head out of the common room and walk in companionable silence until we get outside. It's pretty cold, but the grounds are so beautiful at this time of year. Back home, it rarely gets super cold, so we don't get the vibrant fall colours. Here, the leaves are turning and tumbling from the trees, coating the ground in a carpet of crisp golden stars.

'How was your sailing trip?' I ask.

'It was good. You should really come on the boat . . . for real this time. No pirates.' He grins.

I stop and turn towards him. He stops too, and when he looks at me my heart lurches inside my chest. My God, he really is cute. *A bit of a prick*, as Ivy would say, but definitely cute.

No, Audrey, I tell myself sternly and shiver with the effort.

'You're cold.' He reaches in his pocket and produces a knitted beanie. He tugs it down over my head and curls my hair round my ears, his touch gentle. We're standing very close now.

'I know it was wrong of me to be messaging both of you guys.'

'At the same time,' I add, just in case he'd forgotten.

'Yeah. But I really just wanted to get to know you. And Ivy and I were on a break . . .'

'Still . . .'

'Still, I should have broken it off properly before texting you. But now that it *is* broken off . . . can we get to know each other better?'

'I don't know. Ivy and I have just started becoming friends.' *And I don't want to ruin that.*

'You guys are hanging out a lot, huh?'

'We are. Don't you guys have "girl code" in the UK? It wouldn't be very girl code of me. Plus, you haven't exactly shown yourself to be the most stand-up guy.'

'OK, I understand. But I've been thinking a lot over

half-term. Ivy and I had our moment, and it didn't work between us – even she would agree with that. The thing is, I really like you, Audrey. And I'd really like to take you to the Samhain party tonight.'

A moment follows where the air feels like it changes between us, and that has nothing to do with the cooler temperature outside.

'Oh.'

All of a sudden, it's like we both know what's about to happen, and our bodies seem to lean into each other without any conscious thought. *Oh my God, I'm about to have my first British kiss . . .*

But the spell is broken as something darts between us. 'Jesus!' I cry out as it brushes against my leg, letting out a loud wail in the process.

Teddy and I fly apart and he laughs. 'Oh, that's Shadow – Mr Tavistock's pet. He's harmless. Where were we?' He steps forward.

A black cat crossing my path . . . more bad luck. I feel my phone vibrate in my pocket. 'I'd better check this.' I take a step back, allowing air to swirl between us, dissolving whatever had been drawing us together.

'Are you OK? You look weird,' Teddy asks.

'I have to go.'

'Audrey . . .'

'It's Ivy. She needs me.'

'Think about what I said?'

'You got it.' I spin on my heel and run towards the school, knowing, if I stay a minute longer, I might get drawn back into a situation I don't want to escape.

43

IVY

Audrey charges through the door, her hair dishevelled and her cheeks pink.

'Jesus, Audrey, did you just run a marathon?'

'We can't all breeze a 10k like you, Ivy! You said asap and this is what asap looks like . . .' She slumps down on her bed. 'What's happened?'

'I just had the weirdest conversation with Mr Willis!'

'Ew. I'm not sure I wanna know. Is it the sort of conversation that could end with him being fired?' She laughs, still trying to catch her breath. I throw my pillow at her.

'Um, no! He was talking about Clover, and the podcast. Said he's worried about the next episode and needs to speak to her urgently? He asked me to text her and say he was looking for her . . .'

'That *is* weird,' Audrey replies. 'So, did you message Clover?'

'Yeah, and she told me to say she wasn't back, even though she is.'

'Why wouldn't she want to see him then?'

'She said something about being late with her coursework, but I don't believe that for a second.'

Audrey sits up now. 'Then what the hell is going on? This whole thing is such a mind-fuck. The Magpie Society, the podcast, Mrs Trawley, that creepy crack den in the cliffs behind school . . .' Audrey stops and takes a deep breath. 'Just feels a bit much, doesn't it?'

Which perfectly sums up how I'm feeling.

'It's just . . . I can't believe Lola didn't leave something. If this really was a suicide, I mean. A note? A text? An email? Just to set the record straight once and for all . . .'

'Oh my God . . .' Audrey gradually sits up straighter and straighter, then almost slaps herself in the face. 'I totally forgot!'

'What? What is it?'

She scrambles around for her phone in among the sheets. 'Patrick Radcliffe. He told me that Lola loved to write diaries and letters and stuff.'

'Yeah, so?'

'Well, I actually found a –' Audrey's lips snap shut.

I narrow my eyes. 'Found what?'

She bites her bottom lip, looking like a puppy who's been caught chewing a favourite pair of slippers. She scrunches up her face. 'It was before you and I were friends and I kinda shoved it in my drawer and forgot about it . . .'

'Well, what is it?' My heart's beating wildly.

'A letter.'

'OK, Audrey. What did the letter say?'

'I don't know! I didn't open it.'

'Seriously?'

'I'm not like you, Ivy! I didn't wanna know, honestly.'

Audrey heads for her desk and scrabbles around in the top drawer.

'Here!' She passes it across to me, and I stare at the delicate cursive writing on the front.

To my beloved

I swallow, hard.

'What is it?' Audrey asks.

'This is definitely Lola's handwriting.'

'Oh shit. Guess I should have opened it.'

It takes me a few seconds to process. 'What if this is *the* note? You know . . .' I whisper. I take a deep breath, then reach over to my desk and take out a slim silver letter opener from the porcelain pencil pot.

'Is that a knife?' Audrey frowns.

'A letter opener. It was my grandmother's,' I say, slicing the envelope in one swift movement. 'Saves a lot of paper cuts.' I try to laugh, but it gets stuck in the back of my throat. With trembling fingers, I open the letter.

Dearest beloved,
 This is my final letter to you.
 I know that you say we cannot be together in this lifetime. That there are simply too many walls between us. Too many obstacles standing in our way. You say you wish you were my knight in shining armour, fully prepared to slay the dragons guarding me in my Helios tower, but no armour could stop the arrows that would come your way if our love was revealed.

*I am not Rapunzel trapped in a tower. I cut off
some of my long golden hair to show you I'm not
waiting to be rescued.*

*If we cannot be together in this life, then I will do
the only thing I can – and wait for you in the next.
And I can make only one promise to you: the prize
will be worth the fall.*

*I will wait for you on the cliffs, as we planned, for
our final moment.*

Yours forever,

Lola

'Holy shit, Ivy.' Audrey's eyes are as wide as saucers.
The paper slips through my fingers and drifts slowly to the
ground.

'Where . . . where did you say you found this?' I manage
to ask.

'Behind the wall. I didn't show you because, well, it was
a bit awkward back then . . . and I didn't wanna get
involved . . . and then I just forgot . . .' Her eyes are
wandering all over the place and a flush rises in her cheeks.

'Audrey, shh.' I put my finger to her mouth. 'That doesn't
matter now. Show me.'

She takes a deep breath to collect herself, then heads over
to my side of the room and pulls aside my desk chair.
Kneeling down, she reaches behind the desk and presses one
of the wooden panels, which swings open to reveal a space.

'I was going to mention it when we were in the feathers'
quarters but then I got totally side-tracked by what we
found in the cave. The letter was just in here. The panel

opened when Mrs Parsons locked me in the room, remember? She shut the door with such force it must've dislodged the mechanism. I wasn't sitting at your desk, banging on the wall or anything.' She smiles at me with a coy shrug. 'I'm not going to look at any of the walls in the school in the same way again. Each panel seems to hide a secret passageway!'

I kneel down next to her. 'Is there anything else inside?'

She shrugs. 'Not that I could see.'

'But there might be something,' I persist. 'Like that diary that Patrick mentioned?'

'I guess you're right. Oh my God, all this time . . . I'm so sorry, Ivy.'

I don't reply, but shift forward so that I can get a better look at the secret compartment. Now that the panel is off, we can see the old brick holding the school together. It's chalky like the cliffs, and very crumbly. You can't see how deep the hole is, so I stick my arm in to check.

'Whoa, careful!' Audrey yelps. 'There could be spiders or . . . bugs in there?' Just as my fingertips are as outstretched as I can get them, I feel something. I force my arm in just a bit more and pull it out.

'What is it?' Audrey gawps over my shoulder.

'It *is* a diary,' I say in a hushed voice. A diary written in an Illumen school workbook. I run my fingers over the school crest on the front cover, and the motto – *Alis grave nil*.

'What does that mean?' Audrey asks.

I'm about to roll my eyes at her ignorance, but I stop myself at the last moment. 'The approximate translation is, "Nothing is heavy to those who have wings." '

'Wow. That's beautiful.'

I open the first page and it's filled with tiny little flower doodles surrounding a name: *Lola*.

'I'm not sure we should read this.' Audrey shuffles away, resting her head against the window sill. 'The letter was one thing. But this feels more of an invasion of privacy. Maybe we should hand this to the cops? Or give it straight to Patrick?'

'The police are still convinced this is a closed case. They'll just lock this diary up in some evidence box. Let's check the contents first.'

Without waiting for a reply, I turn the page and, when I look up again, Audrey has moved back next to me.

There's a poem down the centre, and some scribbly drawings either side.

> *Do not take me for what you see of me*
> *I am but a mirage*
> *A figment*
> *A fragment*
> *A half-finished portrait*

'What does that mean?' Audrey looks at me, wrinkling her nose.

'I don't know. I guess it's stream-of-consciousness stuff.' I turn to the next page, but it's just some notes from what looks like science revision. I flick through a couple more pages. Some back-and-forth notes with Jessica about messages they'd received from guys. Then – finally – some diary entries.

Why does this happen to me? Always falling for the wrong guy. He's ignoring me again. It's been a week with no messages, no calls and no eye contact. It makes it so much harder seeing him here every day. He told me he'd leave her. Told me that it will always be me, and that the life that we'll have together will be everything he's always wanted. Yet here I am, still waiting like a fool and hanging on his every word as usual. Am I not good enough? Has he changed his mind?

I just want to know.

I can't carry on like this.

'Christ, I wonder who she's talking about?' I look at Audrey and the cogs start turning in my mind.

'Could this be the mystery guy that Clover talks about in her podcast? Did she have a boyfriend last year at all? Some guy who was playing her and someone else at the same time? Sounds like a douche bag whoever he is!'

'Sounds like Teddy,' I mutter.

Audrey grabs my hand. 'Could it be?'

I pause, then give myself a shake. 'No. Jessica was clear in the podcast it was an older guy, and Teddy's a month younger than Lola was.' I think long and hard. 'I don't remember seeing Lola with anyone else. Not after Alex Winters. They had a big break-up at the beginning of last year. But he wasn't going out with anyone else as far as I know, so he can't be the guy in this entry. But listen – she was a popular girl. She was funny, beautiful and really smart – she always had *someone* interested in her.'

'OK. Maybe a guy from another school?'

'But she says she sees him every day, so he must have been an Illumen student! I guess he's off at uni now.'

'True. Well then, the mystery goes unsolved. Unless she's written his name someplace in here . . .' Audrey takes the diary, and we flick through page after page. More and more paragraphs about this mystery guy and how she feels about him, dates they've shared, texts he's sent, their undying love, but still no name. She's used 'Goofo' as a pet name throughout every journal entry, rant or rave.

'Well, she's one consistent woman . . .' Audrey is nearing the end of the diary now.

'Yeah, she really didn't want anyone knowing who he was.'

Although her diary is filled with very normal seventeen-year-old musings and mayhem, it's clear that Lola was a highly sensitive person. Among pages of love, bewilderment, infatuation and ecstasy are seemingly darker poems about abandonment, heartbreak, depression and loneliness. A side of her I hadn't ever encountered. Many of the poems she'd written herself, but some by her favourite poets litter the pages too. The diary isn't completely full, some pages are untouched, yet I notice a slightly thicker page at the very back. I nudge Audrey to open the diary there and she almost drops it like a ball of fire. Printed out and stuck in is a poem. The final two lines read:

> *Do not stand at my grave and cry;*
> *I am not there. I did not die.*

'Oh. HELL, NO. Fuck this, Ivy. I'm out!' Audrey gets up and runs her hands through her hair, pacing. 'It's a poem about being dead! This is not OK!' I see tears in her eyes and panic on her face.

'Audrey, calm down. It's a well-known poem. *Do Not Stand at my Grave and Weep* by Mary Elizabeth Frye. Lola didn't write these words herself.'

'It's still pretty dark. Maybe she did end her own life after all?'

I feel sick, tears welling up in my eyes. The podcast, and then our investigations, really had led me to believe that foul play had been involved in Lola's death. But maybe we were wrong the whole time. 'You might be right; this definitely proves that Lola wasn't in the best mindset. We should show Clover.' The diary feels very heavy all of a sudden.

'Or Patrick?' Audrey suggests.

Just then, I notice that the corner of the poem is coming loose. It looks as though something is sandwiched between the page and the poem. Using the knife again, I slowly try to peel the edge back.

'Ivy, stop! What are you doing? You literally just said we should show someone and now you're destroying it?'

I ignore her and carry on peeling until the entire poem has come away. A photograph drops to the floor. Audrey picks it up, her hands visibly trembling. The photo is a black-and-white picture of a couple, and it looks like it's been taken on a crap mobile phone, or possibly a shaky disposable camera and scanned in low resolution. You can just about make out that it's Lola. She has her back to the camera, her hair curling against her shoulders. She's holding hands with the guy sitting next to her. We can only see a bit of his profile as he gazes at her.

'Oh my God.' Audrey's hand flies to her mouth. 'That's Mr Willis.'

44

IVY

'OK, I guess it does look like him.' I squint and study the photo a bit harder. 'But it's so pixelated. And it's only part of his face! I wish there was another photo in here. Something clearer so we can know for sure.' I shake the book as hard as I can, half expecting something else to fall out. But there's nothing. A part of me doesn't want it to be true . . . but what if it is? It would certainly answer a lot of our questions.

'Now we have to go to the cops,' Audrey says, standing up.

'No!' I cry out. Audrey frowns at me, and I swallow. 'Let's find Clover. See if it matches with what she's found out already. The more evidence we have, the stronger our case will be, and the more likely that DC Copeland will take us seriously.'

Audrey's blue eyes search my face for a few moments, then she nods. 'OK, let's go.'

We head out of the room, past bedrooms full of giggling students getting ready for the Samhain party. I wish we could feel so carefree and excited. Instead, I'm just a ball of stress.

'I'm not gonna lie, Ivy, I feel like my brain is about to

implode with this information overload.' Audrey rubs her temples as we head down the stairs, dodging people carrying armloads of autumnal-themed decorations. A thought pings in my mind that Araminta is going to be fuming I've missed out on the preparations that I promised to help with, but I bat it away. This is much more important.

'This looks really bad for Mr Willis,' Audrey says.

'We don't know that it's him one hundred per cent,' I reply.

'I know you like him . . .'

'He's a good teacher!' Even I hate how defensive I sound. But we need to find Clover to be sure. We make our way to the entrance of Polaris House and slip in as students are heading out. Clover shares a room with two other girls, and I take the stairs three at a time in my haste to get there.

I give a cursory knock on the door, but open it straight away. 'Clover?'

Audrey steps in behind me. 'Doesn't look like there's anyone here.' The room's a pigsty, with shoes and clothes tossed all over the floor. Only on the night of a big party would it be allowed to become such a tip.

'They must be helping with the preparations. I guess I shouldn't be surprised – I'll leave her a note.' I walk over to her desk, grab a piece of paper and start scribbling.

'Um, Ivy?'

'What?' I look back at Audrey, who's staring down at a brown box on Clover's bed. 'What is it?'

'You need to look at this.'

I drop the pen and make my way to Audrey's side. The package is unopened, the Sellotape still intact. She points at an elaborate logo of PR on the front. PRONTO ESTATES. 'What am I looking at?'

'That's Patrick Radcliffe's company. He gave me his business card when I met him.'

'What's she doing with that?'

'I have no idea . . .'

'Well, we have to open it.'

'What?' Audrey looks at me in alarm.

I pick up the box and inspect it from all sides. 'There's no name on it, so we're not breaking the law. What if it's something dangerous? Another threat?' I tear open the tape with the edge of my fingernail, and Audrey doesn't stop me.

Inside is a brand-new pair of noise-cancelling headphones and a note. Audrey picks the note up and reads out loud.

Clover,

Thank you for your last podcast over half-term. Really intriguing. The payment we agreed should have cleared your account by now, but I wanted to send you something extra as a special token of my appreciation. Your perseverance is paying off and keeping Lola's story in people's minds. Nice touch keeping the threat alive. Who could have predicted the podcast would have taken off the way it did when we talked about this back in July? The more listeners we have, the better chance we have of finding out what really happened.

Do whatever you have to, to keep the podcast going.

Patrick

'Oh my God, Patrick's the one who told Clover to start this podcast.' My jaw drops. I'm shocked – and more than a little hurt. I thought Clover told me everything. Turns out there were even more secrets than I could have imagined.

'And paying her to keep doing it. And "do whatever you have to" . . . Is she making stuff up, just to keep listeners entertained?' Audrey asks.

'Sounds that way. It's all for money,' I say, but my mouth is dry.

'Do you think she even cares about the case at all?' asks Audrey.

'I don't know.'

'So what was her long-term plan? To just accuse someone and see how they reacted? I mean, that could ruin someone's life! Why would she do that?' Audrey exclaims.

'For money and a giant platform? Getting a bit of fame and notoriety before she's even left school? Who knows?' I shrug. I don't want to believe it, yet my loyalty to Clover feels shattered into pieces. 'But now her podcast – as well as her – is completely discredited. There's no way I'm showing her Lola's journal and the photograph.'

'So we go to the cops now?' asks Audrey.

'No. If this is all we have, it won't be enough.' I ball up the half-written note to Clover and toss it in the bin. 'Let's go straight to the source.'

As we storm out of Polaris House towards the staffroom, I only have one thought. *Don't worry, Lola. We'll set the record straight about what happened to you.*

45

AUDREY

The teachers' lounge is down in the basement of the main building, and it smells kinda damp. It's definitely in worse shape than our common room. Well, I guess it is the students' parents who pay the exorbitant fees.

Ivy has the damning photograph clutched so tightly I'm worried it might disintegrate. I can feel the anger rising in her, a hurricane about to hit the shore. My emotions are a whirlwind too – from the revelations in Lola's journal to finding out the podcast was a sham.

She doesn't knock and wait politely to go in. She just bursts into the room, with me following close behind. I scan the lounge, but the only person in it is Mr Willis. He's standing over by the fireplace, trying to coax the embers back to life. The flames cast an eerie reddish glow on his face, and when he sees us his eyes turn from surprise – to fear.

'Ivy? Audrey? What are you girls doing in here? Did you find Clover?'

'Stop talking,' growls Ivy. 'How do you explain *this*?' She holds the photograph right up in front of his face. He takes it from her, studies it for a moment, then covers his face with his other hand. Ivy snatches the photo back.

'Where did you get that?' he asks.

'Does it matter?'

'Look, girls –' he splutters, desperation in his voice.

'No,' I say, stepping forward so I'm beside Ivy, shoulder to shoulder. 'We don't wanna hear any excuses or explanations. We've seen Lola's diaries too. We know who you were to her, *Goofo*.'

Mr Willis's face pales as I say the nickname, as if we hadn't seen enough admission of guilt in his body language. He slumps down into an armchair.

'Did you . . .' Ivy's voice chokes up; she can't finish the sentence.

'Did you kill her?' I do it for her. I watch Mr Willis like a hawk, alert to his reaction.

'What? No! Of course not! No, no, no,' he repeats, shaking his head. 'You don't understand . . . this isn't what it looks like.'

'Let's get real for a minute, *sir*,' scoffs Ivy.

'It's not! Look . . . I'll admit – Lola had made it known that she had feelings for me. I'd tried everything I could think of to put her off, to turn her down, but she was obsessed! And so, so persistent. I was at my wits' end. I thought the summer holidays starting would mean the end of it, but she wanted to meet one last time.'

'When? The night of the party!'

He hesitates. 'Yes.'

'Oh my God,' says Ivy.

'But I didn't show up! I couldn't! I knew it was a terrible idea. I sent her a text saying it couldn't happen. Of course then I heard the awful news . . .'

'How can we believe you? Maybe you let things get too far with Lola, and you needed a way to cover it up!'

'No! And I can prove it.' He scrambles in his back pocket for his phone. He opens it to his photos app, then scrolls backwards until he finds the night of the party. 'Look.' He turns the phone round so we can see. 'I decided I couldn't meet Lola. That would be ridiculous. So I called Carly and we jumped on the Eurostar – a surprise trip to kick off the summer holidays. I was in Paris on the night Lola died.' He sounds almost triumphant as he shows off his proof.

'Did you tell the police about your relationship with Lola?' Ivy asks him as I check the date stamp on the photo.

He frowns. 'No, of course not . . . my reputation . . . and there was no *relationship*. Like I said, she was obsessed with me.'

'That's not what it sounds like in her diary,' I say.

'Oh, you know how teenage girls exaggerate . . .'

I scoff in disgust, and the colour drains even further from his face as he remembers he's talking to two teenage girls. 'That's not what I meant. Lola was different. She was . . .'

'*Don't* talk about her any more,' Ivy snaps. She's staring down at the black-and-white photograph of the two of them together.

'We're going to show this to the cops and then you can explain your alibi. It's not over until they've investigated it,' I say.

'No, please, you can't ask me to do that . . .' He looks from Ivy to me, his hands clasped together, begging, pleading with us not to go to the authorities. But Ivy and I are gonna stand strong on this, because we need justice. Justice for –

'Then leave. Leave now,' says Ivy, her voice cold.

'What?' he splutters.

'If you agree to pack up your things, leave the school, go and start a new life with *Carly* somewhere else and never teach at a school again, then we won't go to the authorities. We won't tell anyone about this.'

'What?!' I cry. Ivy squeezes my hand, but I don't understand.

'But –' He flaps his hands, as if trying to pull an argument out of the air.

'I don't think you're really in a position to argue,' she says, her voice hard.

'No, you're right.' He slumps in the chair and takes a deep breath. When he speaks again, there's resignation in his tone. 'OK. OK. I'll leave.'

'And you won't ever come back.'

He stares at Ivy, his eyes wide but weary. 'I won't ever come back.' He takes one final look at us both, and then strides out of the room.

'Let that be the end of it then,' Ivy says.

'Ivy . . . are you sure about this?' I ask. 'Don't you think we should still go to the authorities?'

'I'm sure.'

And then she does the last thing I expect. She tosses the photo into the flames. It immediately catches, the image of Mr Willis and Lola glowing orange, curling in on itself and finally disintegrating into ash.

46

IVY

Audrey tries to grab the photo from the fireplace. 'What are you doing?!' she shouts.

But I pull her back, not wanting her to rescue it. I feel oddly calm now. 'Don't you see?' I say to her. 'He didn't do anything that night. All that photo could do now is damage his reputation. This way, he can get a fresh start somewhere else, and no one else gets hurt.' I look up at her, meeting her confused stare. 'That's all I want. For no one else to get hurt.'

She bites her bottom lip. Then breathes out in one long exhale. 'But what about the diary?'

'Lola's gone. We can't ask her to clarify her words. We don't know for certain that she's referring to Mr Willis, so the police won't care. And you saw the photographs of him and his fiancée in Paris, the date stamp and everything. He couldn't have been responsible for her death.'

'He's still a predator.'

'And he's gone now.'

'Ivy . . .'

'Drop it, Audrey. Please.'

My phone buzzes in my pocket and I look down to see that Clover has finally replied to my earlier message. I breathe out sharply. She doesn't know that we know the truth about her podcast yet. I spin my phone round to show Audrey.

> I'm in the Tower Wing.
> Room 3A x

'Ready for another confrontation? One down, one to go.'

Audrey nods, and we leave the staffroom, following the meandering corridors to the Tower Wing. Thanks to Teddy, our key cards grant us full access and we race up the stairs. As we pass the art room, I peer inside. It's an absolutely huge circular space, with a double-height ceiling and windows to match. Artwork from students covers the walls, some of it going back years. I spot Mr Yarrow's bald head washing brushes at the sink, but I don't want him to see us – so we carry on, climbing higher and higher, until we reach room 3A. A sliver of warm light filters out from beneath the door. As we approach, we can faintly hear Clover's voice.

'She's recording now?' Audrey whispers outside the door.

I feel my fists clench and I take a deep breath to try and control my rising anger. 'That's a wrap! Or, should I say, that's another bit of cash in your back pocket?' I say as we barge in.

Clover almost jumps out of her chair, her eyes wide with alarm, her arms covering her laptop screen. But when she sees that it's us, and my words register, she chuckles and slowly removes her beaten-up pair of headphones.

'So you found out about Patrick then? I won't ask how

you seem to have got hold of that private information, Ivy.'
She rolls her eyes. How come this girl acts like she's decades
older than fifteen, with absolutely no fear whatsoever? It
almost completely throws me off.

'Clover, what the hell are you doing?' I sit down next to
her and Audrey leans on the closed door behind her. I feel
it's best to give her the chance to admit all this herself.

'Guys, I'm not sure what kind of mission you're on, or
why you think me being paid is even *relevant* when it
comes to Lola's murder, but –'

'*Are you kidding?* Clover, your credibility as a journalist
is completely destroyed by the fact that Patrick is paying
you. How can you sit there, broadcasting stuff you made
up about a girl who's dead, pointing the finger at innocent
people in the way that you are? Haven't people suffered
enough?'

She shakes her head. 'I'm not doing this just to get
paid – honestly, Patrick's money has been helpful to get
this off the ground, but I would've done it with or without
him. Everything I'm talking about and discussing is true. I
did get an anonymous tip. I *do* think something bad is
going on at this school. Plus, I'm not directly naming
names, so no "innocent people" are suffering.'

Clover starts fiddling with her laptop and dragging
audio files into a timeline. 'I just want justice, Ivy. I want
to find out the truth. That's it.' She looks me right in the
eyes, so piercing and meaningful I actually feel slightly
uncomfortable. 'And that means getting this last podcast
out before the Samhain party. So I'm a bit up against it, if
you don't mind . . .'

Audrey and I stare at her, stony-faced. But Audrey is the first to soften. She doesn't have the layers of betrayal of a long friendship that I feel like I'm having to sift through right now. 'So tell us then: who do you think "murdered" Lola? If you're saying you aren't making this up, what's left to talk about? Why not just reveal the person and get the cops involved?'

'I can't do that just yet. There's still a few pieces of evidence I needed to gather in order for the police to believe me beyond any reasonable doubt.'

'So . . . you *don't* know who it is,' Audrey says.

'No, I do! But don't you get it?' Clover's eyes are shining now. 'The podcast has put pressure on this person. They know that I'm *this* close to having incontrovertible proof. They've been careful, oh so very careful . . . but pressure means even clever people make mistakes. And trust me, this person is not only clever and careful, but dangerous too. They killed Lola on purpose and they could easily murder again.' She closes her laptop and stands up, unplugging it from the wall.

'Well, who? What's your evidence? Maybe we can help – apply even more pressure on your behalf!' Audrey asks.

'I don't have to tell you!'

'Don't be so ridiculous, Clover,' I snap, my patience thread-thin. 'Tell us, and we'll tell you what we've found that we think completely contradicts your "narrative".'

'Air quotes aren't cute, Ivy. I'm not interested in what you've found. My "narrative" is pretty much solid at this point.'

'Listen,' I say, injecting more calm into my voice, 'the

police always said that the only thing that made the coroner rule "death by misadventure" instead of "by suicide" is that they never found a note – right?'

'Right,' she says, her arms crossed.

'Well, we found a whole diary's worth of notes. Lola was in a really dark place. She was heartbroken. She was feeling reckless. The change in personality, the abrupt change in hairstyle – all of it,' I say.

'It's all in here,' Audrey says, taking the diary from her bag. 'It's pretty scary stuff.'

She passes it to Clover, who starts flicking through. Then she puts it down. 'Newsflash, Audrey, I'm not sure about the school you were at previously, but loads of girls here at Illumen write depressing-as-fuck poems. It doesn't mean she killed herself. This proves nothing!'

'Fine. I was going to wait to see if you had some actual evidence, but it's clear you've got nothing.' I take a deep breath. 'It's Mr Willis. He's your main suspect, isn't he?'

'Why do you say that?' Clover's eyes dart between us, suddenly sharp.

'Because we know he's the older man you reference,' Audrey replies.

'You do? She names him in the diary?' Now Clover looks excited. She flicks through the pages again. 'Do you know that he was supposed to meet Lola that night?'

'We do know that. But she doesn't name him.'

'So you see? I have to continue the podcast. I'm so close to getting a confession out of him . . .'

I shake my head. 'No, Clover. He has a solid alibi. We've seen it.'

'You *spoke* to him?'

'We did,' says Audrey. 'We saw photographs and time stamps of him in Paris on the night Lola died. He said Lola was obsessed with him. But regardless of whether that was true or not . . . he's left the school. He's gone. He's never coming back.'

'Never,' I say with emphasis.

'So that's it?' Clover blinks several times, then her shoulders slump.

I nod. 'He's not going to teach again. Not here, not anywhere.'

'But wait, he wasn't my only suspect! Just because he has an alibi . . .' Clover drifts off mid-sentence. 'I've just been immersed in this for so long, I can't believe it.' She buries her face in her hands.

I place my hand on her back. Despite everything, she's still my fledgling, my mentee and, most importantly, my friend. 'At least you don't have to worry about anything else happening at the school. No one else has to get hurt, Clover. It's over.'

47

AUDREY

The three of us are quiet as we walk back to Clover's room. 'Will we see you at the party?' Ivy asks her.

Clover shakes her head. 'No . . . I think I'm just going to stay here and sleep. I feel shattered.' She looks it too, her eyes slightly glazed. Ivy fetches her a cup of tea from their little communal kitchen and then we leave her to rest, returning to our building.

'Hey, you did the right thing.' I touch Ivy's arm, pulling her to a stop just before we step into Helios House, and back into the chaos of everyone getting ready for the party.

'Do you think?' Ivy's voice is barely above a whisper.

'Yeah. That creep Mr Willis is gone from the school. And Clover's gonna stop with the podcast. Lola can finally rest peacefully.'

As if it calls to us both, we turn and look up at Lola's portrait. A shiver crawls down my spine. Because, when I look at her face, I'm not seeing Lola any more.

I see Alicia.

'I wish I could've done more for you too,' I whisper.

'What did you say?' Ivy asks as we make our way back up to our room. I feel like I'm strung out on adrenaline.

I shrug. 'Nothing. I guess I just can't believe it's over.' I go quiet, not really speaking much as we return to our room.

Ivy looks at me with concern. 'I don't want to push . . . but I'm used to being the quiet one. You know you can talk to me.'

'It's all just become a bit much. All this focus on murder and death . . . I can't handle it.' I take a deep breath outside of our door. 'I never told you what happened back home, did I?'

'No.' She says it quietly, and doesn't look directly at me. I know she must be curious – I would be – but I appreciate that she's trying not to spook me back into silence. I haven't opened up to anyone about this. It's the last thing sticking between us.

We go into our room. I sit down on my bed and Ivy sits on hers. I hug my knees into my chest.

'I used to enjoy parties too.' I pause. 'Well, I used to enjoy throwing them. Or maybe I felt obligated to, because I was the one with the biggest house and the most money. Anyway, I was having kind of a smallish gathering. Just my "closest" friends, my boyfriend at the time and some of his friends. It wasn't meant to be a big deal. We had lots of alcohol and stuff, but nothing harder. It was just supposed to be chilled.

'I was fighting with Brendan at the time. He was being an ass about something – I can't remember what. But we were so busy yelling at each other that we didn't hear the yelling that was happening *outside*.' My voice drops as I disappear into the memory. No matter how hard I squeeze my eyes shut, no matter how hard I wish it, nothing will change how I acted that night – or what happened. There's a bitter taste in the back of my throat. 'You know, I kinda wish we had some sort of Magpie Society to stop the shit that was happening at my school.'

'So there was yelling going on outside your house?' Ivy gently prompts.

'Yeah. The house is right on the beach – there's a wrap-around porch that literally goes right down to the dunes. It turned out, while Brendan and I were upstairs, another group of kids from our school had walked past the house along the beach.' I take a deep breath. 'A bunch of kids that included Alicia.'

'Who was Alicia?'

'Well . . . if we were the stereotypical "popular" kids, then she was a nerd. I know it's so cheesy to define it like that, but honestly . . . in this case, it was kinda true.

'The other girls in her group made the sensible decision. They ran away when my friends started calling out and jeering at them. But, for whatever reason, Alicia chose that moment to stand up to us. I wish she'd just gone with her friends, but . . .' I bite my lip. 'No, sorry. Scratch that. I'm not gonna put any of this on her. She had the right to be on that beach too.'

Somehow, in the time that I've been talking, Ivy has moved from her bed to mine, and is sitting next to me. 'My . . . friends invited her up on to the porch. Made her feel welcome. They plied her with drink, made her feel like part of the cool crowd for a while. But of course it was all just in the name of joking around. They were bullies.'

'Sounds awful.'

I look up at Ivy, but I'm barely able to see through the blur of tears. I let a few of them fall, then collect myself. I have to honour Alicia by telling the whole story. All of it. Without missing anything out. 'So then they all decided to get into the hot tub.' I say the next part in a rush, as if telling it quicker makes it sound less terrible. I just have to get it out. 'They were fooling around. Playing games. Completely wasted.

'Then it all went wrong. I heard screams – even I could hear them over our fight. By the time Brendan and I got downstairs again . . . Ivy, she was dead. She'd drowned in the hot tub.'

'Holy shit!'

'Lydia was panicking, crying, begging me to call 911,' I go on. 'I finally got the story out of her when she'd stopped having hysterics. One of the guys, Tyler . . . she said . . . she said he held Alicia's head down in the water. That he'd tried to get her to give him . . . well, you know. He said it was a joke gone wrong. A joke he's in prison for now. His trial is scheduled for a few weeks' time. He's probably gonna go away for life.'

'Too fucking right,' Ivy says, but then she snaps her mouth shut as realization dawns on her face. 'That's why you came here.'

'Yeah. I couldn't stand to be there any more. In that house. I was having panic attacks at home, at that school. With those people. The police didn't need my testimony or anything like that. They had my statement. They had eyewitnesses in all my friends who were in the hot tub. My parents said I didn't have to go through the trial. I don't think that I could have. They were moving to England anyway, so I came with them.'

'Oh, Audrey. To me it seemed as if you had the perfect life. You are kind of intimidating with all . . . this.' She gestures at my face and hair, and it makes me laugh, despite everything. 'But I guess you never know what people are going through. Just like with Lola. I'm so sorry. That's really terrible. No wonder you wanted to get away.'

'You're right. This is why I came here. For a fresh start. I admit, I was pretty afraid of being here when it seemed like your school was just as focused on the death of a student as mine was. I felt like I was cursed. But instead I found the best friend I could possibly ask for.' I reach out and take Ivy's hand.

'Me too.' She squeezes my fingers back. 'Audrey . . . it wasn't your fault, you know – Alicia? You weren't even there.'

'I know. But she died in *my* house. I just can't help but think there was more I could have done. Not even necessarily that night. It wasn't like the bullying had started that evening. I was such a stupid, selfish bitch. At any point, I could have just stood up against what I knew was wrong.'

'Like you did with Clover – well, both for Clover and against her.'

'Exactly. It's like I've become my own version of the Magpie Society. I can't stand by any more. Not now my eyes are truly open to the consequences.'

'Me neither.'

We sit in silence for a few seconds. Then Ivy slaps her hand down on top of mine, and grips my fingers tightly. 'My God, the school therapist is going to make a fortune from us!' She laughs, and I find myself chuckling along too. Nothing like a dark joke to break the tension.

'Well, all we can do is keep trying to do better. And we also have to give ourselves permission to live our own lives. So let's do it, right? We've got rid of Mr Willis; we've stopped Clover. It's late. Tomorrow we'll give the diary and the letter to the police. But for now? Now, we've got a party to prepare for.'

48

AUDREY

'So, what are you going to wear to the Samhain ball?' Ivy asks me.

'I have a few options,' I reply. Ivy gasps over each one as I bring it out. My favourite is black and lacy, with a scoop neck, kind of a fancy version of a witch's dress. A very *fashionable* witch's dress, of course. There's also one in a bias-cut navy silk, and another in luxurious bronzes and golds that should make me look like an autumn princess. This is my first chance to properly dress up.

'These are all so beautiful,' says Ivy. I grin. She's like a kid in a candy store.

'What about you? What are you gonna wear?'

'Oh, I'm not great with fashion really. But I found a black dress in a charity shop last week that will work well enough.'

'Show me? I love a good thrift find. I've got some killer vintage pieces back home that I picked up for, like, no money. You get a surprisingly good selection down in Savannah, some really cool old stuff, but the best is if I get up to New York. It's probably one of the few times that Mom and I actually bond . . .'

As I talk, Ivy heads over to her dresser, rifling through

the bottom drawer. I feel a tiny twinge of alarm. What's she doing?

'Ah, here it is,' she says, shaking out a crumpled black dress with ruffles down one edge. For someone who shows such care and attention in most aspects of her life, I can hardly believe that she takes so little interest in her clothes.

'No way, honey, you can't wear that,' I say.

'I could give it an iron?'

'No, seriously. I have a ton of dresses here. Just pick one and go wild.'

'Wait, seriously?'

'Yeah, of course! What are room-mates for?'

'Oh my God, thank you so much, Audrey. I just haven't had the brain space to think about dresses, and this was the only thing I could find that was even vaguely appropriate.'

I grimace. 'I'm not sure I'd even call it that.'

She leaps forward, instantly gathering up my black, lacy dress in her arms. My heart stops for a moment – I'd really had my heart set on that – but I catch myself. I can wear it anytime, and I have dozens more like it at home – in the UK and in the States. I smile. 'It'll look beautiful on you,' I say.

'Thanks! Which one are you going to wear?'

My eye falls on the bronze-and-gold one. With the right make-up, it will be a stand-out look for the party. I run my fingers over the slinky material. 'This one.'

'Amazing. You'll look just perfect.'

We change into our dresses, swapping make-up and chatting. It feels so nice to actually have a proper *friend* again. It's the kind of boarding-school friendship that people write about in books. Ivy's so smart and brave. I feel lucky that she sees something in me, and wants to be friends with me too.

Ivy texts Harriet, and soon our room is a hive of activity as she comes to join us and we throw our bedroom door wide open. I share my vast array of make-up with the girls, and it almost feels like things are back to normal. I curl my hair into big bouncy waves, going full Southern gothic belle. Big hair, dark eyes, a dark lip, a black velvet choker and the iridescent dress. I help Ivy with her make-up too, and we settle on a shimmering gold eyeshadow and spider-leg-thin fake eyelashes to show off her hazel eyes.

'You look amazing. Your skin is incredible.'

'I have my mum to thank for that,' she says. 'She hardly wears any make-up at all.'

'Lucky. And Harriet, I love the colour of your dress.'

'Really? I think it makes me look like a chubby sack of potatoes,' Harriet says.

Ivy tuts. 'Oi, stop saying you're chubby. You have an amazing body that I can only ever dream of. Have you seen your arse? Beyoncé must be quaking.'

'Yeah, you're right,' Harriet laughs, doing an expert booty shake.

'OK, we'd better head downstairs or we'll miss the kick-off,' says Ivy, glancing at her phone.

'But before we do, since it's a party . . .' Harriet opens her purse. With a wicked sideways grin, she pulls out three tiny airplane bottles of vodka.

'Ooh, naughty!' I say in my best British accent.

'If you can't be naughty around Halloween, when can you?' Harriet winks.

Ivy grins. 'Willy Wonka strikes again!' She takes one of the bottles, untwisting the cap with a practised flick of the wrist. 'Cheers!'

'Cheers,' I reply, clinking my little bottle with hers and Harriet's and taking a big gulp. I grimace. 'This tastes like shit. Don't you have any Fireball around here or something?'

Ivy's face is also a picture of disgust as she finishes her bottle, and she gives her body a shake. 'Fireball? What's that?'

My jaw drops. 'You haven't tried it?'

'Uh, no.'

'You're missing out. I'll bring some from home next time. It's like . . . cinnamon whisky.'

'Sounds disgusting.'

I stick my tongue out at her. 'It's freakin' delicious. As warming as a fire on a winter's day . . . not like this stuff. Gross.'

'Does the trick though,' says Ivy. 'Right, are we ready?'

I stand up, towering over my diminutive room-mate. 'Ready.'

'Let's go!' says Harriet.

We giggle, grab our phones and head out the door.

The school looks absolutely gorgeous. Say what you want about Araminta, but she has party planning in her future if she wants it. The banister of the staircase leading down into the great entrance hall is wrapped in autumn leaves, each stair with its own intricately carved pumpkin.

Torches, lit with vibrant flames, flicker along the wall, lighting our way and casting eerie shadows.

What Ivy said about this once being a religious event suddenly begins to ring true; it feels sacred, even now. Although we're dressed up, there isn't a traditional party mood. Instead, there's an almost sombre feeling in the air, a quiet reverence.

'Someone's waiting for you,' Ivy says, nudging my arm.

I see Teddy at the top of the stairs. He looks smokin' hot in a black velvet blazer, dark shirt and slacks. He has a leaf pin on his jacket, with gold curls of vine leaves creeping down his lapel.

I don't need Ivy's approval, but when I look over at her she's grinning, and I smile back. Teddy extends his arm, and I take it – and he leads me down the stairs towards the crowd.

There's a clap of thunder sound effect and flashes of lightning. 'Wow, Araminta's gone all out with this fake storm. Really adds to the atmosphere.' Teddy's voice is low in my ear.

'Right? It reminds me of being back home. We can have some wild storms – nothing fake about those.'

'I'd like to go to Georgia. Sounds like a cool place.'

'It is, although . . .' I look up, once again feeling awed by the vaulted ceiling and enormous paintings hanging all around. With the addition of the Samhain decorations – the elaborate displays of autumnal leaves, harvest foods, candles, torches and wreaths – it looks more ancient and medieval than ever. I can't imagine any place being 'cooler' than this.

'I know. We do go a little over the top here, don't we? I'll go and get us a drink.' He leaves my side, meandering over to the cauldrons bubbling away in the corner, manned by one of the younger fledglings.

Ivy whispers in my ear from behind. 'Don't worry, the non-alcoholic mulled cider is pretty nice.'

'And I can always spice it up for you,' says Harriet, waggling her eyebrows.

'Is it always like this? So very . . . extra?'

'I think our Minty feels she has something to prove . . .'

'I'll say.'

Max and Tom find us through the crowds, Teddy returns with the drinks and, as we all stand around, sipping cider, I realize this is the first time I've felt properly happy and relaxed in a long time. I lean into Teddy's arm and he smiles at me. Ivy is laughing and chatting with Harriet, and I feel a warm rush of feeling run around my body that I think has more to do with friendship than vodka.

Abruptly, the music and sound effects stop, and we all turn as one towards a plinth set up in front of the double doors. Araminta and Xander are standing on top of it, both looking absolutely gorgeous. Araminta is wearing a gold sequinned dress that wouldn't look out of place at the Oscars and Xander looks sharp in a fancy-patterned purple-and-gold tuxedo, his normally spiked hair now slicked back and shiny.

'Welcome, fellow students, teachers and staff of Illumen Hall, to our annual Samhain party! Samhain is a solemn tradition, and we pay tribute to Lord Brathebone, whose interest in Druid and pagan rituals inspired the very first

Samhain party. Although, in keeping with Illumen Hall rules, we have divested from our religious roots in all capacities, that doesn't mean that we can't take a moment to appreciate the turn of the season, the bounty of the harvest and the rich colours of nature.'

'Wow, could she sound any more pompous if she tried?' Ivy whispers to me, and I giggle.

'And now, everyone gather –' starts Xander, but there's a rustle of movement from behind him, and he stumbles over his words, not nearly as confident and smooth as Araminta.

Araminta glances back, confusion on her face. The torches all around us flicker ominously, and there's another huge clap of thunder inside. Some students scream. There's a commotion by the stage, and a dark figure jumps up in between the head girl and head boy. The figure spreads its arms – encased in an enormous set of wings with huge, oily black feathers that shimmer purple, green and blue. The figure has a grotesque mask on with a long, curved beak – more like one of those Venetian plague doctor's masks than the head of a bird. It opens its mouth and lets out a fearsome shriek, then jumps down into the crowd. Just as quickly as it appeared, it's gone.

It's not alone. There's a whirlwind of feathered figures dancing and spinning around us, separating Ivy and me, cawing in my face and chanting. I'm so confused, so desperate not to get caught up in some kind of frenzied stampede, that I can't make out what they're saying.

I feel Teddy's strong hand grab mine. He drags me to the edge of the room, where we press our backs to the wall. Dozens of people dressed all in black, their arms and backs covered in feathers, their faces covered by masks, fill the room. Now that I see it from here, there does seem to be some sort of choreography to their movements, as they move as a group from one end of the room to the other. I see terror on Ivy's face and I push my way back towards her. Some of the teachers are trying to grab and unmask the strange bird-people, and Araminta is shrieking above them all, 'Stop them! This isn't supposed to happen!' But the fake thunder seems timed to drown her out.

All around us, they're simply chanting one phrase: 'One for sorrow, one for sorrow, one for sorrow.'

49

IVY

I look around at the faces of other students for reassurance. Most are laughing, some are whooping and clapping and others are more confused. It's hard to know if this is something Araminta has orchestrated or this flash mob is separate from the Samhain celebrations. If this is some kind of Halloween party trick, it's certainly strange.

From the sound of Araminta's screeching, I don't think she's behind it. My throat starts to close and I can feel the blood pumping through my body. I notice I'm panting and Audrey's lace dress suddenly feels two sizes too small.

Audrey catches my eye, and it's as if she's having the exact same thoughts. Fear and dread are plastered across her face. I notice she's clutching Teddy's hand and, in that very moment, I want to clutch it too.

'Something about this feels wrong!' I try to shout over the noise. But my voice cracks and the two of us look at one another while the room fills with laughter and screams. Laughter and screams that are getting louder and more manic by the second.

'Are they part of the Magpie Society? Why do I feel like we're the only ones not in on all this?' Audrey mouths back. She may have said it out loud, but all I can hear is the buzz in the room and that incessant chanting. I focus so hard on Audrey's lips, but it feels as though she's moving them in slow motion. Just as I feel like bolting from the hall, one of the masked figures swoops past us and, as they do, they lock eyes with me. Their eyes are so dark I can't see the iris from the pupil. My entire body fills with panic. We both freeze and time feels like it's stopping as the figure dances past in the strobe lights. Beneath the mask, I see a sinister smirk.

'Who was that?' Audrey yells above the noise. As I go to speak, my mouth doesn't move and my vision starts to blur. I need to get out. I start running, but I'm not sure where the exit is. Another masked figure swoops in front of me, stopping me in my tracks. I halt abruptly and change direction. I look around for my friends, but I can't see them anywhere. I can't see where the door is, so I start running in the opposite direction, pushing past other students – I can vaguely hear Audrey shouting my name behind me, but I have to keep moving forward . . . I *have* to get out.

But I can't. Somehow I've walked right into the magpie flash mob. Suddenly I'm being pushed until I'm right up against a wall, unable to move, surrounded by a sea of feathers.

There's a terrible crack from above me and I look up. An antique mirror is teetering on its fixtures, shuddering under the weight of the autumnal decorations wrapped round its gilt frame. I know I should move, but I *can't*. I'm rooted to the spot. I close my eyes and brace myself as everyone around me shrieks and squeals in horror, watching the mirror above my head as it starts to fall away from the wall. I feel the air change and little bits of debris begin to rain down on my body. I still can't move. I hear more screaming and can't tell if it's me or someone else in the room.

Out of nowhere, Audrey grabs my arm and pulls me sideways with such force that I fall to the ground, centimetres from where the mirror shatters on to the floor, creating the most insane disco-ball effect round the room. The frame is smashed to pieces, denting the floor with the force of its weight. I look down at my hands and notice they're bleeding. The music and thunder has stopped and the eerie quiet of the room is filled with the faint sounds of people gasping and running, and the growing voice of Mrs Abbott shouting from a distance. I try to move, but shattered glass crunches under me. *Audrey's dress is ruined*, I think. My heart is beating so fast I can hear it.

Audrey pulls me into a hug so tight my ribs almost crack. But all I can see is the reflection of the final magpie to leave the room – his beaked face reflected back a thousand times in the splinters of glass.

50

AUDREY

'That could have killed me!'

Ivy is shaking all over as I finally release her from my arms and help her to stand. The sleeve of my black lace dress has been ripped off, her hair is dishevelled and her face is blotchy red. I can barely look at the blood all over her arms and legs without wanting to throw up. She came so close to being seriously, seriously hurt.

'Oh my God, Ivy, are you OK?' Araminta has rushed over to Ivy's side.

'All right, stand back – give her some space.' Mrs Abbott directs everyone away from the site of the mirror crash, and reluctantly people move away. I can see a dozen phones pointing at us. There were no rules banning recording at *this* party. 'Put those away, please. It was just an accident,' says Mrs Abbott, her tone brooking no argument. Reluctantly, students turn away.

The magpies are gone. Someone turns the music back on and a janitor appears with a broom, and within a few minutes the students have started to get back into the swing of the party.

Everyone except us, of course.

'How could this happen?' I ask. I stare up at the wall,

where part of the plaster that held up the mirror has been torn away. 'Is all this building falling to pieces?'

'Now let's not jump to conclusions about the state of the building,' says Mrs Abbott nervously.

'No, it's not the school's fault,' Ivy says, and the headmistress looks relieved. 'Look at this,' she continues, lifting the chain that held up the decorations-covered mirror. One of the links has been opened, as if with pliers. With the right amount of force, it would separate from its neighbour and cause the whole mirror to come tumbling down.

'Who put the decorations round the mirror?' I ask Araminta.

'Oh my God.' Her hands fly to her mouth. 'I know who did it.' Tears spring up into her eyes.

'For God's sake, Araminta, just tell us!' says Ivy.

'*Clover.* She volunteered to help me today. Said it was to show that she'd put everything behind us and that she was sorry for . . . for accusing me. That things had got out of hand. I was suspicious, but I wanted to be the bigger person. I let her. In fact . . . you were supervising, Mrs Abbott, weren't you? Because she had to go up on the ladder and that required adult supervision.'

Mrs Abbott nods. 'I was. I didn't see anything suspicious of course . . .'

'I should've guessed – after she warned that something was going to happen at the party. She wanted to ruin it! To ruin me!' cries Araminta. She's pulling at her cheeks, her face a picture of horror.

'Um, Minty, I'm pretty sure you're not the one who *almost died* here,' says Ivy.

'Oh my God, guys. Look at this,' says Harriet.

'It's on my phone too.'

I scrabble in my purse for my phone. I turn it over and I see that there's a notification from hours before – I hadn't noticed amid all the party prep. Clover's released another podcast.

THE <u>WKL?</u> PODCAST TRANSCRIPT

EPISODE FIVE

Sound of feedback from a microphone and rapid breathing.

> CLOVER
> I really wish that I could say this was one of my normal podcasts, but it's not.
>
> If you're at Illumen Hall, you're in danger.
>
> Do not go to the Samhain party. Something terrible is going to happen.
>
> I'm terrified. I wasn't joking when I said that I thought Lola's killer was still out there. And now I realize that I haven't been able to find the truth fast enough. I really thought that I could get to the bottom of it in time.
>
> I'm afraid that not only am I in danger, but the whole school is. I'm terrified that the killer will stop at nothing to keep their identity a secret.

Maybe you'll think I've gone mad, but the Magpie Society is real. Only they weren't trying to hurt Lola. They were trying to protect her.

And now they want to protect me too.

I only hope this has gone out before someone else gets hur–

The sound cuts off.

51

IVY

'I've got to go,' says Mrs Abbott, after we've all listened.

'Wait, miss!' I cry out after her, but she tucks her phone away, muttering to herself.

Araminta lets out a long moan. 'This can't still be happening.'

I grab her by the hand. 'We need to find out who's behind the flash mob. Gather everyone outside at the bonfire, then we can see who's missing.'

'OK,' says Araminta through her sniffles. She pulls herself up to her full height and walks away, clapping her hands together, her voice carrying loudly over the music. 'Attention, everyone! Let's go outside for the annual lighting of the bonfire!'

'Teddy and Harriet, can you guys go after Mrs Abbott? Stall her. Tell her we found something out about Patrick Radcliffe and we'll meet her at her cottage,' I say.

'You got it,' he replies, and Harriet nods. They follow the crowd outside.

'Come on,' I say to Audrey. 'If this really was Clover, then she has to be aware of the consequences.' I gesture down at my bleeding arms and legs. 'We need to get through to her before someone really gets hurt.'

'I can't believe Clover would have endangered us like that. She sounded really worried in that episode.' Audrey's right. If it wasn't for Mrs Abbott's confirmation that she'd seen Clover hanging the wreath round the mirror, I wouldn't have believed it myself. But I'm beginning to realize that, no matter what I thought, I don't really know Clover at all.

Adrenaline is pumping through my body, my arms stinging from the scratches.

'When she said someone dangerous was operating at the school, I didn't realize she meant herself. She needs to be stopped.' I push through the heavy doors leading into Polaris House. The school is eerie, the halls echoing and empty – the students are all outside round the roaring fire. I can hear the muffled sound of laughter through the stone walls.

We march through the corridors, opening each door with such force I worry one will come off its hinges.

'She's definitely doing this for her own gain – there's absolutely no doubt about that,' I say. Audrey is following closely behind me and I can sense an adrenaline boost in her too. I feel like we're on the last level of a computer game, and we're heading to defeat the big boss.

'I know she said it's not about the money, but it must be. Regardless, we're going to bring her to Mrs Abbott right now,' I say as I push Clover's bedroom door open.

Audrey states the obvious: 'She's not here.'

'But she said she wasn't going to the party. I just assumed she'd be here. Surely she's not back at the tower?' I wade through the mess on the floor to Clover's bed and sit down, feeling deflated. But then I notice something out of the ordinary. The clothes, shoes and make-up aren't the only things among the mess. There are books, hard drives, the girls' secret phones and pages ripped from workbooks. It looks like someone's been through all their stuff. I turn round and notice that the bedding I'm sitting on is also completely messed up. The sheets are coming loose and the mattress isn't sitting on the bedframe properly. My heart is in my mouth. This doesn't feel right.

'Someone's been in here!' I stand up in a panic and see Audrey staring blankly at Clover's desk. Her face is turning whiter by the second.

'Ivy . . . there's blood.'

'*What?* Whose?' I get up and walk over to the desk, being careful not to touch or stand on anything.

'It could be Clover's?' Audrey whispers, looking round the room. We lock panicked eyes.

I instantly feel the mood shift in the room, and everything seems dark and uncertain, like running up the stairs at night. 'We were wrong. *Again.*'

'Do you think –' Audrey stops and looks around – 'that Clover really did know something about this dangerous person, and she's now their latest victim?'

'Maybe. She might have known too much.' I look at the blood glistening in the low light of the moon and the dim side lamps. There's not a lot, but enough that it looks like someone was really hurt. And it's still glistening. Does that mean it's fresh?

'We need to tell someone. Right now.' Audrey is backing up. She steps on a phone, which cracks underfoot. She hops up as if her foot is on fire.

'Look, Audrey.' I kneel down and snatch the phone. 'The phone's recording. It's been recording this whole time!'

I hold it out so she can see. Clover had a voice-recording app, probably to help with the podcast interviews. I stop it and rewind to early in the evening. There's almost two hours of recording there, and it takes a little while until we finally hear something.

'Get away from me . . . No . . . stop . . . help!' Clover's stricken voice sounds out on the recording. Both Audrey and I look at each other in terror.

'Oh my God!' Audrey's hand flies to her mouth.

'Don't take me! I won't go!' Clover is shouting and then there's a thump as the phone drops to the floor and the recording falls silent. At least, I hope that's what the thump means. I can't think about it any further than that.

Audrey runs to the door. 'Help!' she screams down the corridor. But everyone's at the party. There's no one around to hear her.

I stop the recording, careful not to delete it. Although the screen is smashed, it still works. I swipe to the emergency call number. My hands are shaking as it rings.

'Nine nine nine, which service do you require?'

'Police. My name is Ivy Moore-Zhang. I'm a student at Illumen Hall near Winferne Bay. We think something's happened to one of the students, Clover Mirth? She's missing.' I stay on the phone to the operator for a few minutes, answering the multitude of questions. 'Yes, OK, thank you. We'll get our headmistress and she can meet you at the front entrance.'

I breathe out hard.

'Ivy, come look at this,' Audrey says. Her voice is quiet, and I see she's now standing by Clover's desk. I'm surprised she wants to get that close, what with all the blood.

I walk over, carefully picking my way through the detritus of the room. I stare down at what Audrey's looking at. It's an etching of the words ILLUMEN HALL.

But no. Not quite.

Most of the etching looks deep and a dark brown, as if it had been there for ages, probably scratched by an old student with a compass. But there's a fresh mark, still pale and splintered around the edges. It changes the way the words read. Instead of Illumen Hall, it reads:

ILL OMEN HALL

I shudder.

'This place really is cursed,' Audrey mutters.

'Come on, we need to find Mrs Abbott.' But, as I move backwards, something catches my eye. Something taped under the desk. A small piece of white paper.

Dear Clover,
You are invited to become a part of THE MAGPIE SOCIETY.

Do you agree to uphold the values of the school, protecting it from corruption and keeping it and its students safe, no matter what the cost?

If so, sign here – and await further instructions.

ACKNOWLEDGEMENTS

First of all, our heartfelt thanks to you, the reader, who has chosen this book! We hope you've enjoyed it as much as we loved writing it together, even if our best laid co-writing plans were replaced with Zoom calls, FaceTime and Whatsapp voice notes!

We realize that a lot of difficult topics are addressed over the course of this story, and we wanted to provide some resources for anyone who is struggling – especially with bullying, suicide, anxiety and mental health issues. Please reach out if you need help. There are people out there who want to talk to you – you are not alone.

Anti-bullying helpline
Childline - 0800 1111
www.childline.org.uk

Suicide Outreach
Samaritans - 116 123
http://samaritans.org
Hopeline UK - Call: 0800 068 4141
http://papyrus-UK.org

Anxiety & Mental Health
Mind Infoline: 0300 123 3393
info@mind.org.uk

Even though it's only our names on the cover, so many people have helped us on our journey. First of all, we'd like to thank Penguin Random House Children's for being the perfect home for this series. In particular, Emma Jones, Wendy Shakespeare, Alesha Bonser, Simon Armstrong, Tania Vian-Smith, Andrea Kearney and Anne Bowman have gone above and beyond across editorial, marketing, publicity, design and rights, and we truly appreciate all your enthusiasm for *Magpie*. We'd also like to thank Abigail Bergstrom of Gleam Literary for her hard work in bringing this series to life.

On a personal note, Zoe would like to thank Alfie Deyes, Mark Ferris, Poppy Deyes, Joe Sugg, Sean O'Connor, Danielle Cox, Lareese Craig, Katie Allanson, Tanya Burr, Alexis Main, Holly Macey and Dianne Buswell, for always believing in her and supporting her in all her endeavours alongside the rest of her friends and family! She also wants to extend a huge big grateful squish to Maddie Chester, her partner in crime, her right-hand woman, and to Amy, her co-writer on this exciting *Magpie* journey!

Amy's first thanks have to go to Juliet Mushens, brilliant literary agent extraordinaire and incredible friend. She would also like to extend a special thank you to Tanya Byrne, Shannon Cullen, Kim Curran, Juno Dawson, Holly Harris, Amie Kaufman, Zosia Knopp, Laura Lam, Tom Pollock and James Smythe, for all their help and advice along the journey. As always, many thanks to her parents, Angus and Maria McCulloch, and her sister Sophie, for their love and support. A shout-out to Moose: thank you for being an endless source of joy and puppy cuddles. And to Zoe – what an adventure this has been, and long may it continue!

Never forget . . . *don't cross the magpies.*

CAN'T WAIT TO FIND OUT
WHAT HAPPENS NEXT?

Turn the page for a sneak peek of

THE
MAGPIE
SOCIETY

TWO FOR JOY

PROLOGUE

LAST SUMMER

The night Lola died, we were off on an adventure.

It was her favourite thing to do.

Take me somewhere, she'd say, and I'd be compelled to oblige, meticulously planning each step, making the most of every minute of our time together. We'd sneak off the school grounds, jump on a train and end up at the top of the Shard; we'd go out on to the water to chase dolphins through the white-capped waves; we'd scramble along the cliffs to look for caves to explore on a long summer afternoon.

Then we'd creep back to Illumen Hall and pretend as though we were barely more than strangers.

It killed me at first, the pretence. But she convinced me that it was our little secret. And now the finish line was so near; only one year left until we could be free. I could wait.

In the meantime, we had our adventures. It would have to be enough.

That night was always meant to be special. We'd started at the school, of course. It was the Society, after all, that bound us. I thought she understood that, especially when she let me draw on her back, the tip of the pen following the sharp lines of her scapula, giving her wings. Everyone else was out, getting ready for the party. We had the place to ourselves.

It should have been perfect.

But something was wrong. The adventure wasn't going as I had planned. She said she loved the drawing – how much it looked like a real tattoo – but I sensed she was lying. In the car, she was too interested in her phone, scrolling through her social media, ignoring me. She wanted to go to the beach. She wanted to be surrounded by other people, when she knew full well that I preferred it when we were alone.

When I wouldn't do what she asked, she turned surly, whining about being bored and how much she wished the adventure was over. We arrived at our destination, but she was snappy and impatient, complaining about the wind, the water – things she normally loved. I tried to stay the course, knowing that what I had planned would be worth it, but it was as if the ground were moving, swaying beneath my feet; I couldn't keep her in focus.

She was slipping like quicksilver away from me.

She grabbed a jacket to cover the artwork on her back. I didn't like that. It was as though she was ashamed of it.

Ashamed of me.

'*Can we see the party from here?*'

She stepped closer to the edge and spread her arms wide. I thought of the wings beneath her jacket, a bird about to take flight.

'*Take a photo of me?*' She turned round and grinned at me. She patted the pockets of her jacket. '*Oh, I must have left my phone in the car. Use yours?*'

I couldn't refuse her (though I'd swiped her phone on purpose, locking it in the car so there'd be no more distractions). She removed the jacket, tossing it at my feet, and struck a pose. As she moved position, her foot slipped, and she cried out before starting to fall –

My heart caught in my throat. But, as I reached out to grab her, she righted herself and looked back at me, laughing, the thrill of the near-miss making us both giddy.

I snapped the photo, but no image could do her justice. I wished I could capture her just as she was in that moment. If I had the skills, I would have carved her into a figurehead to guide me – more striking than any sea creature on the prow of a ship.

In the semi-dark, it was hard to see the magpie. But I knew it was there, the wing tips reaching out to her shoulders. A shadow across her back. We'd come so far, and this was the moment I'd been waiting for, the moment I'd find out once and for all how strong her commitment was.

'*Let's go,*' she said, before I could say anything. The wind was so fierce it almost swept away her words. She frowned. '*Didn't you hear me?*'

Things were worse when she spoke.

The reality of what was happening came crashing back.

Our perfect moment wasn't going to last much longer.

The adventure was ending.

'*Help me down from here.*' She reached out her hand to me.

But I didn't take it.

'*Were you serious about what you said earlier? About the magpies?*' I asked her.

'*Come on. You don't really believe in that, do you? It's just a silly myth. A game we're playing. That's all this is.*'

The words were a slap in the face.

'*It's not a myth. Beware the magpies.*' That much I understood and believed.

She rolled her eyes.

She didn't believe. Maybe she never had. She didn't respect the tradition. But, more than that, she wasn't going to *help*. And that betrayal was bigger than any that had come before.

She understood, I think, in that final moment, the impact of her words. But it was too late to take them back.

'*No, don't! Please –*'

I took a step forward.

One shove was all it took.

It's strange. I thought I'd feel sad once it was done. *One for sorrow, two for joy.*

I keep waiting for the sorrow to come.

But instead?

Instead, all I feel is . . . joy.

ABOUT THE AUTHORS

Zoe Sugg is a multi-hyphenate businesswoman, content creator and the bestselling author of the Girl Online series. In 2009, she started her blog and social media channels under the name Zoella and took the online world by storm. She has amassed 25 million followers across her YouTube and Instagram channels, and regularly uses her platform to address important subjects like mental health, cyber-bullying and women's health.

Amy McCulloch is a Chinese-White author, raised in Canada and based in London, England. Amy has been editorial director for Penguin Random House Children's, where she published Zoe's number-one international bestselling Girl Online series, and has written for YA and middle-grade readers in her series: The Oathbreaker's Shadow, The Potion Diaries and Jinxed. When she's not writing, she can normally be found on top of a mountain.